2020
Writing from Inlandia

An Inlandia Institute Publication

2020 Writing from Inlandia
Copyright © 2021 The Inlandia Institute and individual authors.
ISBN: 978-1-955969-01-7
Library of Congress Control Number: 2021941127
All rights reserved. All rights revert to author upon publication.

No part of this book may be used, reproduced, or adapted to public performances in any manner whatsoever without permission from both the publisher and the copyright owners, except in the case of brief quotations embodied in critical articles and reviews. For more information, write to:

Permissions
Inlandia Institute
4178 Chestnut Street
Riverside, CA 92501

Book layout & design: Mark Givens
Executive Director & Editor: Cati Porter
Publications Coordinator: Maria Fernanda Vidaurrazaga

Printed and bound in the United States
Distributed by Ingram

Published by Inlandia Institute
Riverside, California
www.InlandiaInstitute.org
First Edition

2020 Inlandia Creative Writing Workshop Leaders
We are grateful for you!

Library-Affiliated Workshops
Corona: Andrea Fingerson
Ontario: Tim Hatch
Redlands: James Ducat
Riverside: Jo Scott-Coe
San Bernardino: Allyson Jeffredo & Romaine Washington

Bilingual Workshops
Tesoros de Cuentos: Frances J. Vasquez
Colton: Jessica Carrillo

Workshops for Seniors
Joslyn Joy Writers: Mae Wagner Marinello
Poets in Motion: CelenaDiana Bumpus

Virtual Workshops
Food Writing Workshop: Alaina Bixon
Adventures in Chronologyland: Dr. Carlos Cortés
Natural Inspirations: Christina Guillen
Power Plot: Renee Gurley
Poet-TRY online workshops: Stephanie Barbé Hammer
The Art and Heart of Memoir: Dr. Mary Joan Koerper

Adventures in Chronologyland:
This project made possible with support from California Humanities, a partner of the National Endowment for the Humanities. For more information, visit www.calhum.org.

Corona, Ontario, and San Bernardino workshops:
This event is supported in part by Poets & Writers.

All:
This event is supported in part by an award from the National Endowment for the Arts. To find out more about how National Endowment for the Arts grants impact individuals and communities, visit www.arts.gov. This activity is also supported in part by the California Arts Council, a state agency. Learn more at www.arts.ca.gov.

In Memory of

Candace Shields
Morris Mendoza
&
CelenaDiana Bumpus

Contents

Cati Porter
    Introduction: 2020 20/20 15

"Poets in Motion" Class
    A Unity Poem 18

Joslyn Joy Writers
    Thank You, Mae 23

Elisabeth Anghel
    The Soup 24
    A Favorite Cookbook..26

Don Bennett
    The Not-Ok Corral...27
    Big Outing..29

Brenda Y. Beza
    Memory of Silence..31

Georgette Geppert Buckley
    Mystery...38
    The Creature 42
    Back to the Past 44
    Starting Over 47

Alben J. Chamberlain
    Salt Water Ghazal...48
    Ode to Cats..51
    A Tale of Two Retirements 54
    Thirteen Ways of Looking at Sand 58

Natalie Champion
    Coronavirus...62
    City of Blue Tents...63
    Dark-Eyed Junco 64
    Missionary Church 65
    Cyrano 66

Rick Champion
    The Blessing of the Bikes 67

Sylvia Nelson Clarke
- Compassion ... 76
- Miracle in the Rocks ... 77
- Petition in Song ... 80
- Massachusetts Ice Storm ... 81
- Pain, Prayer, and Praise ... 82

Wil Clarke
- Benign Prostate Hypoplasia — 2004 ... 83
- Cycling in Ndola, Zambia 1961 ... 86
- Mountain Passes Near Cape Town ... 89

Amy Clayton
- Darkness and Light ... 91
- In the Garden ... 93
- Creations ... 94

Deenaz P. Coachbuilder
- The Inequality of Masks ... 95
- Believe ... 98
- Timeless Music ... 100

Elinor Cohen
- Ridiculously Delicious Dinner ... 102

Carlos Cortés
- First Night in Copacabana ... 105
- Güero ... 107

Laurel Cortés
- Interview With Laurel Vermilyea Cortés ... 109
- A Walk in the 4 O'Clock Rain ... 115

Barry Cutler
- Barry Cutler, Major League Baseball Player ... 120

Ellen Estilai
- Wonderland ... 127

Andrea Fingerson
- Masks ... 132
- How Much Do You Need? ... 134
- No Signature Required ... 139

Bryan Franco
- A Most Honorable Warrior's Death 141
- The Answer My Friend To Interpreting the Wind 143
- yahrzeit 145
- BEWARE when entering the poetry zoomosphere 147
- 4 Haikus for 2020 149

Meryl Freeze
- My Parents' Uzbekistan Cooking 150

Nan Friedley
- It 152
- Ode to the Lobe 154
- Just 45 Minutes 155
- Six-pack of Senyrus 156
- Pandemic Pants 158

Hazel Fuller
- How Will They Know I Am "Earning My Salt?" 159
- The Catastrophic Flood of 1938 161
- Wanda's Yellow Two Piece Swimsuit 164

Judy Ginsberg
- Mom 168
- Scotch 169
- Food Writing 170

Ragini Goel
- Spunky Little Ragi 171
- Sterilized Muse 175

Michael A. Gonzales
- Guillermina "Minnie" Ayala Gonzales 177

Ralph A. Gonzales
- Remembering My Grandfather — Rosario Ortiz Ayala 181

Richard Gonzalez
- The Deputy Registrar of Voters 188

Mark Grinyer
- Cooking 191
- Sunlight Sinking in the Sea 193
- Dastardly Weather 194
- The Death of Cats 195

Raquel Hernandez
- Valiente 196
- Hope Deteriorates in the Air 199
- Desert Disappearance 200

Richard Hess
- Going Up The Hill 201
- Good Advice 203
- Show Me the Money 205

Connie Jameson
- Bouquets 207
- Wrong Victim 209
- "His rage has borrowed legs" 210

Ann Kanter
- Mrs. Potts' Sad Iron 212

Naresh Kaushal
- Dreaming 217
- I Never Told Anyone 218
- Public Relations. Specialist. 220
- You will find me 222
- The Bus Driver 223

Cleone Knopfle
- Coffee Pleasures 224

Dr. MJ (Joan) Koerper
- The Wrightwood Post Office April 16, 2020 225
- Perspective: Empty Shelves, Riots, & Chaos 227

Jessica Lea
- The Scale 233
- I AM 235
- Standing Outside 236
- Windy Day 237

Nina Lewis
- Smudge 238
- Homing Birds 240
- No Network Connection 241
- Alkaline 243
- Kite 244

Robin Longfield
   Time, Out of Mind 246
Merrill Lyew
   Rising Sea Level 255
   A Night at the Amphitheater 256
Pamylla Marsh
   Thoughts 260
Terry Lee Marzell
   Flash Flood Casualties 261
   The Beauty in a Hundred Mundane Moments 267
Phyllis Maynard
   May 9, 2018 270
   Lovie 276
Thomas McCabe
   Food With My Family 277
Barbara Meyer
   The Best Time in My Life
      Was About Who-With Not What-Had 279
Marvin Meyer
   Beauty 280
Rose Y. Monge
   The Mask Dilemma 281
   In Praise of the Flour Tortilla 283
Mary-Lynne Monroe
   Maybe Dreams Aren't Merciless 286
   Warriors Like Us 287
   Until the Fires Die 288
   Wavering in the Wind 289
   Redefined 290
Roberto Murillo
   En la Sombra Del Águila 292
   Nuestro Pastor 294
Cindi Neisinger
   California Jam 297
   A Tipsy Business Plan 300
S. J. Perry
   MAGA 302

Christine Petzar
   Soapy Dishwater 303
   A Memorable Holiday, Christmas Eve 2019 305

Raymond Price
   My Beef With World War II 309

Cindi Pringle
   Sea Dance 312
   Haiku 314

Randolph Quiroz
   The Hole in My Life 315

Kristine Ann Shell
   On Writing 321

Stevie Taken
   Social Distancing 322

Elizabeth Uter
   What the Builders Knew 325
   Young Girl Meets Boy King 328
   Steal Away 330
   Windows by Souls 332
   No Place To Be 334
   The Stay 336

Gudelia Vaden
   Empty Town 338
   Fears 339
   Silver Dollar Summer 340
   The Outhouse 342
   The Sock Doll 344

Thomas Vaden
   A Clock Stopped 346
   Pandemic Limericks 351
   Pandemic Poems 352

Frances J. Vasquez
   She Showed the Way ~ Reflections of Francisca Valenzuela
      Borboa 353
   My Higher Education Journey 360

Dale Vassantachart
   Autumn 2020 364

José Luis Vizcarra
Time Is Like the Written Word 365
El Último Rollo De Papel Del Baño 366
Cadaver In The Desert 368
The Magic Farm 370
Helen Young
Nighttime Walks in the Neighborhood – a Suite of Four Poems .. 372
Two Triolet Poems 374

Author Bios 377
About Inlandia Institute 389
Inlandia Books 390

Introduction: 2020 20/20

The calendar rolled over from 2019 to 2020. The year began as any other, with New Year's resolutions to diet and exercise more, to quit smoking, to begin a writing regimen, to call our mothers more often. Sure, there had already been whispering on the news about a novel coronavirus taking hold half a world away, but the odds of it affecting us in the United States were slim. Or so we wanted to believe.

In February, the United States declared a public health emergency. In early March, a California cruise ship's passengers tested positive, and, on the eleventh day of that month, the World Health Organization (WHO) declared a global pandemic. Travel bans were enacted. Loved ones were trapped at a distance. Then, on the nineteenth day, California became the first state to issue a state-wide stay at home order. And so our pandemic lockdown began.

You know the rest. I don't need to tell you about the increasing uncertainty that followed, the fear, the job loss and entire sectors of the economy collapsing. George Floyd. Civil unrest and peaceful protest.

Like all of you, I spent the first weeks in a daze. Like you, I, too, turned to writing to help me sort out how I was feeling, and to document this unprecedented period in our shared history.

So, we pivoted to provide all of our programs in a virtual setting. We learned to Zoom — at first tentatively, then confidently. In recognition of the economic hardships many of our members endured, we waived all fees for boot camp workshops, and we added even more workshops. We contributed to collaborative pandemic poetry, wrote through a pandemic spring, then summer. We were inspired by nature, by food, by memoir, by poetry, by story.

The long months that followed were a yo-yo of feelings, giving us much to write about.

Buoyed by seeming progress, we looked forward to the economy reopening, only to have the door slammed again just as quickly. Differences of opinion on everything from healthcare to politics, socializing to social justice, fractured relationships, revealing different sides of ourselves and each other; more often, we were surprised and disappointed by what we saw.

And yet, there has been much good that has come out of this tumultuous year. We've learned what we can live with, and what we can live without. We've discovered that being together, apart, can, paradoxically, shrink the distance between us. Our workshop leaders found creative ways to keep things going, whether that be on Zoom, by email, over Slack, Google Classroom, Facebook groups, and so on. We thank all of you for your dedication and innovation.

Every year we rely on our program partners to support these workshops, and this year even more so. As Mae Wagner Marinello, workshop leader for the Joslyn Joy Writers, all seniors, writes: "We are extremely appreciative that the City of Redlands provided this opportunity to us. Existing writers as well as newcomers were welcomed into the fold. The pandemic was very isolating and frightening— but, every Thursday morning, our group got together on Zoom and knew we were not alone, that we would get through this together."

We couldn't have done it without: Mike Murphy and the Colton Area Museum; Dani Perez-Granado of Corona Public Library; Janis Young, Jana Waitman, and Jon Anderson at the Ovitt Family Community Library; Aaron Espinosa and T.J. Hicks of Rancho Mirage Public Library; Joy Manesiotis of the University of Redlands; the City of Redlands Recreation and Senior Services Division, especially David Jaffe, Recreation Coordinator, Shari Haynes, Program Specialist, and Julie Schneblin, Program Aide, at the Joslyn Senior Center in Redlands; Erin Christmas of the Riverside Public Library; Judith Vails of the Janet Goeske Senior Center; Linda Adams Yeh and Javier Gonzalez of the San Bernardino Public Library.

We also extend special thanks to Jamie Asaye FitzGerald and our friends at Poets & Writers Readings and Workshops (West), and the Riverside Public Library's California Humanities-funded Humanities Hour project, both of which provided direct support for workshop leader honoraria; and the National Endowment for the Arts and California Arts Council, both of which funded staff time to provide critical support to this core program. And lastly, we are grateful for all of you who have so generously donated to keep these workshops free so that they are accessible to all. Your generosity makes it possible.

Again, the calendar has rolled over.

With vaccinations rolling out at a steady clip, we are now on the cusp of recovery. I have real, tangible hope. Grab some of that with me as you read through these pages.

In gratitude and solidarity,

Cati Porter

A Unity Poem
from our "Poets in Motion" Class to the World

In Memory of our Beloved Teacher, CelenaDiana Bumpus

February, 2021

1.
    The world and its confusion suspended
    beyond windows, doors and walls,
    we smile, laugh, and chat
    within our little squares.
    We write and share our writing,
    keeping the panic pandemic at bay
    at least for the time being.

2.
    Talking stamp postcard moments
    it's just like watching tv?

    Real life America shines through
    surreal life corona and I'm just
    sneaking a glance
    into everybody's living room.

    So good to be so close to people so far
    The only holiday I could afford anyway.

3.
>
> Here we are, joined in words that could make an ocean wave,
> and, rain curl back into itself to make the sun warm our smiles.
> We weave unique stories in and out of diverse cultures, a variety of ages,
> as do our experiences in life. We come together 'art' our umbrella, we shelter
> from this *novel tsunami*, sharing creativity, defiant in the face of drums
> tattooing a war song of ravage, our hearts are savage with song,
> passion patterning our tongues. We are community, a unity
> so vast our tuneful heartstrings reach the moon and back again.

4.
>
> This self-imposed isolation for the sake of safety and health.
> This pandemic has become about preserving and finding new community.
> New communities of poets worldwide merging into something altogether new.
> The word zoom is now about more than lightning speed.
> It is a way to share our lives in isolation:
> transforming isolation into community:
> building community from building blocks of poetry.

5.
>
> We will go down in history
> as the ZOOM era, not the pandemic.
> What will be remembered from this time
> for generations to come
> is connection.
> We crossed oceans

through our screens
to reach out to each other.

Zooming to a 100th Birthday celebration
an eighty-eight-year-old wishes the "birthday boy"
from the other side of the globe
"Many Happy Returns!"

"I wish to be at YOUR 100th birthday"
replies the celebrating man.

They vow to each other
a promise written on water
carried through virtual waves.

Amen.

6.
In our group of multi-cultural members
We have had honest sharing; humor, kindness, sympathetic listening;
Exploring emotional truths.

To grapple with poetry means opening the heart to truth.
To struggle to be honest, builds community and healing.
What a privilege to work with others in this effort – to be better people.

7.
Across the oceans we unite,
comfort each other, hold light to the truth
and find positivity in words.
Connect in a time of disconnection,
hard-wire bridges over solitude,
find no gap between us, larger than a pen.

8.
   Paula taught me to Zoom for Spanish sake
      Eager learners now friends to make
   Celena Zoomed class when Goeske us sent
      To lonely lockdown, health-ward bent
   Wedding Anniversary or Birthday
      More friends smile when "congrats" they say
   Than ever did at a local party
      Instead, virtual joys are hearty

9.
   We are a trug! Each strip delicately chosen.
   All witnesses to (the) power, (of)
   Global collaboration and acceptance.
   Strengthening unique voices,
   Celebrating each other,
   Intertwined in hope for one rare purpose.
   To hold (our flower), in spite of what comes.

10.
   Covid, Oh Covid, you're a formidable foe
   But here is something you really should know

   On Tuesday afternoons we pay you no heed
   Zooming to our Sanctuary for all that we need

   Surrounded by creativity and support we hold dear
   Challenged by writing prompts, not by fear

   "Poets in Motion," a respite from worry and care
   We are so grateful that we can go there

11.
>   Coming together
>   On Zoom
>   Meeting old friends
>   Making new ones
>   Uniting us
>   Not just in writing
>   In encouragement
>   Turning the pandemic into
>   Yes! Yeah! Smile

Collaborators:

Pandemic Smiles from Mary-Lynne Monroe (USA)
Welcome Spaces from Naresh Kaushal (UK)
'Art' Our Umbrella from Elizabeth Uter (UK)
Constructing Community Through Poetry from Bryan Franco (USA)
Reflections from Dena/Edna Led (New Zealand)
Hands Across the World from Helen Young (USA)
Interconnection from Nina Lewis (UK)
Zoom Virtuality from Wil Clarke (USA)
To Hold! From Daisy Luma-Haddison (USA)
Sanctuary by Connie Jameson (USA)
Community Is... from Sylvia Clarke (USA)

THANK YOU, MAE

by the Joslyn Joy Writers

T Thank you, Mae, for changing our lives, for
H Helping us bring our stories to life in an
A Atmosphere, caring and strong, where there's
N Never a critic, no right and no wrong. You're
K Keeping us safe in a pandemic, no less.
     We're zooming along, doing our best.

Y You've kept us connected and
O Opened our minds to the joys that exist in the hardest of times.
U Unfettered, untethered, our thoughts
     seem to roam. And we find ourselves

M Missing your brownies and scones,
A And so many parties we've had to postpone.
E Each of us distanced, but never alone.

F From winter to spring, through summer and fall, you're our
R Role model, resource, editor on call,
O Our leader, our mentor, you show us the way, you're just what
     we need, our
M Marvelous Mae

JOSLYN JOY WRITERS

The Soup

by Elisabeth Anghel

Christo: "Grandma you are wearing socks with vegetable designs on them because you like to make soups."

This was my grandson at 5-years-old. He is now 16 and 6-foot-2.

Yes, I like to make soup. It is a filling dish; good cold or hot, clear or loaded with stuff, good for breakfast, lunch or dinner, for regular meals and celebratory meals.

I am famous for my soup. At my house, a soup dish is served for one of each day's meals. Here is my recipe for a basic meat soup.

Ingredients

- Meat, 2 - 3 lb. of any of these kinds of meats with or without bone: beef, chicken, turkey, seasonal lamb
- All vegetables chopped into ½ inch cubes:
- Carrots, 2 cups
- Onion, 1 cup
- Celery stalks, 1 cup
- Bell Pepper (red preferred), 1 cup
- Cabbage, 2 cups (optional)
- Zucchini or other squash, 1 cup
- Fall squash (seasonal), 1 cup
- Potatoes, 2 cups
- Fresh green parsley, 1tbsp
- Fresh green dill, 1 tbsp
- Lemon juice, ½ cup
- Tomato sauce (store bought), ½ cup
- Black peppercorns, about 10-12 kernels

- Bay leaf, 1 - 2 leaves
- Cumin, a pinch
- Salt, 1 tbsp
- Water, 4 - 4 ½ quarts (drinking or purified water) + 1 pint

Preparation

The meat and vegetables must all be washed well before you start cooking.

In a large pot, pour the water and place the meat to cook.

Collect the foam until the liquid boils and stays clear. Continue boiling on low heat for another ½ hour. Remove the meat and set aside on a plate/bowl for later.

Put all the vegetables listed, except the potatoes, in the pot and add 1 pint of cold water. Cook until vegetables are cooked firm and add the potatoes. Continue cooking until the potatoes are done.

To check the "doneness" of the ingredients, take a long spoon, pick some of the vegetables from the soup, place them on a small plate to cool and taste if fully cooked.

Add lemon juice and tomato sauce and cook for another 10-15 min. If you desire, add half of a teaspoon of sugar.

Cut or hand-pull the cooked meat into small pieces and add to the soup.

Garnish with fresh green parsley and dill.

Serve hot and enjoy.

You may enjoy this soup over small-sized pasta cooked separately, or add yogurt, or sour cream, or more lemon juice, or sprinkle a few thin slices of hot jalapeño for a "kick".

A Favorite Cookbook
by Elisabeth Anghel

My favorite cookbook is the classic 1987 edition of *Betty Crocker Cookbook*.

I bought this book when I started living in California to learn about the utensils used in cooking, the ingredients, and the most popular dishes.

The book is in the binder format. This makes it easy to use on a flat surface or on a bookstand. The book is well organized by kind of foods and has pictures to illustrate each dish, along with lists of ingredients and directions to execute each recipe. It also has a very useful index at the end.

Over the years, I have added some of my own recipes and recipes collected from other people and family members. The book has a section at the beginning to organize independent recipes by categories.

In my cooking, I use Betty Crocker's recipes and also recipes from two old Romanian cookbooks. The challenges of using American cookbooks for me are the measurements. I was used to the metric system. Now, after almost 30 years of cooking for my family, I am an expert in measuring and matching recipes and quantities of any kind.

The Not-Ok Corral
by Don Bennett

My first year as a deputy DA in Sacramento, I was assigned to a Superior Court, handling criminal matters on the court's calendar. I was given an office, which in years past had been used for polygraph examinations. There was a fairly large mirror on the wall, which was actually an observation window where people could watch the proceedings from the next room. The office next door was occupied by two investigators, who were both retired policemen. If you've ever seen the TV show, *Brooklyn 99*, you could say they were like the two cops, Hitchcock and Scully. Let's just say they weren't eager to work too hard.

On one particular day, I had three cases to handle. The third case involved a police sergeant from the vice squad. When he came to my office first thing in the morning, I told him I wouldn't be able to handle his case until last, so he could just make himself comfortable in my office until I returned from court. When I left for court, he stayed in my office.

Two days later, there was an article in the Sacramento Bee, about what happened while I was gone to court. The officer became bored sitting there all by himself. He began watching himself in the mirror. Shortly after that, he began practicing quick draw with his pistol, and he was impressed with his gun-slinging abilities. Unfortunately, on one of his attempts, he accidentally dropped his gun on the floor, and it went off, and shot a hole in the side of my desk.

The sound of gunfire awoke the sleeping investigators next door, and they came running with guns drawn. As they opened the door, they observed a large black man kneeling beside my desk. The embarrassed officer was surprised by the two investigators who were pointing guns at him, but then everyone in the room was surprised. It took some time to sort out the situation.

Later, when I returned from court, I not only found the police officer, who was now sitting outside of my office, writing his report, but I also found the lieutenant from the police department's internal affairs division. He had interviewed everybody involved in the incident, and was waiting for me so he could get my part of the story. Needless to say, the whole thing was the talk of the office for quite a long time. I am happy to say that I got a new office assigned to me after that, which had a desk free of bullet holes.

Big Outing

by Don Bennett

One of the very nice things about the home we are now living in is that we can see the hills and the mountains around us by looking out the kitchen window. The weather in the last several months has fluctuated between hot, cold, wet, and, the other day, there was snow in the hills not too far from our house, which was a little unusual. A crystalline blanket.

Since March of 2020, I do not leave the house unless I am required to visit the hospital and lab or to, once every day or two, walk the dog to the mailbox. Our dog, Henry, is quite perceptive, because, if I change from pajama bottoms to jeans or shorts, he will run at full speed to sit in his chair so that I can hook him up to his leash. Then, I put on my hat and my mask, hook a mailbag to the walker, and off we go.

I have the impression that Henry, in a previous life, had been trained as a sled dog, because on the way to the mailbox he will drag me at full speed. Otherwise, he will only stop to visit other dogs on the way. After we get the mail, we start back to our house, and Henry runs again, dragging me along behind him. It takes some effort to get him to slow down enough to allow me to walk at a comfortable pace.

One day, as we walked by a new neighbor's house, he had just come outside. I was all decked out in my hat, gloves, and mask. I said, "Hello," introduced myself and Henry, and continued, "You'll have to excuse me. My wife dresses me funny." He laughed, but didn't comment on the fact that he wore no protection of any kind.

A few of my neighbors have asked me about the odd contraption I wear around my neck, similar to but very different from what a St. Bernard wears around his neck in the Alps. (Just for the record, I don't yodel either.) I reply that I'm a diabetic, and it's just a device for monitoring my blood sugar.

Occasionally, we run into a neighbor who has walked out of his house, and most of the neighbors don't seem to bother much about wearing a mask. Henry has to stop and say hi, and hope that the neighbor's dog is outside, too. On the day that we noticed the snow, the ground was still wet from the rain, and we walked down past the bank of mailboxes because the mailman had just come and he was still loading mail into the boxes. When we came back, he asked me my dog's name and then mine, so he could hand me our mail. I asked him how he was doing, and he replied that he and the mail had been getting wet recently.

On the way back to our house, an Amazon Prime truck passed us, stopped in front of our house, delivered a package to our front porch, and another to our neighbor. Henry and I picked up our package, came into the house, and our big outing was over. Whew. Big outings tire both of us out.

Memory of Silence

by Brenda Y. Beza

> *"The events in our lives happen in a sequence in time, but in their significance to ourselves they find their own order, a timetable not necessarily — perhaps not possibly — chronological. The time as we know it subjectively is often the chronology that stories and novels follow: it is the continuous thread of revelation."*
>
> **Eudora Welty, On Writing**

In the 1970s, the Oil Crisis of the Middle East triggered a massive global inflation. The energy crisis was particularly detrimental to Latin American countries, like Guatemala, who, since the 1960s, had been embroiled in a civil war that led to the Silent Holocaust, the genocide of Mayan civilians. From 1973 to 1974, the economic growth rate in Guatemala slowed from 7.6 to 4.6 percent; and by 1974, the annual growth rate was 2.9 percent. These moments in history created a set of push-pull factors that led to my mother's decision to migrate from Guatemala to Los Angeles, California.

In December 1975, my then 22-year-old mother, Cledia, left war-torn Guatemala with plans of finding employment in California. On January 28, 1975, my mother had given birth to her first daughter, my sister. Guatemala's economic devastation led my mother to make one of the hardest decisions of her life — to leave her 11-month-old daughter with a trusted family member. As my mother embarked on the trek to the United States, she promised her aunt that she would send a monthly remittance for my sister. These historical events and personal decisions made by my mother set the stage for my family chronology — one that began with the trauma and suffering caused by Guatemala's wartime economy and that continued with my parents' memory of silence.

Mamá

My mother departed Guatemala City on December 12, 1975. The day itself was engulfed by a sacred energy, as my mother started the perilous journey on el dia de La Virgen de Guadalupe, a day that celebrates the apparition of Mexico's patron saint to a young indigenous man. Every year, my mother nostalgically remembers this day as she heads to mass. At various points throughout my life, my mother recalled the promise she made to La Virgen de Guadalupe. In exchange for saintly protection, she promised to someday visit La Basilica de Guadalupe in Mexico City, one of the most important pilgrimage sites for Catholics. My mother swears that all the suffering in her life, post-1975, stems from that unkept promise.

As my mother crossed the United States-Mexico border, she grappled with a life-altering migration that would transform her roles as mother, sister and (grand)daughter. To embark on the journey, she borrowed money from a friend to pay a coyote, a person who smuggles immigrants across the border. She recalls that crossing the border in the mid-1970s was not as dangerous as it is today. Once she arrived in Tijuana, she remembers the coyote handing out documents to each individual in the group. The coyote asked that each person take on the role of a Mexican citizen. For instance, my mother was asked to step into the role of a Mexican woman who had birthed 12 children. She distinctly remembers that the personal identification of Mexican women at the time indicated the number of children a woman had birthed. "The immigration official will not believe I am this age or that I have 12 children," my mother said to the coyote. As my mother looked at the photograph of the woman she was role-playing, she became increasingly nervous — there was no physical resemblance whatsoever. "Look, this is the role you're taking on and this is the backstory — you have 12 children and you're crossing the border into San Ysidro to do some Christmas shopping at the local market center. It's a simple day trip," the coyote said to my mother. Ultimately, this was the role and story that facilitated my mother's crossing into California on December 18, 1975.

Papá

While my mother settled in California, my father, Luis, a man she had yet to meet, was living in San Salvador, El Salvador. In 1976, my paternal grandmother, Yolanda, made the decision that she and my father would move to California. My Tío Manuel's desire to attend medical school was the impetus for this major decision. The cost of medical textbooks and tuition were too costly for my grandparents. My father had no desire to leave El Salvador. By age nineteen, my father had already gained seven solid years of employment experience working in the textile sector. His godfather, who was from Palestine, owned the textile factory and had employed him at the age of twelve. My father reluctantly left his stable employment for the uncertainty he would find in the United States. Like my mother, my father also borrowed money from family and friends to pay the coyote, specifically from his godfather and his then girlfriend's aunt.

As the economic and civil unrest escalated in El Salvador, my father and grandmother departed to California. They settled in the city of Costa Mesa, California with a Guatemalan friend named Patty. Soon after settling in Orange County, my father and grandmother found employment in Newport Beach, California. My father was employed as a bus boy at Coco's Bakery Restaurant at Fashion Island and my grandmother as a housekeeper. A year after their arrival, my father and grandmother had active social lives as they connected with various networks of friends and family from Central America who were also finding migration as their only option to surviving the civil wars and economic instability caused by U.S. intervention in the region. Additionally, natural disasters, such as earthquakes, further devastated regions like Nicaragua and Guatemala.

Mamá y Papá

By 1978, my mother had already lived in California for three years. She had been working odd, short-term jobs until she found a more stable position as a seamstress in downtown Los Angeles's Fashion District. My mother led a bustling social life on the weekends as she reconnected with friends who were making the trek to California. As fate would have it, my mother was friends with Patty, my father and grandmother's friend and roommate. My father was the only one in the household with a car, so he ended up having to chauffeur my grandmother and Patty around Southern California. It was on one of these weekend car rides that my father and mother met.

On September 21, 1977, my mother turned 25-years-old. She held a small gathering of friends to celebrate her birthday. Patty was in attendance and she introduced my father to my mother. "After that, your dad kept calling me and we started dating," my mother recalls. From the outset of their relationship, my mother was transparent with my father about having a child in Guatemala and that bringing her to the United States was one of her long-term goals. By summer of 1979, my parents were expecting their first child and decided that they wanted to raise their family in Orange County instead of Los Angeles County.

La americana

I was born on March 28, 1980 at Mercy General Hospital in Santa Ana, California. As the first-born in the United States, my life has been marked by a number of firsts. I was the first to be raised in a truly bicultural environment, the first to learn English, to graduate high school, to attend a 4-year university, to earn undergraduate and graduate degrees, and the list goes on.

I was raised in a neighborhood that was a predominantly white and conservative. We were the only Latino family living on Charloma Drive in Tustin, California. My father always worked at least two jobs to ensure that we could live in middle-class neighborhoods, even if our family was strictly working-class. And my mother worked from our home either running a daycare and/or running an informal catering business on top of being a housewife. From a young age, I observed my parents' strong work ethic.

The importance of obtaining an education was instilled in me as early as age six. I distinctly remember practicing my letters on newsprint handwriting paper while sitting at the formal dining room table. I do not recall the context of the conversation, but I remember my parents saying to me, "Our job is to put food on the table, clothes on your back, and a roof over your head. Your job is to go to school." Those words were etched in my memory from that moment on and it became a mantra of sorts. I took this sentiment all the way through K-12, undergraduate and graduate school. I literally never stopped attending institutions of formal education until my early thirties.

As a daughter of undocumented Central American immigrants, I had a unique experience in my formative childhood years. This development occurs for all human beings based on our childhood response and interaction between genetics, environment and experience. For the first three years of my life, I was raised in a household full of adults. Throughout the 1980s, my parents hosted extended family and/or friends who were making their way from Central America to Southern California. I was privy to all sorts of adult conversations where my brain soaked up certain terminology. At age four, I knew what "la migra" meant and I knew that it was something to be feared. During this stage of child development, I was also introduced to the word "hermana." This word was foreign to me prior to 1983. My mother recalls my first words being "mamá" and "papá." However, at nearly the age of three, they introduced the word "hermana" (sister) into my vocabulary when they revealed my sister's existence.

Hermana

The Arrival

Without warning, mother's secret appeared behind me in flesh and bone
She arrived with invisible wounds sustained over the first eight years
She was born out of an encounter that had no love or foundation
Born into and left behind in a war zone, she survived the battle
Her arrival into my playroom marked the beginning of her war

On January 25, 1983, my sister arrived in Santa Ana, California with the assistance of a coyote. As my mother and I compared memories of that night, I asked her why it had taken eight years for my sister to enter as part of our family unit. My mother explained that she had saved the money to pay for the assistance of a coyote. By 1983, the cost of paying a coyote had increased to approximately $1,250 per person. Over the course of eight years, my mother had made three attempts to send for my sister. However, her aunt refused to send my sister, as she knew that my mother would no longer be sending a monthly remittance. "Me la dieron ya que estaba bien jodida tu hermana," my mother explains. The heaviness of that comment sat in my heart's center as I processed my mother's perspective and feelings about the situation. By the time my mother's aunt decided to release my sister, she had undergone much abuse at the hands of extended family in Guatemala.

At eight-years-old, my sister arrived in my playroom. I had an hermana. As she walked in, I was pouring imaginary tea while standing at my pink kitchenette. The innocence of that playroom is trapped in time. Life was never the same after that day. My sister's arrival slowly unraveled a memory of silence that was only truly known by my parents for years to come. Mamá, papá, hermana — I wish it had been that simple. Instead, the push-pull factors that led to my mother's departure from Guatemala caused highly dysfunctional family dynamics. My sister came of age feeling profoundly abandoned, as well as resentful of the fact that our mother was physically present in my childhood.

This memory always appears fragmented and comes to me as a series of American sentences, an American haiku. The creator of the American sentence, the Beat Poet Allen Ginsberg, used to say, "One sentence, 17 syllables, end of story." In between those 17 syllables are gaps of silence that carry the weight and burden of the human experience, the immigrant experience. It's not "end of story." Instead, those gaps of silence are a call to action. May we begin to excavate these memories from their silence. May we begin to transform them into life-affirming stories that move forward our collective consciousness and understanding of one another within and without our family units.

Mystery

by Georgette Geppert Buckley

Sweet deep rosy
Buds mystically spiraling
Teetering on bending
Forest green stems
Cheerfully unaware
Of the big bad
Virus a la Corona

Overdriving Mind
Heart racing
Hypothetical
Biological Geriatric
Genocide purging
Earth of the weakest
Links

Gone wrong as
The first baby
Succumbs
Perishing
All ordered
Stay at home
Lessen exposure

Waiting and watching
For signs
While locusts plague

Earth trembles
Calling
Texting
Zooming

Hoping for health
Hoping for TP
Hoping for
Freedoms
Postponed
All gatherings
Cancelled

Watching Mass Online
Praying through Our Lady
Of Perpetual Help
For enough respirators
Others post
Drinking
Corona Beer

Dreaming…
of a simpler way
Self-sustainable
To colonize
Another
Planet

Alarmingly
Friends of the Family

Succumb
One perishes
Memorial
Six months later
Six feet away

Keeping busy
Crafting
Painting
Phrasing
Walking
The weeks
The seasons

As another innocent
Rose blooms
Walking past
Six feet away
From friends
All seeking connection
Vitamin D
Immunity
And Gnocchi

And repeat
As the second wave begins...

And repeat
As the second wave begins...
Whom I miss most is Celena

who called to check on me
We laughed about being OK
As long as there were
No zombie bunnies
We texted admiring
Amanda Gorman's
Awesome
Inaugural Poem
As I was recovering
From COVID
Celena's last text:
"I have a head cold but
Am fighting it fiercely."
She may always be
Mysterious
I searched her poems
For clues of her life
Searched Ancestry
For clues to her
Relatives
I searched my soul
For answers
Why I didn't
Make contact
With Celena
Yet her spirit lives on
We will meet again

The Creature

BY GEORGETTE GEPPERT BUCKLEY

In the last stage of birth, with one last excruciating push, a huge creature crawled out of me. My husband, children, midwife and I stared in disbelief. It had a huge, translucent, grey, shellfish back, kind of like an armadillo or a shrimp. And were those tentacles? This baby must be over 20 pounds! Exhausted from a long, grueling labor, motherhood guilt set in. Had my shrimp cravings caused this?

It sputtered around the bedroom and walls and then leapt up and started nursing. I was repelled. I was so not bonding with this strange unnamed thing. The creature jumped away as if knowing my thoughts. It jumped into the hands but not the hearts of my children who ran away screaming. Extended family was already on the way. I cried in horror and disappointment. I let them observe for themselves. They all left speechless as if it was contagious. I never heard from them again.

About three months later, I really needed to get out of the house, so I took the creature to the beach. It was off season so stares would be sparse. It enjoyed jumping frantically and shooting sand showers in a whirl. Then suddenly, it dived into the ocean splashing and diving by instinct. The few surfers paddled away in terror. It came out, digging and slurping up sand crabs like sushi. The young, muscular lifeguard stood bewildered as the creature grew twice its size.

With increased appetite, it started snatching and gulping any food left out by faraway picnickers. I had already packed up my belongings when it was in the ocean, thinking it had returned to its natural habitat. Unable to control it, I jumped into the car. Unfortunately, it jumped onto the back of the car and rode home. People pointed and swerved away from us. The creature had grown as tall as me by twelve months, still a total nightmare! Then one night it jumped upon my back as I slept, its tentacles puncturing me. I screamed in agony as my temperature rose and my devoted husband froze... Awoken and inspired I typed on my tablet.

Back to the Past

BY GEORGETTE GEPPERT BUCKLEY

Growing up in Southern California, I never knew anyone with my first name. My mother would tell me that there was a little bit of French in the family; I assumed it was only in my name. The only family we visited lived in Illinois or Missouri and certainly didn't speak French. After I was married, I finally met someone with the same name when I was 22.

My paternal second great grandfather, Franciscus Barciszwski, his wife, Barbara, and their two small children left Posen, Poland, and arrived on the ship Laura in Baltimore, Maryland in 1871. They settled on a farm in Posen, Illinois and raised a large family. Frank was naturalized in 1876. They were eventually laid to rest At Our Lady of Perpetual Help Cemetery. Interestingly, my husband and I now live near a church with the same name in Riverside. The latest update of my DNA shows 26% Eastern Europe and Russia with a concentration in the area of Pomerania which is the verified location of my Polish ancestors in my family tree.

Several generations grew up farming in the area of south-western Illinois. My dad and his siblings literally walked miles to a one room schoolhouse, kept warm by the potatoes in their pockets. They were lucky when it snowed because their dad would pick them up in his horse drawn sleigh. My parents met in high school and were married for 48 years.

After much researching, building, sharing and connecting family trees, I found out that my maternal twelfth great grandpa, John Turner, and two of his sons, came over on the Mayflower in 1620 and signed the Mayflower Compact. They settled in Scituate, Massachusetts. According to the list etched in granite on the National Monument to the Forefathers, they did not survive the first year. Fortunately, another son Humphrey, born in Kent, and his wife Lydia Gamer from Essex, England arrived on the Mayflower in 1632 and settled in the same town. Humphrey was a tanner of hides which lasted only one season a year. So he held a number of positions in the community. So, looks like my 12% English DNA checks out.

According to the U.S. Revolutionary War Rolls 1775-1783, my 5th great grandfather, John L. Turner was a drummer for the Virginia Continental Troops. By 1794, he was a captain in the squelching of the Whiskey Rebellion. Apparently later he moved to Tennessee, as The Daughters of the American Revolution of Dickson County immortalized his name in their Bicentennial Memorial.

My mom's paternal line of Turner travels backwards in time from Illinois to Cape Girardeau Missouri, where my grandpa, William L. Turner, grew up on a farm near two creeks. That was why decades later he loved to reply, "I'll be there if the creek don't rise." He found arrowheads as he steered the cantankerous mule drawn plow. He crossed the Mississippi River and courted my grandma, Pauline Johnson. He attended college and then became the manager of the Kroger store. He valued education and gave each grandchild (all females) a savings for their college education.

So, my great grandpa John Jason Turner married Mollie Arminta Ramsey Mabrey. Great grandpa had built a large two-story home for his large family digging the clay from the soil and firing them into bricks in the kiln he fashioned. The Mabrey name changed from the English Marbury. Anne Marbury Hutchington, my ninth great aunt, was born in England 1591. She immigrated aboard the ship, The Griffin, to the Massachusetts Bay Colony in the year 1634. Having read her preacher father's books and Bible, she was highly educated for her time. Now known as a symbol of religious freedom and the first female preacher in the colonies, there stands at least three statues of her in Massachusetts.

Although in her time, Anne was banished from the Bay because of her 'anabaptist' doctrine. She and her husband, William Hutchington, co-founded the new colony of Rhode Island. Anne is listed as Scotch-Irish. By the way, my DNA reads 11% Irish and 6% Scottish. Anne's mother's, Bridget Dryden's, line goes back through her great grandpa, Sir John Cope, Knight, my eleventh great grandpa.

Go backwards in time past more generations of English Knights, and we come to my seventeenth great grandpa, Richard Talbot, the 4th Lord Talbot. Backwards yet again to my twentieth great grandpa, Humphrey de Bohun, Earl of Hereford and Essex who married Elizabeth of England. "Who is her father?" you may ask. None other than Edward I, King of England. Continue to bow down through Kings; John I, Henry II, (aren't you glad I didn't say VIII) and King Geoffroi V (Plantagenet). Interesting to note, the next previous King, Henry I, married Matilda, Princess of Scotland. This Royal and Noble Pedigree completes with William the Conqueror, my twenty-seventh great grandfather crowned in Westminster Abbey in 1066.

My mom's Maternal line of Johnson traversed from Illinois back to Missouri to Tennessee, under the Name of Walton, to Williamsburg, Virginia under the name of Maupin. And then on to France, where a Maupin marries a Capet. His father, my ninth great grandfather, Anthony Capet, wed Elizabeth of Pomerania. (Remember my Pomeranian ancestry and DNA?) His father is King Henry III of France and Poland, whose parents were King Henry II of France and Catherine de Medici of Italy. This line of royalty goes back all the way to Charlemagne crowned emperor of the Roman Empire in 800.

Amazingly, the descendants who fled Europe to America for religious freedom so strong they gave up their right to any ancestral estates, castles or claims in Europe. These family connections are true as far as three years of research have shown me at this time.

Starting Over

by Georgette Geppert Buckley

Amazing as our
Fore parents are
They say that your genes
Are really from your last
Four generations

But then wouldn't they
come from their last
Four Generations
Of fore parents
And so on?

Some didn't survive
The turbulent
Ship crossing or
The first year

Some freedoms
Weren't realized
For hundreds of years
Some still need

To be practiced
Life is a series of
Starting Over…

Salt Water Ghazal

by Alben J. Chamberlain

This beach is a battleground between
    dry land and salty sea.
Its sands are alternatively pounded
    and caressed by the eternal sea.

I walk through the wet sands
    of this long, crowded shoreline
watching endless waves form and break
    on the edge of this foaming sea.

I'm here among so many people drawn
    like moths to this ribbon of beach,
for nothing seems to attract humans
    more than the sight of our mother sea.

She has at least a hundred ways
    to kill us if we let down our guard.
Still, people are here mesmerized
    by the sight of this shimmering sea.

Lovers stroll hand-in-hand while
    children build up their sand castles.
Their joy is freely provided by
    the churning, tossing, restless sea.

I discover smoothed stones, tumbled
    seas shells, and sculpted driftwood here,

daily gifted to scavengers who follow the tides
    on the shore of this shifting sea.

Pelicans glide, gulls soar and swoop,
    and sandpipers wade in the foam;
all seeking their daily sustenance from
    the natural bounty in this provident sea.

Well-muscled young people play
    volleyball, or throw frisbees on the sand,
Heedless of the steady assault on the land
    by this sometimes violent sea.

Sunbathers, glistening with sunscreen,
    repose on blankets on this beach,
caressed by the steady, soft breezes
    and mist from this murmuring sea.

Surfers like dark seals in wet suits paddle
    out to the surf-line on boards,
hoping to catch one epic wave
    generated by this unpredictable sea.

Vigilant lifeguards upon their towers
    scan for beach-goers in trouble,
for trouble and constant danger are
    daily provided by this capricious sea.

In this busy coastal city, houses go down
    to the very last foot before the sand,

for humans long to live within sight
>   of the seemingly endless shimmering sea.

As the sun lowers it illuminates the sails
>   of the many vessels riding the tide,
for salt water is there to rock a poor
>   or a rich man upon this calming sea.

When the sun slips toward the western
>   horizon, I get out and use my camera,
because sunsets are always more resplendent
>   on the face of the burnished sea.

At last Alben's day is over, yet I still face
>   the long and weary drive to my home.
The time and expense was worth it for me
>   to have these memories of God's sea.

Ode to Cats

BY ALBEN J. CHAMBERLAIN

Fat cats, skinny cats.
Yellow cats, black cats.

Sly, slinky Siamese cats.
Proud, puffy Persian cats.

Sassy, survivalist alley cats.
Pampered, elitist house cats.

Prowling, predator yard cats.
Snoozing, lazy couch cats.

Tabby cats, calico cats.
Black and white cats.

Big cats, small cats.
Tranquil and nervous cats.

What do you suppose
they have in common?

They don't provide any
useful goods for us.

They don't cook food
or wash the dishes.

They never plant seeds
or weed the garden.

They can't clean up
or put away clothes.

They sleep and slumber
when chores need done.

They kick back while
I pay the bills.

They wander all about
when I must work.

They beg for my
attention when I write.

They become our friends
whenever they get hungry.

They purr and cuddle
when they want attention.

They want to snuggle
when they are cold.

They're our pals whenever
they get their way.

They like being stroked
when they need affection.

They greet us whenever
we return from work.

When useful, they give
us their undivided attention.

They know how to
push our emotional buttons.

They have us cat-lovers
wrapped around their paws.

Cats have we crazy
humans all figured out.

A Tale of Two Retirements
A Pro and Con Poem

BY ALBEN J. CHAMBERLAIN

It feels so good not having
to wake up to an alarm.

It feels so fine to not have to get
up so early and go to work each day.

I no longer have to seek employment
to earn a paycheck to survive.

It's peaceful now with no noisy
children running about the house,

We're free now to travel to all the
places we wanted to visit and see,

There's time for interesting hobbies
pastimes, leisure, and recreation,

Still, it's hard to find ambition
lying in a bed so snug and warm.

yet the camaraderie of friends and
coworkers are worth as much as pay.

Somehow, I must adjust to living on a
fixed income for the rest of my life.

but it's just too quiet and lonely at times
for just me and my spouse.

though both of us feel too old and worn
down to travel all around comfortably.

so why are we stuck on Facebook worrying
about other's lives around the nation?

Cooking meals for just two people
is certainly no big deal.

Still, we mostly can't agree about what to
eat or when to prepare a meal.

It feels fine to be independent and
free from meeting the needs of others,

so why do I often feel unwanted, ignored, or
unneeded, except by sisters or brothers?

It feels good to stay up late to watch
the news, to read, or to write.

Still, I miss out on the morning hours when
I wake up long after the first light.

There's less pressure to stay focused
and be productive at work or at play.

Why does everything seem so random
with no game plan for the day?

It's nice not getting children or
grandchildren ready for school.

Forgetting to take morning medications
makes me feel like a fool.

Now, I have so much less stress,
hassles, deadlines, and strife,

but I often feel redundant or
abandoned by life.

I finally can check off items on
my bucket list one by one,

though I live in constant fear of
leaving most of them undone.

I'm able to get out to see the world,
enjoy life, and to play,

though my vision, hearing, and mobility
are rapidly fading away.

I have time to organize all my rooms,
kitchens, closets, and halls.

Then, I ask myself, "What do I do next?"
as I stare at the unchanging walls.

I can step away from the demands of
the workplace and still pay my bills,

though I no longer feel special or needed
for my knowledge or skills.

I need no agenda, pressures, or
plans to get through the day,

though feeling unfocused and unproductive
is the price I must pay.

Not needing to be in charge or the
authority for the first time in years.

Sadly, this makes me feel unneeded and
diminished by children and peers.

I had big plans to spend more time
and do more things with my friends,

then the vile COVID-19 Virus came
and put those plans to an end.

It's wonderful to take naps after lunch
while there's still daylight.

though it's not so marvelous when I
can't fall or stay asleep at night.

I had big plans to walk more in

order to get back in shape,

I thought I'd be able to help

others at any time at all.

It's the best of times and the worst

of times as you can see,

It feels so good knowing we've

survived so long under the Sun.

so why can't I seem to find the time

in the day, for Heaven's sake?

Now, it's lonely babysitting the iPhone

waiting for someone to call.

though whining about the bad parts

won't make it better or set me free.

It's frightful reading obituaries as

friends and peers pass away one by one.

Thirteen Ways of Looking at Sand

A Perspective Poem

BY ALBEN J. CHAMBERLAIN

1. The overly-ambitious man
   clutches at vain power,
   yet as it slips through
   his feeble fingers he realizes—
   he's only clutching sand.

2. The ill-advised politician spent
   six-hundred million dollars
   on ads to plead for votes.
   Then, on Super Tuesday,
   the elections' results proved
   he had only purchased sand.

3. The extravagant man built
   an enormous luxury home
   in which to spend his days.
   He forgot that the foundation
   was laid upon common sand.

4. I tried to pile up
   knowledge and wisdom
   to impress my peers.
   In the end, I discovered
   I was only piling sand.

5. The actress built up her
   reputation and fame upon
   half-truths and image-making.
   It didn't take long,
   in this cruel world,
   to crumble down like sand.

6. My neighbor traveled through
   more than a hundred
   nations-storing up memories.
   Then, at age eighty,
   dementia struck — turning his
   cherished memories into sand.

7. A young man,
   struck by Cupid's arrows,
   spent huge sums of cash
   to buy his fiancé diamonds.
   After five years of marriage
   she found another lover.
   His investment turned into sand.

8. My friend, an entrepreneur,
   spent eight years, his savings,
   and uncounted working hours
   to build a successful restaurant.
   Then, a pandemic struck
   and cruel financial realities
   turned his dream to sand.

9. Alexander, King of Macedonia,
spent his thirty-three years
conquering and building the
largest empire in human history.
In the grasping hands
of his four generals,
it turned into shifting sand.

10. While hiking one day
I jumped between solid boulders.
They trembled beneath my feet.
Intuitively I sensed
they feared their inescapable
transformation into sand.

11. To realize his dreams
a young professor
rejected God to gain
the approval of men.
He advanced in academia,
but passed at sixty-two.
After this unexpected departure
his legacy sank into sand.

12. An aspiring führer,
through promises and lies,
gained enormous power.
He vowed to build up
a thousand-year reich.

Then, after twelve violent years,
it all turned to sand.

13. Sand itself is fearful
sensing in its being,
that given time,
heat, and pressure,
it will be converted,
through nature's cycles,
once again to solid stone.

Coronavirus

BY NATALIE CHAMPION

Coronavirus on the loose- run!
Sheltering in place - no fun
Missing friends and family
Chatting on Zoom - barely
Remembering days basking in the sun

City of Blue Tents

BY NATALIE CHAMPION

City of blue tents in a lonely park,
Nowhere to live,
Hope to thrive,
Les Miserables,
The forgotten ones,
Product of excess,
Tech success,
Even Robin Hood can't save them,
Les Miserables,
The forgotten ones,
A death kiss,
The ones no one will miss.

Dark-Eyed Junco

by Natalie Champion

Dark-eyed junco in a cherry blossom tree singing
"Come, come outside why don't you?"
Escape from hiding indoors
Beckoning balcony doors
May tempt us, but
Do not heed dark-eyed junco's call.

Missionary Church

BY NATALIE CHAMPION

Eight mourn,

Silent plague creeping,

Seeping through veins,

Unbeknownst

Legal order "shelter in place,"

Too late for some,

Death takes toll,

Silent poll,

Angels watch.

Cyrano

by Natalie Champion

I once had an entertaining parrot
called Cyrano de Bergerac
I really want him back
He thought he was a *Hound Dog*
He was canting and swaying as he jumped up and down on his log
Thanks to Elvis, he was a class act

The Blessing of the Bikes
by Rick Champion

Los Olivos

Los Olivos might have been, at one time, a working olive orchard. The soil was sandy and rocky, brought down by floods from the San Gabriel mountains. Or the olive trees could have been planted as landscape when a government agency built affordable duplexes. Whatever their origin, the trees provided summertime shade. The trees dropped small black and bitter fruit. In Spain and Greece, I learned that the olives had to be aged in brine to be edible. The trees felt at home in Upland.

Los Olivos was Upland's barrio. I rode my bike from home to home leaving newspapers on doorsteps. Mrs. Hernandez insisted, "Come in. I won't pay you unless you come in." I was shy, but I wanted to be paid. When I crossed the threshold seven daughters were lined up oldest to youngest. Seven giggle attacks. As I took my money and ran, Mrs. Hernandez scolded, "You scared him." I understood Spanish.

The barrio was surrounded by "the field," a dry patch of desert weeds. There was also cactus; the kind that were round and tall, and the short flat ones. Jack rabbits and dogs loved the field, as did kids. As I rode down the block, I noticed a dark Mexican man with a straw hat sitting on his kitchen porch. He had a bucket of flat cactus and he was cutting out the stickers one by one. I thought, "He must be really poor to eat cactus." Now my wife and I buy nopales, already spineless, from a Mexican store in San Francisco's Mission district. We follow the recipes passed down from my wife's mother and grandmother.

Parking places in Los Olivos were crowded with classic Fords and Chevys, all lovingly decorated. They had moon hubcaps, lots of chrome, fringe in all the appropriate places, and bobbing hula dolls with lights that flashed red. Occasionally, there were orange and yellow flames painted as if coming from the engine. Some cars were muffler free, announcing their presence like roaring lions. The cars were products of the vocational arts program at Upland High School.

As I continued my bicycle journey, I noticed an old truck with splintery plywood side panels and benches in the back. A hand lettered sign announced, *Salida*. I had learned a new Spanish word, "Exit." I sensed that the men worked in the orange groves. I sensed heavy work under heavy sun. The men lived in the broken-down houses that were on the dirt streets outside the barrio. Their homes were surrounded by cactus forests.

My last stop was at Rosa Gonzales' house. I watched her drop a tortilla on the gas flame, and then nimbly flip it without burning her fingers. I could not imagine what possessed her to do such a thing. It made more sense when she dropped a spoonful of beans in the tortilla and then another spoonful of nopales. When I make a taco snack, I add a bit of cheese and a sprinkle of chile. Rosa was older than me. I was too young to recognize her beauty. She was always out of money, so I had to come back several times to get paid. I did not worry overly much because I knew what being broke was all about. My dad was often broke. But after Rosa got way, way behind I stopped dropping newspapers on her porch. Many months after, the newspaper supervisor handed me an envelope of cash. "Pennies from Heaven. Rosie paid her bill." So, she was honest as well as beautiful. I remember Rosa's pleasant personality.

I rode across the line from Los Olivos to the Anglo part of town.

Christmas

I had graduated to a bike. My dad promised to take off the training wheels as soon as I could ride. That was two days later.

My dad took airplanes apart so that they could fly. I wanted to be like my dad, so I got into my dad's toolbox and started to take apart my bike. He was annoyed that he had to do extra work, but he was proud that I took an early interest in his craft.

The car's engine was emptied out. Car parts were spread across the garage floor. My dad explained that he was doing a complete overhaul. He was hoping that the car would last for another hundred thousand miles. My dad had buckets full of parts for all kinds of mechanical devices. He could have restarted the Industrial Revolution with what we had in our garage.

My dad had a bicycle frame stripped down to the bare metal. Later he explained, "The paint is baked on, just like for cars. And this is an old sprocket with new chrome." He showed me how to squeeze grease around the ball bearings. It was gross, but I understood that the bearings had to roll so that the bike could go.

On Christmas Eve, my dad took me to the garage. He lifted me onto the bike. My mom was upset because I could not reach the pedals. I would grow into it. My mom did not know how to take things apart and put them back together.

Benito Juarez

El respeto al derecho ajeno es la paz. Peace is the respect of the right of another.

Benito Juarez emphasized *ajeno*, which might be translated as "*another person*," "a foreigner," "a stranger," or as "an alien." None of these choices are as strong as they need to be. In Spanish *ajeno* is poetic and politically powerful. "Respect" is an easier word, but we should think biblically, respect for our neighbor.

The seeds of these thoughts were sown when I was in fifth grade at Upland Elementary School. There was a mural by the Works Progress Administration (WPA) on the outside wall of the auditorium. It showed men hefting large boxes of oranges in a grove, and a surveyor dividing the land. The surveyor was dividing land that had been taken from people who did not want to give it up. All the people in the mural were Anglo; none were Mexican – people who had come from Mexico or who had been here since before the Treaty of Guadalupe Hidalgo. There was probably a small inheritance from the California indigenous peoples.

The Mexican store was across the street from my school. We could not go there during the school day, but the sun was dropping to the horizon. We rode our bikes into the orange grove, which was shady and much cooler than by day. The wagon track led to a small gray store with splintered plywood walls and a porch. The store was labeled *La Reforma* which led me to believe that something had been reformed, but what?

Grandma had pigtails and looked like the indigenous women in Diego Rivera paintings who sold flowers, but I did not know that at the time. We bought Abba Zabas (three cents each), licorice (two cents), and little wax bottles with sweet juice (one cent). I got the impression that Grandma and Grandpa did not speak a word of English, but candy selling does not require high foreign language skills. Grandma worked a hand pulled adding machine. Urban legend said that Grandma never tore off the used receipts. A snake of paper tape coiled on the floor. Our bikes got us home before dark.

Before leaving, I looked back at the sign, *La Reforma*. Once again, I wondered what was being reformed and why.

Grandpa George

Grandpa George had come to America from Paris around 1895. He was not thrilled with school. My great grandmother gave him an ultimatum: school or work. George and a friend rode their bikes from Los Angeles to the Mojave. After a few days, the friend returned. George stayed. He was self-supporting from age thirteen on.

Grandpa traded bike repair for rabbits and chickens. My auntie said that the family always had food, even during the Depression. In 1932, Grandpa bet that Roosevelt would win. George won a big, green, seriously industrial truck. A black collie, Skipper, always occupied the passenger seat.

When freezing temperatures came, the orchard owners lit smudge pots. Someone had to fill the pots with noxious oil that, when burned, would heat the air enough to save the harvest. This explained why Grandpa's truck smelled of oil, and why there was a smelly work shed on the back lot, and why there were old fashioned, broken down kerosene pumps in the yard. My auntie said that she dreaded the smudge pots.

I had saved enough money to buy the latest advance in bicycle technology: a ten speed. It had two gears in front and five in back with a derailleur to switch the gear combinations across multiple sprockets. The bike cost eighty dollars, which for me was a lot of money. I rode from home up the mountain to Baldy Village, and then, took advantage of the downhill slope to return. Along the way, I flipped but landed in a pile of sand; no damage to me or the bike.

The French have the *Tour de France* which I consider to be part of my heritage. The ride to the top of Mount Baldy was much shorter. An early version of the bicycle, a *Laufmaschine* "running machine" made its way to Versailles where it created a sensation when it was run across a drawing room. This story may be apocryphal, but then Versailles was known for sensation.

Bike Messenger

My friend Jill was Wonder Woman. After the Bay to Breakers, she asked how we were going to get home. I was about to collapse, so the MUNI was the obvious choice. "No way that I'm going to spend money. I can run home," which is exactly what she did. I ended up walking — slowly. MUNI was packed.

Jill had a job as a bike messenger. I came home to find that Jill had gone to a poetry reading in Mill Valley, which led me to mistakenly believe that she had a ride with someone. She had ridden her bike across the Golden Gate Bridge, up over Mount Tam, down Mount Tam, and then across town to the poetry reading. She came home along the same path, except in reverse order. She was a candidate for the *Tour de France*.

Jill took pride in her bicycle repair skills. Her disassembled bike was laid out on the kitchen floor. "I've fixed it and I'm going to put it back together, just like David." I asked innocently, already knowing the answer, "Jill, can you take apart and reassemble the derailleur?" After a moment of tense silence, she admitted, "No, only David can do that, but I'm going to learn." Jill was angry that a man could do something that she could not.

Bikes have a natural enemy – the car. As Jill was zipping down Market Street, a car door opened. Jill ended up at UC Med. She claimed that the orthopedist's name was Dr. Crusher, information which I received skeptically. Now broke and unable to work, she asked with great irritation, "You know what this means?" I let her tell me. "It means that I'll have to go home to my parents. Yuck." Jill had one good hand to steer with and one hand on the mend that could work an automatic transmission.

Jill got a drive away car. The two hands working carefully together could build a campfire. Jill stayed at National Parks until Mom and Dad took her in.

Critical Mass

Roaring trucks monopolized the road. Undefeated, the bikes crept along the margins, tactfully encouraging the trucks to alter their path by a few centimeters. As more bikes gathered courage, the trucks grudgingly gave way. The tactic was Critical Mass, a phrase taken from physics. Critical Mass originated in China and crossed the Pacific to San Francisco.

Bikes first tried the democratic process, but without success. Cars had a firm grip on power. Bikes demanded their natural right of safe, free movement. Cars refused compromise, so bikes turned to guerrilla action, meeting at the Embarcadero on the last Friday of each month. As the bike crowd grew, bikes began to circulate randomly. They began to gather like an amoeba that extended pseudopodia up the streets until cars forced them back. When the critical mass became large enough, it captured first one block, then another, and finally an entire street, a victory that *guerrilleros* from around the world could appreciate.

Any car with common sense would take cover during Critical Mass hours. One limo was a failure in the common sense department and was captured by Critical Mass as if in quicksand. Mayor Willie Brown was unhappy. He demanded an event more to his liking, insisting on meetings with the leaders of Critical Mass. What the mayor overlooked was that Critical Mass had no leaders; it was self-organized. The mayor appeared at the Embarcadero to show that he was still in charge. He was not well received. The warring parties agreed to an armistice.

Blessings

It was a bright day in San Francisco, October 4th, the Feast Day of Francis of Assisi, and the day on which the animals were to receive a special blessing. The priest was vested. He was assisted by an altar server in black and white robes who held a silver bowl of holy water and a silver sprinkler.

People began to gather with their pets – reasonably well behaved – on the steps of Mission Dolores. Under his breath the priest commented, "I can't believe that so many people still come to these, but since everyone is here, I'll do it." The priest began with a reading from Genesis. Then he opened the Book of Blessings, and continued:

The animals of God's creation inhabit the skies, the earth, and the sea. They share in the ways of human beings. They have a part in our lives. Francis of Assisi recognized this when he called the animals, wild and tame, his brothers and sisters. Remembering Francis' love for these brothers and sisters of ours, we invoke God's blessing on these animals, and we thank God for letting us share the earth with all His creatures.

The tradition of the Blessing of the Animals has spread from Assisi to many of today's denominations. My Alabama cousin reports that:

Many years ago, the Catholic church held a Blessing of the Animals on campus in the outdoor amphitheater. People came from miles around with horses, chickens, and whatever. At the time we had a bull mastiff puppy that was incorrigible, and we felt she needed all the blessings she could get. So, these good Methodists (now Presbyterian) took Honey Bear down for the event. She got blessed and nearly knocked over the pastor. I think he needed a blessing for being there.

Catholics go beyond blessing animals. Unabridged books of blessing offer prayers for the fishing fleet, as well as implements of agriculture such as plows. In Mexico, I saw a blessing of a brand-new pick-up truck. The proud new owner insisted that the priest lift the hood to bless the engine.

There are also blessings of the bikes, usually attended by exercise enthusiasts and bicycle messengers. I have never seen a bike blessing, so I presume that they are rare. However, the internet suggests possibilities if you are eager to take your bike across America.

I have, however, seen a blessing of the motorcycles. I was at mass when a herd of bikes roared by and then kept circling. I thought, "How rude!" At the end of the mass there was a phalanx of guys in black leather and helmets in the back of the church. I thought that we were in for a rumble. The leader politely approached the priest and explained that they were recreational.

The priest accepted their apology and offered an impromptu blessing which they gratefully accepted. The bike leader suggested that since they were roaring through California and visiting Missions along the way, perhaps it would be appropriate to bless their bikes, too. The priest sent for a bowl of holy water and the silver sprinkler. He blessed bikes and riders that they might have a safe journey.

Compassion...
by Sylvia Nelson Clarke

Comes from an
    Omnipotent God's
        Marvelous
           Patient
                Attributes and
                    Saving
                        Self-sacrifice
                            Intended for
                                Our
                                    Needs —

And is
                      Grounded in LOVE!

Miracle in the Rocks

BY SYLVIA NELSON CLARKE

"Mom, can you sit up?" Julia's words penetrated my confused brain. Where was I? Why did I hurt? I slowly opened my eyes. Above me, huge granite boulders blocked the view. Lifting my head, I saw sunlight streaming through a couple of gaps and filling the level I was on with daylight. At my daughter's urging, I struggled to sit up and slowly moved to my left onto a rock where I could rest my back against a wall. "You fell, Mom. Where do you hurt?" Julia snagged my attention again.

Julia, my husband Wil, and I were in Joshua Tree National Park scrambling on the rocks with Wil's brother Elwood, his wife Kathy, and grandson Seth. The climb was familiar to the two brothers, but it was my first attempt at this place. We chose to do one climb before lunch. The last thing I remembered was looking for a good handhold near a hole in the rocks so I could get out of a crouched position and move upward.

Now, in spite of the pain, I found comfort in the fact that our daughter Julia, a trained first responder, stood near me, shielding my face from the sun. She had debated whether or not to go with us on this excursion. I thank God she did. Soon she was joined by A.J., a young woman trained in emergency response that Wil met in the parking lot on his way to get the car to drive for help. A.J. volunteered to help and kept me talking while more emergency personnel gathered.

Our family has visited Joshua Tree National Park hundreds of times over the last 30 years, starting when it was still a Monument. The huge rock formations reminded Wil and Elwood of the ones they climbed in Rhodesia during childhood, so it became a favorite area for a day of picnicking and climbing or hiking. We often brought others with us to enjoy the spectacular scenery and invigorating climbs up different groups of rocks and invested in shoes with special soles that helped us — and them — stick to the rock surfaces.

As I sat under those huge boulders, fading in and out of consciousness, I knew God's protection had been with me in my fall because I was still alive. I smiled as I told those who began to gather in the space near me, "My angel must have guided my fall, or I'd be dead." [The next day, brother-in-law Elwood returned and measured the distance of my fall — 30 feet!]

Meanwhile, Wil drove to the Hidden Valley area where, on our way into the park, we had seen Search and Rescue volunteers promoting their organization. That was providential since we had never seen them there before. When Wil interrupted, "Excuse me, but my wife has fallen!" one of them immediately picked up a radio and called the rangers and helicopter. Had they not been there, Wil might have needed to drive to the park entrance gate, another 20 to 30 minutes away.

God must have known Kathy needed to go with Wil. She knew the name of the parking lot near where I went down, Wil didn't! So the woman on the radio could give the location of my accident. A nearby park ranger heard that call and pulled into the parking lot just after Wil. He was able to give me aid in addition to what AJ had done. Later, I learned that before long two fire trucks and an ambulance showed up. When it arrived, the helicopter also landed in that lot because the pilot found no place nearer.

Little by little, more people climbed down into the space near me. My dear Wil even had a chance to come and tell me, "At first I thought you were dead!" and rejoice that I wasn't. Soon, however, the EMT sitting in front of me sent Julia and Wil away to make room for those who would help get me out of there. Wil disappeared, but I watched Julia successfully climb up a difficult way, thankful her muscles and shoes kept her from falling. She told me later that at least five people waited along the route where she had entered, so she tackled the more challenging exit.

Time meant little to me in my injured state, especially after the medicine those wonderful emergency individuals gave me took effect. In all about three hours passed before the responders had me fastened to a board and handed me off to those waiting inside and outside the rocks to rescue me. Only snippets of memory stay with me:

Blue sky above as I emerged into the open

Strong arms holding and guiding me down to the ground

The smooth ride as several carried me away from the rocks

Glimpses of desert plants along the path toward the helicopter

Sliding into the middle of the helicopter near its ceiling.

Once on our way in the helicopter, I really noticed the name on the shirt of the EMT who had been in charge — S. Clarke! "That's my name! Sylvia Clarke — Clarke with an E," I exclaimed. His seat in the helicopter faced me, and I learned his name was Stephen Clarke. *"Wow,"* I thought, *"Isn't that just like God to send someone to help with the same last name as mine!"*

Post Script: When he learned I had lost my glasses during my fall, Elwood returned a week later. His daughter Sonya found my glasses — intact, under a rock about five feet below where I landed. Talk about miracles!

Petition in Song
by Sylvia Nelson Clarke

How can I praise You, Lord?
    How can I raise You, O Lord,
        where You belong
        in heart and song?
    How can I please You today?

Come, Lord, and fill my mind
    with Your gentleness so kind
        so all I meet
        I'll surely treat
    As Your children on the way.

Your love runs very deep,
    Your power able to keep
        my steps aright
        both day and night
    Strengthen me now to obey.

May I be quick to hear
    slow to anger and fear
        Guard what I say;
        teach me to pray.
    Forever friends let us stay —
Forever friends in Your sway!

Massachusetts Ice Storm
by Sylvia Nelson Clarke

Day three — weighted, brittle —
    Fantasy fairyland glitters
    Powerlines, road signs
    Drip icicle fringes

Crystal branches bow low
    Buds all encased in icy coats
    Tree chandeliers
    Reflect surrounding lights

Cars wear white moustaches
    Houses slipping toupees
    Dogs slither on slick snow
    To their favorite trees

Pain, Prayer, and Praise

by Sylvia Nelson Clarke

When we lived in Massachusetts, one of my sweet friends was Agnes, a grandmother who volunteered in her granddaughter's classroom at the school our daughters attended. Like Wil and I, she and her late husband had served as missionaries in Africa, so we had much in common. I always enjoyed my visits with her. I recorded the following story in my journal after she told it.

Agnes Vixie called this morning to tell me she will be gone for a month to stay with a dear friend in the South somewhere. Among other things, she shared an experience she had recently. During spring break, when her granddaughter and family were in Florida and her daughter and husband in California at a convention, she came down with the flu. One night painful cramping in her toes and lower legs jolted her awake. She struggled out of bed and walked around her apartment for a while, praying, "Lord, take away the pain — please!"

When she lay down again, her whole legs began to cramp, and the pain was worse than ever. "Oh Lord, if you don't want to take the pain away right now, just help me to bear it," she prayed. A Bible text popped into her mind, "Sing unto the Lord"[1]. So in her pain she began to sing "What a Friend We Have in Jesus."[2] By the time she had sung the very next line, "All our sins and griefs to bear", the pain was gone.

"Maybe I'm childish," Agnes confided, "and some would call it just happenstance, but I believe God took the pain away when I sang!"

"I agree," I replied. "I'm sure this is one way God wants us to be like little children, humble and trusting[3] — believing He does help."

1   Psalm 96:2
2   John M. Scriven, 1855
3   Matthew 18:3, 4

Benign Prostate Hypoplasia — 2004

by Wil Clarke

Grampa came to live with us around 1950. I remember that he suffered from BPH. He would typically take 20 minutes to void his bladder. As a child, I would stand in the bathroom and watch the painful procedure. He explained it as an old man's disease.

His problem hit me just about the time I turned 50. It only got worse and worse until at one point I couldn't pee at all. Sylvia took me in to the ER. They inserted a catheter, and I got instant relief and an intimate knowledge of a catheter.

My urologist at the time was Dr. Sidharth Avatar (name changed). He explained to me that I had several choices. I could have the TURP procedure, have microwave treatment, or take lots of drugs. Dad had had the TURP procedure, which he referred to as "Roto-Rooter." That didn't sound very exciting, nor did the drug treatment. So, I hemmed and hawed until Dr. Avatar said, "OK, I'm scheduling you for a microwave treatment next Friday!"

Friday, I showed up and dressed in the usual hospital "gown." I lay on my back on the table, and Dr. Avatar and his nurse spread my legs and inserted a device and thrust it in the same way one uses a catheter. He positioned the narrow end almost into my bladder and turned it on. He then instructed me not to move and walked out. His nurse remained with me. I lay on the table, legs spread, uncovered from the waist down and feeling the heat building.

Pretty soon several other women from the office area, including the receptionist, the appointment clerk, the cashier, and the recorder, walked in for the show. They were all less than half my age. They jostled each other to get the best view of my nether regions as they sat on chairs or cabinets chattering merrily with each other. They reminded me of Romans gathering in the coliseum to watch a lion devour a Christian.

I was mortified and humiliated. My attention was focused on the almost unbearable pain I was experiencing as this device slow-cooked my insides. I knew it would be this way for 20 long minutes. I also knew I had the full attention of the women: Every time I made the slightest move to try vainly to ease my suffering, they would call out in chorus "Don't move!"

The minutes crept by like hours. It seemed every cell in my body was screaming in pain. My audience loved every wince or moan. I was making their day. I imagine they went home that evening and described to their significant other every twitch and groan; how every red hair started to glow and smoke from the heat; how my very privates wilted and shriveled.

After it was over the doctor pulled out the instrument of torture and shoved in a catheter. He told me to leave the catheter in place and empty the urine collection bag as needed. My audience melted away. He then told me to come back on Tuesday and he would remove the catheter. I crept out of there as though I was a little boy who had just been caught in the women's restroom.

On Tuesday, I came back as instructed. Without ado, he told me to drop my pants. Then I stood astride a pan. Using scissors, he niftily cut the tube that secured the catheter in my bladder, and it slithered silently down into the pan.

Smiling broadly, he told me in triumph, "You'll be happy to know that I have just obtained a new microwave device that is entirely painless! No one else will ever have to feel the pain."

He looked into my face expecting a great sharing of his joy. Instead he saw my face screw up in fierce wrath. He watched me clench my fists and saw the extreme mental anguish I was having trying to resist hitting him very hard. I started to yell, "Why the

…" and bit my tongue.

Avatar suddenly realized the needless, inhuman, torture he had wreaked on me. He understood that he was in personal danger from my anger. Quickly changing the subject, he started to give me further instructions. Needless to say, I heard nothing he said and stormed out of his office in unrequited fury.

Cycling in Ndola, Zambia 1961

by Wil Clarke

During the summer of 1960-1961, I was a colporteur, selling books in the city of Ndola, Zambia to earn tuition money for college the next year. A generous stranger heard of my project and that I needed wheels to get around. He offered to lend me his bicycle since he planned to be out of town that summer.

It was a really beautiful racing bike made of ultralight aluminum. The handle-bars reached out and then curved down in true racing style so that when I wanted to go fast, I could clutch the lower parts, bend my whole body to make the least wind-resistance, and put the most force on the pedals. I carried samples of my books in a leather briefcase. I would hook the top of the case over the crossbar and latch it on the other side. The case would nestle securely on the two frames below so it couldn't be moved without my unlatching it.

The pedals were permanently in high speed mode, making climbing hills tough but regular street riding fast. One time I was riding down a street where cars were going fairly fast. I rode along with them, and out of curiosity, I pulled into the center of the street and rode up next to a car going my speed. I peered into the window at the car's speedometer. I was doing over 40 mph. The driver looked up and about had a heart attack to see a cyclist overtaking him and close enough for him to touch.

The extra light rims and tires were very narrow and rounded so that I could lay the bike over for cornering, and they wouldn't let go of the pavement. One time I needed to turn across the oncoming lane of traffic. I should have slowed down, but I sped up, and as soon as the oncoming car went past me, I laid the bike over really hard. Ahead of me the curb came at me with blinding speed. I slammed hard on the rear brake, expecting the wheel to lock and the back tire to skid around so I wouldn't hit the curb head on. Indeed, the back wheel locked but clung tenaciously to the tar. I crashed, taking a bunch of skin off my arms and legs. Then I looked at the bike. The rear wheel had bent almost at a right angle.

"Oh no!" were my first thoughts. "What's the owner going to say about my wrecking his bike?" I sat on the curb with the wreck in my lap. I was a long way from my apartment, and I didn't want to carry the bike and the briefcase all that way. I grabbed the rear rim with both hands and stuck my knee into the hub. Then I pulled with all my might. Being of that light material, the wheel straightened out nicely.

No! Not nicely. But it straightened out enough so that it would actually turn. Part of the time it would rub on the left rear fork and part of the time on the right rear fork. I picked up the briefcase, repacked the books and latched it on the frame; then I got on, and it held me. I found I could ride it. It wound a snaking trail down the road, squealing and squeaking, but at least it made progress. I went directly home. My landlady took pity on me, washed and bandaged my wounds, and served me tea.

The next day, I took it down to a bicycle shop. The mechanic looked at it in dismay. Then he put it in a vice and got out his spoke tool and spent an hour tightening and loosening the appropriate spokes to bring the wheel back to true form. Finally, he gave me back the bike.

"That's the best I can do, Boss. You need a new wheel."

"Well, do you have a new wheel?" I queried, knowing full well I didn't have enough cash to pay for one.

"No, Boss. That is a very special bicycle. But it will go now without rubbing on the forks."

Thanking him, I paid him, and snaked the bike back home. I continued selling books for the rest of the summer but rode much more sanely and carefully from then on. It was through my landlady that I had borrowed that bike.

I never met the bike's owner. When the summer ended, I left the bike with my landlady with a note of thanks to the bike's owner and an offer to pay for fixing his bike. He responded that he never rode the bike anymore and didn't really want to ride it again. He didn't want me to pay him for it. I have eternal gratitude to both my landlady and the bike's owner.

Mountain Passes Near Cape Town

BY WIL CLARKE

In 2008, we spent about a week with Lincoln and Rosemary Raitt who live near Cape Town, South Africa. On one day Lincoln suggested we should take a six mountain passes tour of the Western Cape. Two of these passes are on 4-lane highways. The other four are very scenic winding mountain roads.

The first pass we took was Sir Lowry's Pass on the 4-lane national road N-2 going east out of Cape Town. A viewpoint at the summit of the pass, usually frequented by a rather pesky pack of baboons, provides a great view of Helderberg Mountain where I grew up, the Hottentots Holland Range, with Cape Town and Table Mountain in the distance. The second pass, called Viljoen's Pass; is probably the least strenuous pass and goes through lush Western Cape fynbos flowering plants and shrubs. The third is the Franschhoek Pass and affords a magnificent view of the local wine country.

Lincoln suggested that we eat at a high-end restaurant near the Huguenot Memorial in Franschhoek at the bottom of the Franschhoek Pass. Although it was midwinter, the sun was warm, and we seated ourselves at an outdoor table and looked at the menu. Sylvia ordered a vegetarian salad. I said to her, "I think I'll order the springbuck — South Africa's National Animal." The waitress took our order and disappeared into the kitchen.

After a bit, I asked the folks sitting at the next table how long they had been waiting for their order. "Almost an hour!" the woman sighed. The servings, delivered on huge plates, were rather meager in quantity but very artistically arranged.

An hour later, the waitress showed up with Sylvia's order. It too was somewhat meager but very artistically presented. I was getting rather chafed under the collar at this whole palaver. I suggested that Sylvia not start eating until I had been served. She understood my feelings.

When my plate arrived, it had one thin slice of springbuck and a few vegetables. I looked at it and felt instant revulsion well up in my stomach. The meat was completely raw! It had never seen a flame.

I called the waitress back and pointed out that if I had known she wasn't going to cook the meat, I wouldn't have ordered it. She argued rather brazenly for a few minutes until I demanded that she take the plates back.

She said, "Wait!" and disappeared into the kitchen.

Five minutes or so later she came back and reported, "The maitre d' said, 'Well, you'll just have to order something else!'"

I looked her in the face and said forcefully, "And wait another hour — No! I won't!" and we got up and left.

It was mid-afternoon by this time, and all the restaurants in town were closed. We finally stopped at a grocery store in Paarl and bought a few provisions to tide us over until supper.

We drove on up Du Toitskloof Pass on the 4-lane national highway N-1 going to Johannesburg. It delivers a magnificent view of Paarl Mountain where the Afrikaans Language Monument stands, probably the only monument in the world to a language. It also provides a great view of Cape Town and Table Mountain in the distance. Then we headed over the very narrow and poorly maintained Bain's Kloof Pass down into Wellington. Finally, we drove down over Helshoogte Pass into Stellenbosch and from there back to the Raitts in Kuilsriver.

Our experience just reinforced my determination to beware of touristy-artsy places. When he heard our dinner story, Lincoln was apologetic, remarking, "I've never tried the place. I just thought it looked interesting."

Darkness and Light

according to

Moses, Job, David, Isaiah, John, Paul, Mohammad, and Madeleine L'Engle

BY AMY CLAYTON

Let there be light
There was morning
The first day
Take the wings of the morning
The darkness did not overcome it
It covered the face of the earth
Surely the darkness shall cover me
Settle at the farthest limits of the sea
The darkness has brought on blindness
The darkness of indifference and evil
Whoever hates another is in darkness
Hold us fast
We were formerly darkness
Woven in the depths of the earth
Those who lived in a land of deep darkness
Walk as children of light
On them light has shined
The true light is already shining
The life was the light of all people
A living fire to lighten the darkness
Light upon light

In a glass, the oil of the olive tree gives light though fire does not touch it

A brightly shining star, a lamp in a niche

Where is the way to the dwelling of the light?

In the Garden
by Amy Clayton

Lug dirt and hose, mud
Making transplant
Shocking deep
Watering

Mixing browns and greens, soil
Making life changing
trash into

Hope keeping mind
Heart circling
Yard checking
Salvias inhaling

At the sink
Brush and soap
Smudged and sweaty
I stand

Creations
by Amy Clayton

Emerge through evolution
chilly darkness to healing warmth
Sources swirl now
A timeless pursuit cycles within
Packed, crumbed, flowed in hand
Elder lore and lab science dance in practice

The Inequality of Masks
by Deenaz P. Coachbuilder

The first facial mask was invented in England during the 18th century by Madame Rowley for women to preserve their complexion. Even the ancient Egyptians, conscious of keeping skin moist under the burning sun, kept serum in their tombs to ease their journey into the next world. Virginia Wolf wished for women to have "a room of one's own", a space that no one could invade, where one could, if one desired, exfoliate to one's heart's content.

Being naturally oily of skin, I follow in their footsteps by using a charcoal mask once a week, luxuriating under its cool touch upon my skin, as an aroma of lavender hovers around me, lying in bed so the liquid does not drip into my collar, reading, for twenty peaceful moments. My grandmother kept sachets of dry lavender flowers among her linen. When we spent summers with her as children, I would bury my nose into the pillow on my bed and float away in its fragrance.

In order to stay as far away as possible from the COVID-19, I remain at home, do not visit grocery stores as advised, nor socialize with friends. My son and husband secure some of our provisions. Necessity is the mother… so I have learned to order online via Instacart, a most useful service, or the grocery stores' delivery systems.

Where we live in Riverside, California, masks are mandatory when stepping outdoors, no matter the purpose. I have a white mask, light, soft, easy to wear, it hooks over my ears. My husband Pheroze' is black. I keep mine in a plastic bag. But these are functional, not cosmetic masks. The only time I wear this mask is when the two of us take our daily walk. We step onto Breckenridge Avenue, a quiet cul-de-sac. Turn left onto Overlook Boulevard. The street is tree lined: crepe myrtles, eucalypti and oaks. The landscape winds around walkways decorated with rock rose and Indian hawthorn bushes bordered by violet colored society garlic.

My mask covers my nose and mouth. I hardly notice it as we walk downhill. Uphill is different, as my breathing becomes strained. When I approach the upper bend that turns right towards home, I slip the mask a bit lower, allowing the air to flow into my impatient nostrils, my heart thumping. Our mid-morning walk is often a solitary one, only Sundays brings out the venturesome. The sound of an occasional car as it saunters uphill breaks this serenity.

To help mitigate COVID-19 transmission, and focus medical resources on emergency patients, the State of California cancelled all elective medical procedures. They have now, in April 2020, been allowed to resume. A dear friend Harkeerat Dhillon, M.D., who has recently recuperated from a serious illness, will commence performing orthopedic surgeries at a clinic a few miles away. Clad in protective garb, he will be in physical contact with his patients: caring for them, medically and emotionally. He tells me he will be as careful as he can and "leave the rest in the hands of God". Another very close friend, Khushro Unwalla, M.D. is assigned to San Bernardino County Hospital, in Colton. He has a severe upper respiratory problem.

I worry about them and all responders present when ambulances wail, working with loved ones, parents and grandparents — the keepers of our memory, our youth, our children. They speak to us of the pain and hubbub surrounding them. We pray for their safety.

As we shelter in place, I find myself texting and making more phone calls than ever before. "Are you wearing your mask?" I ask. "Why not have the grocery stores deliver," I suggest. First responders hook on their masks as they step outside their door in the early morning, until their return at night. Pheroze' and my masks are worn for a short half hour.

As we walk, the fragrance of newly awakened buds is everywhere, Mary Oliver's "wild high music of smell…"

Believe

by Deenaz P. Coachbuilder

Soon,
Americans
will fall in love again
as Americans.
Soon,
there will come a time
when the air
that surrounds us
is no longer turbulent
but calm.
We will not be
worn out
before the sun
lights the sky at noon
nor wonder what
news the dawn brings.
That treadmill
will halt
its dusty
rust-clogged tracks,
gradually covered
with the verdant
freshness of a
new
before.

We have been awakened
to the pain of inequality,
the despair of injustice.
We long for
and recognize
the beauty of the ordinary,
an ordinary
that will transform
into the extraordinary
to include
all
as America's wounds
are made whole again.

Soon,
the soul of the nation
will return
to its
beating heart.

Written on October 23rd. 2020 as Americans prepare to vote for the next administration, and amid the scourge of COVID-19.

Timeless Music

by Deenaz P. Coachbuilder

It was Seattle in the summer, when the city is a magnet for entertainment of all kinds. Downtown celebrates the culture of its residents, the traditions of immigrants from India, Turkey, Sweden, Somalia, and a multitude of other countries; their food, music, dance and literature. Lovers of ballet throng to enchanting evenings presented by the Pacific North West Ballet. The weekly theater productions are so numerous, it would take a page to count them, from community presentations to the superb displays of professional performances in storied halls like the Paramount Theater and 5th. Avenue.

My favorite is the Seattle Symphony that is a permanent inhabitant of the truly beautiful Benaroya Hall. It takes my husband Pheroze and I half an hour to get from our condo to our seats, well before curtain call. It was 2016. The Music Director was Ludovic Morlot. The opening piece of the recital was said to be the Overture to Wagner's Tannhauser, according to the program that I had perused. The overture is one of my favorites, and I was looking forward to the evening. We stood respectfully for the national anthem, then settled comfortably into our seats.

The overture opens with a very slow sustained crescendo. It represents pilgrims approaching, ever louder, as they journey towards Rome. Suddenly, tears well into my eyes and start coursing down my face. Embarrassed, I try to wipe them away, unsuccessfully. I am instantaneously transported on the wings of music across a span of decades, to a quiet family dinner in our Mumbai, India home. My father Barjor, my mom Freiny, my brother Shahrukh, and I are beginning dinner, seated at the long black glass topped dining table where sprinkles of light drops reflect the chandeliers above. Ceiling fans cool the evening. No noise from the garden outside disturbs us.

It is my responsibility, one that I delight in, to select and arrange about four long playing records that the record player will play sequentially. That night the first musical piece is Tannhauser. We cherish these weekday dinners as a family. This is a time when we share the experiences of our busy day, and feel a sense of closeness. I was back again in the arms of my family, nostalgia staining my wet cheeks, with the musical chords of that familiar overture reverberating in my soul.

Why was I crying? It is hard to tell. There was a deep sadness that filled every pore of me. Perhaps I missed the family togetherness of those days. My father introduced me to the world of classical music. We had explored Wagner together while reading *the Lord of the Rings*. I left India in 1967 on a journey to the U.S. with the goal of continuing my studies. I did not know that I would never see my dear twenty-two-year-old brother and only sibling again. He was my trusted and best friend. His was an accidental death in Yenna Lake, Mahabaleshwar, in 1968. Over the years, I returned to Mumbai with my own family, my husband and two sons, to spend the summers with my parents. I missed his presence. Perhaps it was a recognition of the long journey I had taken, like Tannhauser's pilgrims, halfway around the world to the other side of the planet.

Back at Benaroya, I succeed in choking back those tears, patting my face with a now soaking tissue, and reaching out to hold Pheroze's hand for comfort.

Ridiculously Delicious Dinner
by Elinor Cohen

We pulled up in front of the restaurant and realized we were in for a long wait. This spot was hot! The location is fantastic, famously "just 8 doors down from the Venice Pier" at the beach, practically right on the sand. After dodging the valet and finding a place to park two and a half blocks away, we joined the line in progress. Hungry, eager, our stomachs began to rumble and shout. "Feed me!" I could hear mine yell among all the gurgling. Just then, an angelic boy wearing a crisp collared shirt appeared holding a tray of glistening garlic knots. "Killer Garlic Rolls?" he asked sweetly. OMG yes. Marry me, garlic bread boy? When we were seated at last, our server explained the red wine honor system. We'd help ourselves from the spout on the wall, and keep track by marking our paper table cloth with crayons. Yeah, we drank wall spout wine. Like some kind of barbarians. The wine was hearty, robust, a bit thick, warm going down the throat. What did it taste like? House Red. I drew a cartoon self portrait on the edge of the tablecloth with a stick figure arm holding glasses of wine to mark my drunken momentum. I only got to two glasses. Don't worry, despite having green and blue crayons at my disposal, I colored the wine glasses red, nothing too radical or avantgarde.

Looking around, the decor was nice, casual, crowded, well-lit. Murals of old Italy painted on the walls, with smiling signoras hanging laundry on balcony lines as ivy and white lilies climb up around them. More signature garlic rolls arrived to the table, then salad with an unfortunate number of iceberg lettuce spines, see-through and grayish, layered beneath slices of vine-ripened tomatoes and sweet Maui onion. I was really getting down with the balsamic vinaigrette dressing. But then came the sing-a-long.

Service stopped cold. Laminated song lyric sheets were passed around, and from speakers hidden in the ceiling, the familiar cooing of Dean Martin, doing his best Louis Prima: When the moon hits your eye like a big pizza pie, that's amore. Did you hear me? That's amore! They're all singing. All of them. Then comes the clapping of hands, thunderous clapping, and the, wait is it some kind of line dancing?

Finally, it's here. Rigatoni in a vodka cream sauce. The waitress says something but I don't hear her. She's holding a plastic magic wand that explodes fresh parmesan from its mouth. I nod excitedly and watch the cheese pieces rain down like tiny meteorites. Come on out, parmy, join the party! Then, I take a bite. This sauce is so goddamn creamy, it's like a warm hug. Around my taste buds. Like wearing a cable knit sweater on a cool cloudy Nantucket day (no, I've never actually been to Nantucket. I think it might be in Massachusetts or Rhode Island?). The color — it's sunrise over the ancient Mayan temple ruins of Tikal (yes I've been there! It's in Guatemala! For real!). (Side note, I ate weird spaghetti marinara in rural Guatemala at the one and only restaurant serving food during the daily siesta. It came with plantains and black beans.) But the sauce… a coral pink hue with darker swirls of salmon pumpkin cantaloupe. The rigatoni: ever so slightly al dente and just right, like when you cook it exactly one minute longer than the package suggests. Each hollow noodle tube heavy with swirly sunrise sauce. But where's the vodka? Can't taste it. Promise it's in there?

The fresh basil: cut with scissors, not torn by hand, shaped into perfect little rectangles and squares. So tangy and tart, almost refreshingly minty. I can smell it, savory and sweet. (Did you know that humans can only decipher five basic tastes like bitter, sour, salty, and sweet, but we can recognize like millions of aromas? I bet maybe you did know that.) Anyway, this portion is huge. Absolutely no room in my belly for Chef's Classic Tiramisu dessert. I'll have lunch leftovers tomorrow for sure. Will I have the patience to wait and warm it up in the toaster oven or will I scarf it cold straight from the foil-lined paper container?

Were this a traditional restaurant review, I would mention that C+O is open for lunch and dinner seven days a week, plus breakfast on weekends and holidays. They accept all major credit cards, have a beautiful outdoor heated patio, and they threw damn good catered parties before the pandemic.

Confession: I ate here probably five times before I learned that C+O stood for Cheese + Olive. How splendid.

First Night in Copacabana
by Carlos Cortés

I'm thirty-three-years-old, and my wife and I are just moving into our Copacabana beach-front apartment in Rio de Janeiro. We've rented it sight-unseen from a U.S. Embassy official who has been assigned to Europe for two months. As we ride the cramped elevator to our eighth-floor apartment, I'm relishing the idea of the afternoon view from our balcony.

Oh . . . my . . . God! The enormous golden horseshoe of sand curving endlessly in both directions. The Atlantic Ocean pounding relentlessly into the beckoning enclosure. Hordes of surfers, sun worshippers, and volleyball players, punctuated by occasional capoeira dancers demonstrating their African-infused fighting skills for Sunday viewers. And, of course, packs of young, bikini-barely-clad girls — not yet women — pouring over from nearby Ipanema Beach.

I can't bring myself to unpack. No use wasting the sunshine. Should I go down and join in the festivities? No. It's too glorious just looking down. So I open a bottle of pre-mixed caipirinhas (Brazil's national drink, a margarita cousin) and settle in for hours of eye-balling.

As the sun sets and the sea of bodies begins to evaporate, I take stock of our setting. The modest, comfortably-furnished apartment — one bedroom, a small living room, an even-smaller kitchen, and a bathroom — is situated near the right edge of the oft-photographed Copacabana arc. To my left, the sand curves endlessly until it comes to a halt near Pão de Açucar, the majestic Sugarloaf Mountain jutting up sharply from the ocean. Less than fifty yards to my right sits fabled Fort Copacabana, a surprisingly tiny structure that still houses several handfuls of soldiers to protect Rio against...well, who knows?

The next morning, I will spot a group of soldiers playing volleyball on the beach. Although hesitant to disturb them, I will don a t-shirt and shorts and ask if I can join them. With classic Brazilian hospitality they will welcome me, and this break-of-dawn game will become a daily event before I head out to explore historical archives and interview Brazilian politicians. A great way to wind up my twenty-months of doctoral dissertation research in Brazil.

But that first night calls for a seafood dinner at a nearby oceanfront restaurant. It turns out to be muqueque de peixe, a succulent strip of whitefish smothered in a thick, spicy Bahaian cream sauce, with the sounds of bossa nova wafting down from a nearby bar. Accompanied by more caipirinhas, obviously. Who can turn down a good belt of cachaça, Brazil's potent fermented sugar cane liquor?

I sleep well. That is, I sleep well until I wake up at 3 a.m. to a deafening sound through my window. I go out onto the balcony and look down. An accident? A fight? A protest march against the military dictatorship? Nothing. Just the famous black-and-white curved mosaic sidewalk stretching the entire length of the beach. Then I realize the source of the noise. The ocean.

Its voice masked during the day by bumper-to-bumper traffic noise and the screams of reveling beach-swarmers, the ocean has now taken over with a vengeance. Erupting from unknowable distances, then funneled sharply into the compressed Copacabana horseshoe, the ocean emits an incessant roar as wave after wave pummel the beach and echo up the cement canyon of wall-to-wall hotels and apartment buildings that cover virtually every inch of the beach's elongated curve.

How can I sleep with this constant noise? Two months later I will be asking, how can I ever again sleep without it?

Güero

by Carlos Cortés

It hasn't always been fun being a güero. But it's been an interesting ride.

Güero is a Spanish term for a light-skinned Latino. That's me. It's what I get for being the son of an American-born Austro-Ukrainian mother and a Mexican immigrant father who insisted on naming his first son after himself, Carlos.

This meant walking around the rest of my life clad in white skin and bearing the name Carlos Cortés. Although my ethnically-proud father imbued me with pride in my Mexican ancestry, people who don't know me simply view me as some white dude. Most of the time I don't pay much attention to this clash of identity and perception. But every once in a while I find myself in situations where the clash is palpable.

Like those years at the University of California, Riverside, when I would walk into the first day of my Chicano History class knowing full well that many of the students would look at me with a mixture of puzzlement and dismay when I turned out to be the listed Carlos Cortés who was supposed to expose them to the experience of Mexican Americans.

Like teachers in school lounges prior to some of my multicultural education workshops, bitching in front of me about having to waste an hour listening to some Mexican and then dropping their jaws when that Mexican turned out to be the strange white guy who had been sitting in their lounge.

Like the emcee on a nationally-televised panel who thought he was being oh-so-clever when he said to me, "You don't look Mexican," a lazy remark I had heard only four thousand times before, to which I responded, "I guess you don't know many Mexicans."

Like the guy who invited me, sight unseen, to speak at a state-wide education conference and then, when I introduced myself, couldn't restrain himself and allowed the unedited words, "Oh, I was hoping for someone darker," to slip from his tongue. This permitted me to respond with a retort I had been saving for such an occasion: "This year I'm working on younger. Next year I'll work on darker."

Which leads me to a conundrum. What if my parents' ethnicities had been switched and I had been anointed Hoffman, my Russian immigrant grandfather's surname? Would I have grown up with an Eastern European Jewish identity? Would I have been appointed chair of Chicano Studies at UCR? Would I have become the Creative/Cultural Advisor of "Dora the Explorer?"

Maybe I would have just wandered through life as some ordinary white dude, without any güero stories to relate. How boring!

Interview With Laurel Vermilyea Cortés

BY LAUREL CORTÉS

Hi, I'm Carol Woodward. I'm here to discuss your work! I'll start with this question: Who is Laurel Vermilyea Cortés?

Wow. That's a hard one. But I guess in memoir it all starts and ends with that question. I'll take it literally. I've written about the fun I've had being named Laurel. I've also written a great deal over the years about my family name, Vermilyea. The *noir* master Raymond Chandler once dubbed one of his female characters, "The Vermilyea." I love that — "The Vermilyea."

Because I write mainly memoir stories, Vermilyea serves as topic or background to many of my pieces. As for Cortés, I have carried that name for the second half of my 80 years, having married my smiling best friend and trivia partner in 1978.

But who are you and what gives you the impetus to write on the topics you do?

To answer the last question first, I often write on a subject when I have three stories to join together. For instance, in *Soap Opera* I write a short history of soap and add a couple of soapy anecdotes from Istanbul and Meru National Park in Kenya. In *The Best-Fed Monarch*, I explore and compare the fascinating diets of Queen Elizabeth II and Henry VIII of England and Moctezuma II of the Aztec empire.

I write about family, food, music, the ocean, travel, life in the forties and fifties in Carlsbad…

And Oceanside.

Ah yes, my high school years — class of 1955! I lived in Carlsbad, which had no high school until 1958. (My brothers went to Carlsbad High as soon as it opened.) The oldest five siblings, all girls, went to Oceanside-Carlsbad Union High School. As is turned out, that became an important divisor as we grew up.

Why is that?

Well, because Oceanside is adjacent to Camp Pendleton, the town was much different from quiet, quaint Carlsbad — three miles to the south. The tattoo parlors, the bars — and at the beach, Marines! Surfing, beach volleyball, miniature golf, fishing off the Oceanside pier — the bus station (don't *ever* look in the telephone booths!); even the kind of movies offered were not family-oriented — lots of cowboy flicks, dramas, and war movies.

And O-C High was fully integrated. Our friends were Marine brats. They came from every social status, ethnicity, religion, from all over the country. Our friends were Japanese-Americans who had been in the interment camps as children. Our fullback hero was black: C.R. Roberts, who was high school All-American, College All-American (at USC), and part of a great trivia question, "What backfield in professional football was comprised of players with initials as names?" Answer: The San Francisco 49ers' R.C. Owens, C.R. Roberts, Y.A. Tittle, and J.D. Smith.

C.R. became a high school football coach in Long Beach.

So back in high school, C.R. always dedicated his third and fifth (of a consistent seven) touchdowns to me; his second and fourth to Gloria, his classmate.

You said that was a divisor regarding your brothers. How so?

Carlsbad is to this day pretty much a white enclave. We were surrounded by so many different ethnicities in Oceanside; I just think it must have made a difference in our natural attitudes. It interests me. But in that era O-C High was an anomaly. There was segregation, rigid or unspoken, in many schools of that time, just ask my husband from Kansas City. Total segregation there. I feel very lucky, but at the same time, I envy the boys their grounding in the more peaceful atmosphere of beautiful Carlsbad.

Who were your parents, since we're dealing with memoir?

My mother, Natalie Anderson, was half German, half Swedish, and the eldest of seven children. She was born and raised "middle-class" in Omaha — a classmate of Henry Fonda — but was whisked away to a homestead shack in Wyoming when she was twelve. It was a shock.

She grew up to admire the law, and she believed that individual rights — if it came to that — should give way to the needs of the state. Not totally fascist, and I have probably overstated it to contrast it with my father who, as a Wyoming cowboy, naturally favored anarchy. Veblen Platte Vermilyea was at heart a nineteenth century country-loving cowboy married to a twenty-first century city-loving techie, and they "enjoyed" a rockin' and rollin' relationship in that middle century, somewhat alien to them both. That's my take on them.

They neither smoked, nor drank, nor cussed. My mom was a political junkie; my dad did not vote. When he exasperated her, she'd say, "It's a good thing you kids got your dad's looks and my brains, 'cause the other way around…I don't know." He was actually sharp as a tack — if unschooled — and she knew it. They're fun to write about.

What's your educational background?

I started to read right out of the womb, since I was the fourth girl and there were books everywhere. I was in kindergarten at age four and skipped second grade, so I was in third grade at 6-years-old and graduated from high school at 16. I attended junior college in Oceanside for a year, and then, at 17, flew down alone to Mexico City to attend the University of Mexico. I lived with a wonderful family named Villaseñor in Colonia Roma, across from Chapultepec Park, for six months, July to December 1956.

February of that year, when I was then eighteen, I enrolled at

San Diego State as a Spanish major and Comparative Literature minor, working my way through college in a dormitory kitchen and a pharmacy.

What then?

I married my college sweetheart in La Jolla at age 21, lived there for four years (that was eye-opening!), and moved to Riverside with my husband and two kids in 1965. I went to work at UC Riverside in the Spanish Department, which later merged into the Department of Literatures and Languages, and I became the large department's office manager, or MSO. I toiled there for 28 years, until that "golden handshake." (They made me an offer I couldn't refuse.)

So you see, my life actually has had great symmetry, stemming from my initial fascination with the Spanish language. Everything came from that. I worked in the exact place that suited my interests.

Meanwhile, my marriage failed amicably, and I took up with my present husband, Carlos Cortés. We had already been friends for 10 years when we married in 1978, and our friendship continues.

Carlos and I have travelled through seven continents, each of them more than once (even Antarctica!), except for Africa. We want to go back there. We're going up the Amazon River on a 3-week Viking Cruise in January 2021. It's "free"; Carlos will be a Lecturer, delivering eight different lectures on the sea days.

So, after eighty years, what do you make of all of it?

Good question. I think I've been lucky in that my life has had an ever-broadening aspect, not only for my body (ha ha), but also for my view of the world. It's been true every step of the way, from my upbringing in a great place with a large entertaining family, an education that was inclusive and filled with positive images of diversity, to going to Mexico City and coming back with an expanded view of the world and well-defined interests.

Nowadays, our travel, our love of music, languages and the arts offer an ever-widening perspective.

Wait. Tell me something about your experience at UCR.

To describe one aspect of my job, I'll tell you this. In the Department of Literatures and Languages, with students and faculty from ages 17 to 70, from every country and background, there was not a single sentence you could utter that would not outrage someone. I'll give you a small example that you will think extreme, but it isn't.

We were consoling two young students at the counter who were literally sobbing over the murder of John Lennon. Into the office came a soon to be retired 70-year-old German Professor (an Austrian Count, by the way), who, upon learning why they were crying immediately said, "Ach, they should have assassinated him long ago." He left. I had to remind my staff, before they blew sky high, that what we had there was just life, that's all. "That's just this department in a nutshell."

Oh, that's priceless.

We used to categorize people this way: you were open-minded, broad-minded or narrow-minded. You could cross over, and someone would say, "I'm surprised that you are so narrow-minded about this." But basically, we know who we are. Open-minded, me? No. There are things I can't stand. I can't stand going into Best Buy and seeing them sell dangerous drones as if they are toys. I can't stand long intrusive TV commercials about intimate health items or drugs. I can't stand the thought of the legalization of marijuana and what that portends.

I will continue to strive to be broad-minded. I do read about other points of view and have often sought out and embraced experiences outside of my normal comfort zone.

And even now, because I essentially have a sister-like relationship with my children and sometimes even with my grandkids, I am learning soooo much! And they have let me know that they treasure my stories.

I feel like I've known you all my life. Thanks, Laurel.

Thank you, Carol. You must be tired.

July 18, 1956

A Walk in the 4 O'Clock Rain

BY LAUREL CORTÉS

Dear Mom and Dad and all of you rascally rascals:

Well, I'm 17-years-old and I'm taking an after-dinner walk out across the wide Paseo de la Reforma to Chapultepec Park in Mexico City. Soon I'll head up the hill to Chapultepec Castle, which is now the National Museum. I'll be out of breath when I get up there, but it's good for me, no?

I found out that the Marine Corps hymn that starts out "From the halls of Moctezuma" [to the shores of Tripoli] refers to the battle for this castle during the Mexican-American war (1846-1848). At the end of those two years (I'm reading this), Mexico dropped its claim to Texas; ceded rights to California, Nevada and Utah, major areas of Colorado, New Mexico and Arizona, plus parts of Oklahoma, Kansas and…Wyoming! In return, Mexico received lots of money and cancelled debts. I don't know the particulars.

I'm looking forward to revisiting Emperor Maximiliano I and his second cousin and wife, Empress Carlota. Their larger-than-life portraits hang on either side of the entrance to the grand hall of the castle. I don't quite know why. After all, Maxi, at the age of 34 was executed by a firing squad in 1867, when Napoleon II — who sent him there — abandoned him, and Benito Juárez reasserted his Presidency. Charlotte was 27 when she returned to Belgium, and she ended up in an insane asylum. I don't mean to be flippant, but why be so nice to them now?

I guess the curators of this museum are like you, Mom. If you have a picture, you hang it on the wall, no matter what it is or who gave it to you…*haha*.

Anyway, at the palace I visit all the great halls, the bedrooms, dining room, and the Presidential office. It's like Versailles. The magnificent view from the rooftop of the castle is like the view from Paris's Arc de Triomphe — you can see the whole city from all sides. There is a wonderful, fragrant garden up there, where I go every time I visit — when it's not four o'clock.

* * * * *

I travel by bus three times a week out to the beautiful campus of the Universidad de México, where I take three classes in Spanish and Latin American literature. I have one teacher who sits the whole hour facing us at a desk adorned with three ashtrays, each featuring a lit cigarette. The ciggies get him through the hour as he drones on, interrupted only by his ritual drag/expel/cough. Smoky/smoky! I like his reading list, though.

Today is Thursday, not a school day. We finished dinner and cleanup at about 3 o'clock, and I took my usual walk around the neighborhood in Colonia Roma. But I always end up in Chapultepec Park, one way or another. It's an oasis, and only two blocks from our home. Sometimes I like to walk in the 4 o'clock rain, other times I find shelter. I always carry an assigned novel with me.

As usual, the capitol city seems hot at 85 degrees, because it's closer to the sun than I'm used to. It's 1.4 miles high, 7350 ft. to be exact, much higher than Denver or Tahoe. I sure run out of breath faster here, as I did on my FIRST WEEKEND HERE when we drove 30 miles out of the city to Teotihuacán, and climbed up to the top of the Pyramid of the Sun. Wow. With the sun beating down and the altitude, I almost didn't make it up all those rocky "stairs." But I did! And got back down too!

* * * * *

The everyday 4 o'clock summer rain cools things down. It lasts for about a half-hour, but it's often a heavy rain, not the sprinkly kind we have in Carlsbad. A half-hour a day is just long enough to keep the park green and sparkling. When I'm through at the castle, I'll walk around the lake, taking in the after-rain smell of the beautiful flowers. Occasionally, I chat with other strollers, but usually I sit in the shade and read.

Now that I've been in Mexico City for about three weeks, I'm really getting to know my way around. I like to get on a bus (an accomplishment in itself!) and get off wherever it takes me. I'm not afraid. But the family I live with gets freaked out when I tell them *which* bus I took and where I ended up. *DON'T TAKE THAT BUS!!!* It cracks me up, because the people here, even on the overcrowded buses, are nothing but gracious.

Much of this district, Colonia Roma, is inspired by the French. The wide boulevard, Paseo de la Reforma, patterns the Champs-Elysées. The Castillo's style is neoclassical, and Chapultepec Park — gigantic and fascinating. Emperor Maximilian I built or remodeled it all in the three short years he ruled here.

As I wrote you last week, the Villaseñor family is funny, smart, and kind. I am so fond of each of them. We eat dinner at 2 p.m., when the father comes home from work. He takes a nap, then goes back to work from 4 to about 7. Then at 8 p.m., family and friends stop by to visit and have a coffee. It's like Spain.

I have a new story to tell you. The joke's on me.

Last night, I suffered my most embarrassing moment since I've been here. The Villaseñor's eldest daughter, who is married, visited as usual. She stayed after all the other visitors left and took me aside. Esther said, "When our friends come to visit and you greet each one of them with 'mucho *me* gusto,' they don't know what to say. Because instead of saying 'mucho gusto', which means 'I'm very pleased to meet you', you say 'mucho *me* gusto,' which means, 'I please myself very much'. I think I know you well enough to tell you now. Just say *'mucho gusto!'*"

I can't imagine what my high school Spanish teacher, Mrs. Rosemont, would think if she knew that I speak Spanish all day but still forgot the basic greeting in the Spanish language! She would shriek! And every night for three weeks!!!

[Remember? Mrs. Marguerite (*Margarita*) Rosemont married a U.S. Marine pilot she met in her native Spain. They got stationed at Camp Pendleton and El Toro, and liked the area so much they just stayed in Oceanside. Doesn't everyone? Señora Rosemont grew up in a beautiful home, that just happened to be A CASTLE IN SPAIN. Education: a governess! No kidding! She used to separate the class into two warring factions for our language contests. One team she called her "leetle bingo-bangos" and the other team, her "leetle oog-'n-oogs". She was so much fun. She turned me on to the Spanish language. She's why I'm here.]

Guess what? I have a job! Because I give the Villaseñors most of the fifty dollars you send me (they are so happy to get it) I need some pin money. A family friend who comes to visit in the evening works for Sanborns, the largest department store in the city. She's going to pay me to be a house detective! She'll give me some pesos and send me into whichever department she's chosen. I'll take my time and purchase something (or not), then write a report about how I, as a foreigner, was treated by the clerk. Or I can comment on whatever else I observe. I think it'll be fun. You know me, I always find a job.

I like to stay out until about 6:00 pm, but I promised my "roommate" Gloria (15-years-old) that I would go with her to the mercado and help her set up the café and bolillos (rolls) for this evening. They have no refrigerator, so everything here is fresh.

Luckily, Mexico is all fruits and vegetables, beans and rice, and a bit of meat. The outdoor markets are fantastic. Here at home, people eat pretty much like we do, +beans+rice+tortillas. Tacos and burritos are like hamburgers and hotdogs back home, just snack food. I'm already feeling slightly broad in the beam, but I walk a lot, as I do at home.

Mom and Pappy, I'm seventeen, I'm a sophomore in college, I'm learning things I never expected to learn, and I'm happy that I'll be here for six whole months. Thank you so much for letting me come to beautiful México. I love you and all of my family.

Laurel

P.S. That's my news — what's yours?

Barry Cutler, Major League Baseball Player

(Or –Why Not?- The Greatest Story Ever Told)

BY BARRY CUTLER

Until the Dodgers arrived in Los Angeles in 1958, I didn't know a baseball from a soccer ball, and a soccer ball was a hell of a lot easier to hit. Although I had been listening to the drug, Vin Scully (the Dodger's play-by-play announcer and the greatest sportscaster in the history of sports –shut up, don't argue, your guy wasn't even close), the first professional baseball game I ever saw was at the L.A. Memorial Coliseum in May of 1959. The Coliseum contained the oddest shaped baseball field in the history of the game. From home plate to the left field fence, it was only 250 feet. But what a fence! A screen, actually. A screen more than 40 feet high. (The U.S space program was just revving up and the Dodgers traded for a former mathematics student named Wally Moon. He soon used his math skills to figure out a bat angle that would pop lots of home runs over that towering screen. Scully quickly labeled those homers "Moonshots.") The right field fence was a ridiculous 440 feet away. It took a Mars shot to hit a home run to that field. The seating capacity of the Coliseum was some 93,000.

And every one of those seats had an ass in it on Roy Campanella Night, an exhibition game between the Dodgers and the despicable New York Yankees, and the first game I ever attended. Campanella had been the great Brooklyn Dodger catcher (and future Hall of Famer) who, tragically, in January of 1958, having never played in L.A., crashed his car and was paralyzed for life. Between the fifth and sixth innings, Pee Wee Reese wheeled

Campy to the pitcher's mound and all of the lights were turned out, as the public address announcer asked us to light matches. As at every Dodger game for decades to come, thanks to the thousands of transistor radios, Vin Scully could be heard calling it "a sea of lights at the Coliseum; perhaps the most beautiful and dramatic moment in the history of sports . . ."

After only a year of listening to his exploits on the radio, Sandy Koufax had already established himself as my favorite baseball player of all time. Following in my footsteps, he was left-handed and Jewish and I was absolutely certain that I would someday be the next Sandy Koufax. t was inevitable. At that time, he was an imperfect but exciting player. In 1958, he struck out 131 batters in 158 innings. He also walked 105. He was a little wild. In fact, in that very same year, he led the majors with 17 wild pitches. Yes, just a little wild. Roy Campanella Night was the first time I ever got to see him in person. The despicable Yankees got some 13 hits off him and a couple of other pitchers in that game. They beat the Dodgers pretty badly. Big deal! It was just a stupid exhibition game.

But enough about the Dodgers and more about me. I began working on becoming the next Sandy Koufax. Every day, after school, having paced off sixty feet, six inches from our backyard brick wall, I would throw strikes at the rectangle I'd chalked on that wall. So what if it drove the next door neighbors out of their minds? I was the future of baseball. As I improved, so did Sandy. It wasn't long before he was the greatest pitcher in baseball history. (Shut up. Don't argue. Your guy wasn't even close.)

I, on the other hand, hit a wall. But, no, not the brick wall in our backyard. We had a swimming pool in our yard; surrounded by TIKI torches, the whole works. With three children in the family, my dad decided to put a fence around the swimming pool. It wasn't forty feet high, but it was enough to destroy my aspiring baseball career. I'm a southpaw. The fence was to my immediate south. There wasn't enough room between the fence and the house to move further north. Hence, I could no longer throw sidearm without ripping open my knuckles against the wire fence. Hell, I couldn't even throw at a three-quarters angle. Everything had to be directly over the top. Sandy only improved the more he began pitching directly over the top. But, as Sandy lost his wildness and became the greatest control pitcher in history (shut up, don't argue), I lost all control. I knew Sandy Koufax. Sandy Koufax was a great pitcher. Cutler, you were no Sandy Koufax.

I began looking into a lame career as an actor.

I stopped playing baseball for many years. I was just a fan. I was, of course, the greatest Sandy Koufax fan in history (shhh…), but just a fan. Aside from that time he intentionally missed the first game of the 1965 World Series because of Yom Kippur, he could do no wrong. (I'm a bad Jew. I pretty much stopped being a Jew the morning after my Bar Mitzvah, when I realized everybody had just been kidding and, at the age of thirteen, nobody was really going to treat me like a man. I don't give a drek about Yom Kippur.) On September 9, 1965, my eighteenth birthday, I went to see Sandy pitch against the Cubs at Dodger Stadium. He pitched a perfect game. For my birthday. Obviously, he knew I was there.

The following year, Sandy retired due to an arthritic elbow. He'd only pitched for 12 seasons, but those 12 seasons made for the greatest pitching career in history. Shortly thereafter, I began getting my first jobs as an actor. I was a little wild at first, but after a while, I settled in.

In my early thirties, I returned to baseball. Or, rather, softball. And I was no longer pitching but tucked away safely in right field. There was no fence where we played so, in a way, our right field stretched much further than right field at the Coliseum, where it had been nearly impossible to hit a home run. However, with me playing right field, it became quite possible. I played sporadically with a group of actors. I had fallen so far from baseball, I didn't even have my own glove. I had to borrow one from a player on the opposing team. One day, our pitcher landed an audition and had to leave. The team captain asked me to pitch. This was the first time I had pitched since I was constantly striking out the brick wall in our backyard, nearly two decades earlier. I took to the mound against the actor Charles Martin Smith. A little guy. No power, I figured. There was, of course, no fence surrounding a swimming pool, but I still couldn't pitch sidearm because, well, this was softball, damn it. I pitched the ball. Charles swung. He hit a hard line drive back toward my head. I raised my glove for an easy catch. At that moment, I almost had time to realize that the webbing on the glove was very loose. The ball flew through the glove and hit my nose. I went down. My nose began bleeding.

Everyone ran to surround me on the mound as I tried to stand up. "No, no," they all said. "Stay down, your nose is bleeding."

I was embarrassed. I told them it was nothing because I had always suffered from stupid nosebleeds since I was a kid. But the blood wasn't flowing from my nostrils. It was pouring from the bridge of my beak. Eventually, the bleeding was stopped and a lovely actress, who had come with me to watch the game, drove me to a hospital and had me stitched up. It was humiliating. I didn't return to play again for many months. When I did return, I slid into third, trying to stretch a double into a triple, and tore every damned ligament in my left knee. That was it. I hung up my spikes. Well, not having any spikes, I just limped around for many months and never returned to the game.

Until . . .

The 2020 major league baseball season was the oddest of seasons. Thanks to a pandemic, each team played only 60 games. For most of the season, due to the dangers of COVID-19, very few fans were allowed in the stands. The Dodgers decided to take advantage of that and charge fans up to $299 to have cardboard cutouts of themselves in the stands for the entire season. As I was still a big baseball fan, I bought one and I was lucky enough to get my cardboard cutout a seat right behind home plate. And, then, toward the end of the regular season, when the Dodgers held a contest for several lucky fans to attend the final game in person, I was one of the winners.

So, on September 27, 2020, in a game against the Los Angeles Angels at Dodger Stadium, I was there. In person. All the Dodgers had to do was win that one game to end up second in the Western Division of the National League. However, if they lost, they would be out of the competition for the championship.

Eighty-four-year-old Sandy Koufax threw out the ceremonial first pitch! And then — then! — he sat in the stands, socially-distanced, six feet to my south!

The game was a real nail-biter, only, of course, nobody was biting their nails because of the virus. The Dodgers went into the top of the ninth inning leading the Angels by only one run. With one out in the top of the ninth, the Angels had the bases loaded. The batter lined the ball toward the pitcher. While the pitcher managed to catch the ball, he tripped and fell, as he lobbed the ball home to prevent a run from scoring. There were two outs in the top of the ninth and the bases were loaded. The Dodgers were one out away from winning the division. But the pitcher had been injured. He had broken his leg stumbling to catch the ball.

So, this was the problem. The virus had run rampant, throughout the season, badly impacting on every team. For the Dodgers, it had wiped out every pitcher but the one who had just been injured. There was nobody left to try to get the final batter out. Except, sitting six feet to my left, there was SANDY KOUFAX, the greatest pitcher in baseball history.

Manager Dave Roberts approached and said, "Sandy, we need you. It's only one batter. Will you pitch for us?"

Sandy turned red, looked down at his feet and muttered, "No, I can't."

"Why," asked Roberts. "I've seen you out there before the games, training our pitchers. You've still got it. Please!'

"Sorry," said Sandy, "I just can't."

"Why?" Roberts pleaded, at the very same moment I turned to Sandy and asked, "Why?"

"Because," said Sandy, "it's Yom Kippur."

"No," I cried, "not again!"

Sandy looked at me, kindly, and asked, "Are you Jewish?"

"I was Jewish. Just like you. And I'm a southpaw. Just like you. But I'm an agnostic now."

"Funny," he said, "you don't look agnostic."

"Well," I replied, somewhat embarrassed, "I am."

"Well, then," said Sandy, "Well, then. Why don't you pitch, kid? Hand him the ball, Dave."

And I climbed down out of the stands. And Dave Roberts handed me the ball. And, over transistor radios, strategically placed throughout the ballpark, I heard Vin Scully say, "Roberts is walking a young seventy-three-year-old guy named Barry Cutler out to the mound and giving the kid some last minute advice. Every other fan in the stands, all twelve of them, are lighting matches as he takes the mound to face Mike Trout, the best player in baseball. Cutler looks in for the sign. He checks the runners. He sets. And he throws directly over the top, exactly like Sandy Koufax!"

And Trout lined the pitch straight back, directly at my head. I raised my glove, shouting, "Oh, shit", and my words rang through the empty ballpark, echoing into television sets across the land.

"And Cutler catches the ball!" Scully shouted from the transistor radios. "The Dodgers Win! The Dodgers Win!"

Sandy jumped out of the stands and embraced me. I had, indeed, followed in my hero's footsteps. The entire Dodger pitching staff quickly recovered (it turned out that day's pitcher had just twisted an ankle), and the team went on to win their first World Series since 1988.

The day after the final game of the series, at the same hour, on that same day, Sandy and I died of the virus we had shared during our embrace. But we died…Happy!

Wonderland

by Ellen Estilai

Yazd, Iran, October 1971

Shortly after I arrived in Iran as a new bride, my husband Ali and I made a pilgrimage to the ancient desert city of Yazd. It was not to a mosque or that city's famous Zoroastrian fire temple, but to a *shirini foroushi*, a pastry shop, *the* pastry shop, the one by which all others were judged. The Haji Khalifeh bakery had been a mainstay for desert travelers since 1916. Everyone in Ali's family stopped there on their way to or from Kerman, stocking up on the pastries that are an essential part of Iranian hospitality, as important as religion, maybe even a religion in itself.

When Westerners think of Iranian food, they think of kebabs, colorful rice pilafs, or khoreshes — those braised stews with artful combinations of meat, herbs, vegetables and often fruit. But to get to those delights at a traditional Iranian dinner party, one must first have tea, fresh fruit, and *shirini*. And I do mean *must have*. You can *ta'arof* a little, begging that you don't want to cause any inconvenience. *Please, upon my children's souls, I really shouldn't. Why did you go to so much trouble? Your hand should not hurt.* But to refuse the host's repeated ministrations is bad form — and of course, the pastries are ultimately irresistible.

When someone is the recipient of good fortune — a new job, new baby, new house — it is his or her responsibility to give *shirini*. *Shirini* can be shorthand for throwing a party or taking friends to lunch, but it can just as easily mean bringing a box of pastries for co-workers to enjoy in the break room.

Every good Iranian host has a massive supply of *shirini* on hand, tucked away in tins in the pantry and arranged artfully on the coffee table awaiting the inevitable drop-in guest. I was not a good host. I had no coffee table, let alone *shirini*. Fresh out of university in California, we had arrived in Tehran with two suitcases each, mostly filled with books, and were dependent upon the good graces of Ali's friends, who installed us in their upstairs apartment and lent us a dining set and a bed. We had little furniture but we still had visitors. They perched on the unyielding dining room chairs and waited politely for the trays of shirini to appear while I scrounged frantically in the kitchen. I hadn't yet gotten into the rhythm of preparing for guests. I was little more than a guest myself.

I was still in guest mode on our way back to Tehran after spending a week meeting my new in-laws in Kerman. Ali had come home after six years in the States with both a PhD and a new bride, so that week was one long progressive party, an endless tablecloth streaming from one living room carpet to another, with steaming platters of chicken in tomato-saffron sauce, mounds of saffron-scented rice, bowls of fragrant stews, yogurt with cucumbers or spinach, and plates of *tahdig*, the crispy rice at the bottom of the pot, placed conveniently near us because we were the guests of honor. Little children vied to sit next to us so they could be near the *tahdig*.

And of course, there was always *shrini*, mostly the delicate Yazdi versions, but often the hearty Kermani confection, *kolompeh*, a heavy, embossed cookie filled with ground dates and almonds. We had *shirini* with mid-morning tea, before lunch, in the afternoon with tea and melons, and before dinner. And when it was time to head back to Tehran, my sister-in-law prepared a tray for us to pass under to ensure our safety on our journey. It held a Koran, a glass of water, and *shirini*.

Winding through the tree-lined streets of Yazd in the dwindling light, we glimpsed traditional homes, surrounded by high walls and lush, fragrant gardens. Many of these homes had the distinctive Yazdi architectural feature, a *baadgir*, or wind catcher, a tall brick tower that captures the breezes and guides them down to a pool in the center of a stone floor, where they skim the water and infuse the thick walls with their coolness. These pools and gardens were fed by *qanaats*, a subterranean network of wells that channel water to the lower elevations. In such a cool shelter, on a hot summer day, a weary visitor might be treated to tea and melons and, of course, trays of *shirini*.

My brother-in-law, Ahmad, pulled up in front of the bakery, and we all got out, stretching our stiff legs. Tired and wobbly from the bumpy roads, we slowly made our way into the shop. As we opened the door, the warm, heavy scent of fresh pastry, a yeasty, heady mix of sugar, rosewater, almonds, and cardamom, enveloped us.

The bearded, middle-aged owner beamed as the three of us entered the empty shop. He waved us in with a flourish and bowed slightly, his right hand on his heart. Happy at the prospect of business so late in the day, he was eager to make us feel at home.

"Welcome," he said. "I am at your service

Ahmad explained our mission. "My brother, here, is just back from the United States with his American wife, and they want some of your very best *shirini* to take to Tehran."

The shop's bright fluorescent light bounced off the gleaming white tile walls and well-scrubbed mosaic floors. Neatly stacked pyramids of Yazdi specialties crowded the display cases: *Nan-e berenji*, rice cookies garnished with poppy seeds; *nan-e nokhodchi*, chick-pea cookies; *sohan-e asali*, honey almond brittle; *toot*, mulberry-shaped candies; and *ghottab*, crescent-shaped cookies filled with ground walnuts.

There were also trays of *baqlava* — not the honey-coated, flaky Greek variety, but the dense, candy-like Yazdi version, thin layers of dough sandwiching a grainy paste of cardamom and ground walnuts, laced with rosewater syrup, dusted with pistachios, and cut into glistening diamond shapes.

We were sampling the wares when I glimpsed movement in the back room, a blur of white, and some laughter. Leaning closer, I saw that there were four men dressed in immaculate white uniforms and crocheted skull caps sitting on short stools arranged in a circle around a large tinned copper tray. On the tray was a shiny, taffy-like ring of white sugar paste. The men grasped the ring and pulled it back and forth among them, stretching it, their bodies rocking rhythmically to and fro, their cheeks turning rosy with the effort.

They noticed me looking at them and smiled at each other, amused that a foreigner would find this at all interesting.

"Go ahead, Khanum," the shopkeeper said. "You are welcome to watch."

"What are they doing?" I asked.

"They're making *pashmak*," he explained.

I had eaten *pashmak* in Tehran, but I had no idea how it was made. In the same family as spun sugar, or what the British call "fairy floss," its literal meaning is "little wool." The *pashmak* makers would work for hours this way, like jolly elves in some fairy tale, until the sugar reinvented itself. Its molecules rearranged, it was transformed from a slick, gooey mass to long, dry, flaky filaments — looking like fine, creamy white mohair yarn.

"Try some," insisted the shopkeeper, flaking off a sample from the large brick stashed in the display case and depositing it in my hand. When a brick of *pashmak* is liberated from its densely packed tin and pulled apart, it's like wisps of insulation material. I pinched some of the long strands between my fingers and put them in my mouth, where they melted magically.

Thirsty from all this sampling, I asked for some water. The proprietor disappeared into the back room and emerged with the largest glass of water I had ever seen — a fluted Picardy tumbler about ten inches tall. The oversized glass only added to my sense that I had somehow fallen down a rabbit hole.

As he tied up our purchases with brown paper and string, the shopkeeper asked me where in the States I was from.

"Ah, Kaleeforniaaa," he said, nodding. "My son is a student in Chicago. Maybe you know him."

Like that enormous tumbler, his sense of scale was off, but there in that pristine shop, the rosy-cheeked men laboring happily in the back room, it was entirely possible that America could shrink to the size of Kerman or Yazd, where everybody seemed to be a few degrees of separation from everybody else.

Alas, we said, we did not know his son, but we wished him well in his studies.

We thanked the shopkeeper and gathered up our purchases, ready to return to Tehran, still with no coffee table but one step closer to being good hosts.

Masks

by Andrea Fingerson

Stay in place.
Maintain your space.
And cover your face.

That is the advice, repeated
On electronic street signs,
Robo calls from my district,
And flyers posted, well,
Everywhere.

As if I need a rhyme
To know how serious
A pandemic is.

Schools are already closed
Students and teachers alike, sent home
Without answers, textbooks, or a foreseeable future.
Unsure what the questions even are,
We know that businesses are next on the list
On the chopping block that has already decimated the world

Like so many others, I'm trapped at home
Forced to binge watch tv and break out the puzzles.
Early morning grocery shopping
Has become the highlight
Of my week.
Even if that means

Waiting in the rain
At seven am.

But now I have to wear a mask
Each time I step outside
To escape this prison quarantine
That has become my life.

They, whoever they are,
Promise that it's only for my protection
And those I love.
And I believe them
I think
But it's hard to think
When it's hard to breathe
And my mask is blocking the air
Preventing oxygen
From reaching my lungs
Or the gray matter
That is overwhelmed by a new normal
It doesn't want to accept.

I don't, can't, know what will happen
But I want to come out of this lockdown
With more than a new accessory
Added to my daily routine.

How Much Do You Need?

BY ANDREA FINGERSON

How much do you need?
In a lockdown
In a quarantine?
How much do you really need?

I don't know,
And I'm scared to be wrong
So I'm at the store
Again.
It's not even seven in the morning
And it's raining.
And I'm unsure of
Everything.
Should I touch the grocery cart
With my hand
Or with a scarf?
What unknown germs
Invisible threats
Are waiting for me to take them home?

"Thanks for hoarding,"
Barks the man.
He's approaching the line
My line.
Getting close,
Too close

For anyone's comfort.
And he's not wearing a mask.
He trails along the front of the grocery store
Heading for the end of the line
Which has now become his too.

I'm not even in the store yet,
But in his eyes
I am one of them.
A hoarder.
Someone who takes more
More than they need.
At least according to him.
But how much does one need?
That stranger that can't see my refrigerator
Can't see my pantry
Or freezer.
Can't see the empty spaces
That my fears are filling up
With dread
He can't know that I am feeding not just myself
But two parents
And a grandmother.
Occasionally a neighbor.
All of whom have to stay at home
Because they are high risk.

That man can't know that I am high risk too.
That asthma makes my breathing tricky

Even when I'm not existing
In a pandemic.
But I am the only one
The only one who can go out
The only one who can decide
How much we need.

But how do I know
How much I'll need?
How much we'll need?
Let alone
How much she'll need?

The Hoarder
I see her when I make it through the door
Finally
The sliding doors that are guarded
By sanitizer
And an exhausted grocery worker.
I see the woman with two cartons of eggs, eighteen each
With six tubs of wipes, 100 or more per container
The antibacterial kind
That I haven't been able to find
(They were gone
Before I made it inside
Taken by her
And who knows how many others.)
She also has three
Gigantic bags of toilet paper

That she couldn't possibly use.

Or can she?
Maybe she does need that.
ALL that.
Maybe she has kids.
Teenage boys or girls.
Maybe her husband is sick
Battling leukemia or heart disease.
Maybe she's wearing a mask
The medical kind
The kind you are called selfish for using
Because she can't risk bringing home germs
Even of the normal variety
Let alone the novel kind.

How much does she need?
Really?
I don't know.
I can't know.
And honestly
I'm not sure I want to know
Just how much
The entire world will need
In the coming days?
Weeks?
months?

So I buy what I think we'll need

To survive

This week at least.

Toilet paper- yes

Paper towels- no — only one paper product each is allowed

Hand Sanitaizer- I wish

Yogurt- easy

Cereal- we've got plenty

Red meat- chicken will have do

Frozen vegetables- so they won't go bad

Whipped cream- check

Angel Food Cake- check

And a pound of bright red strawberries- check

Because tomorrow is my birthday

And strawberry shortcake is something

I need

And something I can get

At least for today.

No Signature Required

by Andrea Fingerson

Neither snow nor rain
Nor heat nor gloom of night
Stays COVID-19
From the slow completion
Of its appointed rounds.

Its microscopic droplets
Will arrive at every open doorway,
Every fleshy nose and unlatched mouth,
Transported by loved ones
Groceries and unsanitary fomites,
Those carriers of bacteria, and viruses,
And infections you cannot see.

Nothing can stop its arrival,
Except social distance
And hand soap.
But even then
It finds a way
Determined to infect
As many as possible.
But, hopefully,
As slowly as possible.

To flatten the curve
We hide in our homes

Wear masks
That don't protect us
And try to discover a new normal.

Seven weeks have passed
And Spring is almost behind us.
Victory is close at hand
Because sunshine destroys
COVID's deadly spread.
Unfortunately, the parks are still closed
And you can be ticketed
For walking on the beach.

But COVID's deadly march is still on
And no one knows
When it will be delivered to their doorstep
Knocking for entrance, no signature required.

A Most Honorable Warrior's Death

Dedicated to CelenaDiana Bumpus

BY BRYAN FRANCO

So many poetry people I know
have said poetry has saved their lives.
The same story is told
in a million different voices
around the world.
Poets are warriors.
Poets are fighters.
Poets are Olympic pugilists.
Our enemies,
our nemeses,
our sparring partners
are simultaneously
our mirrors and our pasts.
Our present tense existences
are fleeting moments
in which we contemplate
lives,
decisions,
relationships,
families.
Our words run
through veins

to hearts
and through nerves
to brains.
We spit them out as poetry
exposing them to the elements
sending them
to a glorious death
memorialized on page
to be read
both out loud and in silence
not only by us but also others
who have experienced
pieces of our lives
in their separate lives.
Our epitaphs
become their epitaphs.
Our poetry
is a graveyard
that transforms
death into life.

The Answer My Friend To Interpreting the Wind

by Bryan Franco

I'm at my wit's end with you, Wind:
the way you blow through conversations.
I have tried to comprehend your tongue.
I've been told there is no language
outside your repertoire.
Your general style of communication
is a cluster of weather patterns.
I am enamored, though, with how
your breathy spring breezes
help erase winter doldrums.
Your soft summer exhalations
that spread the seductive scent
of magnolia blossoms
after late-afternoon rainstorms
feel like love letters
from a hopeless romantic.
But hopeless romantics don't celebrate
autumn by destroying whole coastal towns
with various categories of hurricane gales.
Why do you choose to spend winters
assisting the snow by blowing it horizontally?
Is it just so someone will call you BLIZZARD,
and maybe, a high school will name
a sports team after you after they rid themselves

of an offensive tomahawk-waving Indian.
I think you are not so much multilingual,
but potentially burdened with multiple personalities.
There is no shame in taking a sabbatical
from the weather and getting help.
Dr. Josephine Gaia is a climate psychologist
in Berkeley, California who offers
her services on a sliding scale.
She has helped many natural disasters
turn their lives around.
One famous tornado transformed itself
into the most popular waterslide park in Nebraska.
She helped a family of forest fires find their way
to start an artisan custom organic charcoal briquette factory
using tree branches from people's yards
and utility company trimmings.
Maybe you can finally realize your dream
of opening that string of B & B's
that look like Tara from *Gone with the Wind*
with multiple magnolia trees surrounding
the property, a perfect place to hold
small intimate weddings and go for romantic getaways.
After all, you are a hopeless romantic.

yahrzeit
by Bryan Franco

A yahrzeit candle burns
for twenty-four hours.
The candle is encased
in what looks like
a twelve-ounce water glass,
the type diners use
to serve milk or a large juice.
It is filled with white paraffin
that has a faint odor of petroleum.
The aroma doesn't permeate a room,
but it is the kind of aroma
that seems slightly disturbing.
This candle will burn itself out
with no danger to anyone.
At the end of twenty-four hours,
a burnt wick attached
to a small metal washer
sits at the bottom of a glass
with traces of burnt-wax residue.
One could clean and scrub
and wash the glass
then use it in the bathroom
for taking aspirin
or rinsing after brushing teeth.
As if it did not represent

the life of a relative.
As if Kaddish wasn't recited
as it was lit.
As if no one knew the glass
they drank their juice from
or the glass that held milk
they used to dip Oreos in
held paraffin that slowly melted away
representing memories and history
and a life that lives on.

BEWARE when entering the poetry zoomosphere

by Bryan Franco

A friend invites you
to watch her read poetry
on zoom for the first time.
You say, "I don't think I'm a poetry person."
You humor your friend
and decide to watch,
but remember, for a poet,
sitting in a chair hunched over a laptop
isn't as comfortable as
standing on a stage
which allows for
more movement and expression.
It's all about the poetry.
Listen to the carefully crafted words,
rhyme, rhythm, flow, and verbal acrobatics.
Don't be afraid when
you hear nonexistent music behind a poem.
It's not uncommon when a poet
is thinking or writing a poem
to hear a jazz combo
accompanying his or her piece:
the steady bum-bum-bum of an upright base,
the perfectly placed wahhhh-wahhhh
of trumpets and trombone during pauses,

even some whispery drum tapping.
If you find yourself swaying to a poem
like it's a good folk song,
you can now call yourself a poetry person.
Welcome to the poetry zoomosphere.
Put pens and brightly colored comp books
on your shopping list
because one day soon
something out of the blue
will trigger poem in you.

4 Haikus for 2020
by Bryan Franco

The meaning of life
is not about breathing, but
deciding to breathe

Cynicism is
an acquired attitude
no one is born that way

Optimism is
more than just an idea;
it can be mantra

Twenty-twenty-one
is the year of the poet
because it makes sense

My Parents' Uzbekistan Cooking
by Meryl Freeze

My parents were born and raised in Tashkent, the capital of Uzbekistan. I grew up in Woodland Hills, California. I've always associated Uzbek food with family, old world culture, and celebrations with huge feasts covering the table from corner to corner. I've had good bonding moments shared over food with my parents as well. Uzbek food is definitely my favorite cuisine. I love the feeling of anticipation when a dish is being prepared. That very first bite of intense flavor zapping your tastebuds and scrambling your mind while you try to figure out what amazing food you are eating never gets old.

Uzbekistan cuisine is very similar to the cuisines of Mongolia, Uyghur, and other Middle Asian countries. Uzbek cooking is fairly easy to make, and the list of ingredients needed for recipes is not extensive. Even though many Uzbek recipes share the same ingredients, their tastes are very different from each other. The main spices used are cumin, red pepper, barberry, and peppers. Uzbek dishes can have a lot of vegetables and greens in them to help digest the meat and add flavor. A great thing about Uzbek cooking is that all the ingredients are fresh, and when you eat them, the food gives you a lot of warmth inside and makes you feel invigorated. You should be sweating with the energy the food gives off! That is what my father calls the mark of a well-prepared dish.

Uzbekistan's signature dish, and vastly its most popular, is called *plouf*, a dish consisting of rice, carrots, and lamb. Chickpeas and raisins are usually added for special occasions such as weddings. *Plouf* is made in a *kazan*, an oven set over coals in the ground. All the ingredients are added in a big cauldron and cooked together. *Kazans* can get so big, a whole cauldron can feed 1,000 people. My father said the dish originated when Alexander the Great needed a meal that would be easy to make and keep his army moving.

Manti are dumplings made with lamb, onion, and lamb fat. They can be eaten with a side of sour cream and topped with butter. Steaming is the main way to cook them. A kind of bouillon develops inside the *manti* while they're cooking. The combination of soup enclosed in dough is interesting and delicious. Two soup dishes that come to mind are *Lagman* and *Shurpa*. Both are lamb and vegetable-based soups. The biggest difference is that *Lagman* has noodles while *Shurpa* has potatoes.

Samsa are meat pastries filled with lamb, onions, lamb fat, and spices such as cumin. You can think of them as a type of samosa. Uzbek *samsas* are baked in an oven called a *tandyr*. Other Uzbek food made in a *tandyr* can be lamb and *lyposhki*, which is fluffy and moist Uzbek flatbread. You stick the *samsa* onto the inside walls of the *tandyr* to bake them. The result is a flaky and crunchy crust with a moist and tender filling. And they are very filling! To add a creative touch, my parents sculpt the *samsa* into various shapes such as roses or snowflakes.

Uzbek people are very big into drinking hot tea. Usually green tea is served with every meal, without milk or sugar, although in Tashkent, black tea is more popular. Uzbeks drink hot tea all year round, even in the middle of summer. According to my father, this is because drinking tea helps a person retain more water than by just drinking water.

When I got married two years ago, my husband was introduced to my parents' cooking. Now he loves it as much as I do!

It
by Nan Friedley

launched from a loaded
sneeze on a
Chewy cat food order
carried to my porch by
typhoid Mary
in a brown uniform

I felt fine
as I tried out several carts
no wobbly wheels
no jammed brakes, but
no wipes by the door
for my Walmart handlebar

I felt fine
as I scanned the produce
touching, smelling, searching
for the best plums
to bag in plastic
closed by a green tie

I felt fine
as I picked up a basket
dodging other customers
sharing eye contact at Rite-Aid
standing on a red line
six feet from each other

I felt fine
as I walked my 1.5 mile
neighborhood route
giving a wide berth
on a narrow sidewalk to
fellow walkers

I felt fine
but maybe I'm a super
spreader who passed it on in March
a maskless typhoid Mary
unaware of the potential of
it

Ode to the Lobe
by Nan Friedley

Lobulus ariculae
fleshy lower part of an external ear
Some dangle, unattached free spirits
liberated to wag in the wind
by a common inherited trait

fewer are attached directly to the head
small, hangless lobes
belong to introverts
always looking to the future

either kind is a handy
place to hang silver hoops
pierce to post diamond earrings
pearls to pass down from grandma

Just 45 Minutes
by Nan Friedley

Arrived 45 minutes early, self check-in
Plenty of time for a Starbuck's latte
Santa Ana airport dressed for the holidays
Departure board, ORD flight on time

Settled into a seat by the bathroom
Started chapter two in my recent read
Beginning chapter three, ticket agent announced
45 minute delay due to freezing rain in Chicago

By chapter four, another 45 minute delay
Now I'm looking at my itinerary, doing the math
Could the pilot make up enough time, could I push
My way down the aisle, run to my next gate

When we landed, my 9:25 PM connecting flight
had already departed, 45 minutes ago
Door closed, ticket agent moved on, empty seats nearby
Last flight of the day to FW, standby at 6:30 AM tomorrow

By now, O'Hare is getting dark, stores have closed
Restaurants are cleaning up, janitors mopping, lights out.
Backpack pillow, I stretch out on a row of hard plastic seats
Tossing and turning till the airport wakes up in the morning.

Probably slept about 45 minutes

Six-pack of Senyrus

by Nan Friedley

Limit One

Eyes above a mask
Search barren shelves for that last
Roll of paper towels

Through his Window

Happy birthday dad
Celebrate 92 years
In your room alone

Flight 1412

Sitting between two
Masked men, wondering which one
Tested positive

New Normal?

Waiters wearing masks
Fine dining in parking lots
Tables under tents

Zoom School

Checkerboard children
Microphone muted, eager
To wave hello

Halloweenless

Trick or treat cancelled
No COVID candy for me
Still wearing my mask

Pandemic Pants

by Nan Friedley

in my COVID cocoon
comfort has replaced fashion
with leggings, spandex stretched
to its limits, "black goes with everything"
my new casual, formal, all the time wear

ideal for quick trips to Target
drive-thru at McDonald's
walks in the neighborhood
easily adaptable for formal wear at
zoom meetings and FaceTime

as the coronavirus continues
I find myself eyeing those
gray sweatpants with drawstrings
post pregnancy fat pants
in the back of my closet

soon I'll be one of those Walmart
shoppers in pajama bottoms
stocking up on junk food
searching for bigger pants
until LA Fitness opens again

How Will They Know I Am "Earning My Salt?"

by Hazel Fuller

How will they know I am earning my salt? she asked one day.

As facilitator of the Creative Writing Workshop at the Joslyn Senior Center you are certainly "earning your salt." Before the March 2020 pandemic lock down, you got up, dressed up and showed up at the Senior Center on Wednesday mornings. You brought objects to share, a small Buddha, a box of Cracker Jacks, an apron, magazine and newspaper articles to share. You gave prompts, set time limits for writing, had us read what we wrote, cut us off if we went on and on, praised our work, encouraged us to submit to Inlandia and other publications. Just part of your "job" as facilitator. You assigned prompts for homework which we could do or not. You kept us on track with due dates for Inlandia submissions, helped us pull together to assist members without computers to get their stories typed and submitted to Inlandia. You brought doughnuts, brownies, cupcakes and other goodies, and stuck birthday candles in them to celebrate our birthdays. For some, the workshop was like a therapy session, a place to share good times and bad. You encouraged us to write childhood memories and histories for our families. And every Wednesday as we left you gave each of us a hug, an encouraging word, "earning your salt."

That was when we met inside at the Joslyn Senior Center, before the pandemic. Then, March 2020 and COVID-19. No more meetings at the Center. But did that stop you? Oh, no! You went zooming along, continued the workshop on Zoom, facilitating the Zoom meetings, sending emails to members with a prompt and a link. Problems? Oh, yes! But no problem for you. There was no link for the February Zoom meeting. You texted. You made phone calls. You left voice mails. Finally, you got not one but two links. Part of the group was on one link, part on another link, one member was unable to log on, and there were three new Zoomers! But you handled it, got everyone connected. That's what you do, "earning your salt."

In ancient times salt was very expensive and labor intensive to harvest in large quantities. Salt was highly valued and its production was legally restricted. It was considered a valuable commodity. Salt is essential for human and animal life. Salt is used in many ways. Long used for flavoring food, it was the primary method of preserving food before the invention of canning and refrigeration. It is used in tanning, dyeing and bleaching, in the production of pottery, soap and chlorine. It is used in the field of medicine and in the chemical industry. Used on roads to melt snow and ice. In ancient times salt was expensive. Today salt is cheap and plentiful, a one pound box costs less than a dollar, but it still has great valuable.

The word "salary" is derived from the word "salt." Some sources state salt mine workers were paid in salt. Hence, the idiom "earning his salt." To say someone is "earning his salt," is to acknowledge he is competent and deserving, valuable, worthwhile and deserving of pay." In my opinion, and I think others would agree, you are all that: competent, deserving, valuable, worthwhile and deserving of pay. We know you are clearly — no ifs, ands, or buts about it Mae — you are definitely, positively, absolutely, indubitably, and without a doubt, "earning your salt."

The Catastrophic Flood of 1938

by Hazel Fuller

In the afternoon of Wednesday, March 2, 1938, I was in the kitchen with my mother and siblings, two brothers and five sisters, including my nine-month-old baby sister. The power line to our house was down, the whole house dark without electricity or sunlight. Voices were hushed, worried, concerned, waiting for Daddy to come home. Outside the sky was black with rain, storm clouds blocked the sun, rain soaked the earth. Why had Daddy gone to the store in this downpour? We lived on a farm. We had a cow and chickens. Had milk and eggs, a cellar full of canned food my mother and sisters had "put up" during the summer. We did not need food.

Daddy finally returned home with a cardboard box filled with groceries from Gerrards Grocery store in Redlands. Mother quickly looked in the box and found what she was looking for: candles. Oh, of course, that's why Daddy went to Gerrards — to buy candles. Mother lit and placed candles on the kitchen counters and table. The yellow glow brightened the kitchen where we sat at the long table and waited while Mother and my older sisters prepared supper. Mother made delicious tamale pie in her cast iron Dutch oven on top of the yellow and green, four legged, oil burning stove. Maybe we ate tamale pie, maybe home made cream of tomato soup and corn bread. We were warm, together, eating supper by candlelight.

As we ate, the rain continued, loud on the roof, against the windows. Thunder clapped, then lighting flashed, and violent wind lifted a strip of corrugated tin on the roof of the shed where Daddy parked his car, lifted, then banged it down again and again, a nerve-racking noise. Nervous, anxious adults, frightened children. I was three-years-and-three-months-old, unaware of the coming storm and the catastrophic flood of 1938.

The storm pounded the area from Sunday, February 27, to March 4. At first a light rain, nothing unusual as that time of year is the rainy season in Southern California. The showers intensified, then for a few hours on March 1 there was a break, then a second system delivered a steady downpour with the heaviest rain on March 2. The first storm, February 27-28 dropped over four inches of rain, the second system, a torrential downpour, over eleven inches flooded the counties of San Bernardino, Los Angeles, Orange and San Diego. This was the third powerful storm in Southern California since December. My parents and siblings must have been aware of the danger of flooding. I was not.

March 2 was different from previous days. Everyone was home. In the house. Not at school or work. Not outside milking the cow or gathering eggs, or tending the garden, but inside warm and safe in the glowing candlelight. I remember Mother taking a bag of marshmallows from the box of groceries, giving me one, my first marshmallow, the soft sweet ball of fluff filled my mouth. I wonder why Daddy bought marshmallows. The country was in a depression. Money was tight. Marshmallows were a special treat.

Our house was located on Mountain View Avenue in Redlands, one block south of the Santa Ana River. Was my family in danger? No radio. No telephone. There were reasons for concern. We were close to the river. If it overflowed would the house be flooded? Washed away? And while some of my relatives lived in Redlands others lived in San Bernardino, north of the Santa Ana River, cut off from us and in a floodplain. Were they safe? Were we?

The rain stopped sometime on March 3. The sun came out and so did we. We walked north on Mountain View Avenue to where it once continued on to San Bernardino. But on that day it ended abruptly, the road washed away by a torrid of water in the Santa Ana River. I remember standing on the pavement looking at the wide, raging, angry river, debris hurled end over end, trees, lumber, large boulders, maybe a car or two. I have an image of Daddy's dark green, 1928 Dodge touring car hanging off the undercut riverbank by its back wheels. Was it his car? Did it belong to someone else? Or was it only my three-year-old imagination?

A Google search states approximately 115 people lost their lives, more than 5,600 homes were destroyed. Runoff from the mountains washed out countless roads, bridges and railroad tracks across the counties. More than 30 inches of rain were recorded at Lake Arrowhead from February 27 through March 2. Google's aftermath images show flood damage: the National Orange Show, the Rubidoux Bridge, a house floating in the Santa Ana River, the train repair shop in Colton, train tracks twisted, trains buried, hundreds of cars throughout the area buried, telephone poles down, highways undercut, badly damaged. That was the local damage. Other pictures show the horrific destruction to cities in San Bernardino, Los Angeles, Orange and San Diego counties.

What I remember about March 2, 1938 is the constant rain, the muddy, debris filling the Santa Ana River, family being together, safe and warm, glowing candles in the kitchen and marshmallows, sweet, soft, chewy, fluffy, puffy marshmallows. A special treat from Daddy during the catastrophic flood of 1938.

Wanda's Yellow Two Piece Swimsuit

by Hazel Fuller

If one was to compare our bodies to a tree, Wanda would be the round sturdy trunk, Esther a long slim branch, and I, a skinny twig. We attended Redlands Junior High School and in the summer of 1946, between seventh and eighth grade, Esther invited me to go to the beach with her and her church friends. I wanted to go but had two problems, the first was that I had to ask Mother. She might say yes, no, or you will have to ask your Daddy, who I knew without asking would say NO. And I didn't have a swimsuit.

Summers on the farm where I lived were hot and chores began early in the morning before the sun got to hot. Feeding chickens, gathering eggs, cleaning eggs, weighing eggs, crating eggs for the egg man to pick up, crates and crates of eggs. Picking fruit from our trees, apricots, peaches, pears, plums, picking vegetables from the garden, okra, green beans, lima beans, tomatoes, and canning those fruits and vegetables. All that in addition to the usual chores — cleaning house, cooking meals, washing and ironing clothes — in a house without insulation, air conditioning, or a fan, sweat running down my face, peach fuzz on my arms. And the work was never done. Same thing day after day, except Sunday, all summer long. I looked forward to a day at the beach. My chances of going were slim to nil.

I worked up enough nerve to ask Mother and by golly. She. Said. Yes! My first trip to the beach! I wasn't sure what that meant — go to the beach. I had permission to go so first problem was solved. Second problem, the swimsuit. I knew there was no money to buy one so I asked Wanda if she had one I could borrow. She did and I could. Wanda was 14-years-old, a little chubby, very well developed with boobs and hips. I was 12-years-old, skinny, with neither boobs or hips, and no sign of either in sight. I borrowed Wanda's yellow two piece swimsuit. I was all set.

Esther and I, along with chaperons and classmates boarded the church bus for the hour long drive to Corona Del Mar State Beach. My first view of the Pacific Ocean was from the bluffs above the beach, a breathtaking view, the cliffs covered with ice plants, their dark green stems covered with purple and yellow blossoms, the beach, white sand dotted with people and umbrellas, people and surfboards in the water, huge rolling waves crashing against a rock jetty snaking out into the ocean, sheltering the beach and a cloudless blue sky. Beautiful! Over the years to come I would return to Corona Del Mar Beach many times with family and friends.

Many years before my first day at the beach, at the beginning of WWII, the government ordered a ten percent reduction in fabric used in women's swimwear. Fabric was needed for military uniforms, parachutes and other war efforts. Fashion designers economized fabric by designing two-piece swimsuits that looked like a one piece swimsuit cut in half, the top half shortened to looked like a bra, with thin shoulder or halter straps. The bottom, shorter and tight, covered the hips from waistline to a little below the buttocks. Wanda's swimsuit was one of those creations. I am sure with her hips and boobs it fit her perfectly. But on that summer day after arriving at the beach, I realized I should have tried on the swimsuit before leaving home.

Esther and I changed into swimsuits in the restroom located near the snack bar and rental shack. Her one piece suit was cute and fit her tall lean body. Wanda's two piece yellow suit was way to big for me. I could adjust the bra-like top by tying the straps tight at my neck and the bust line. I had nothing to fill the cups! The bottom half I could not adjust. It was stretchy fabric. I needed it to shrink not stretch. I held onto it to keep it from falling down. Once I was in the water I'd be okay, I thought.

On the way to the water, we stopped at the rental shack where Esther rented a boogie board. Obviously, this was not her first trip to the beach. The boogie board was an inflated canvas like mattress about two feet wide and three feet long, four or five inches thick. She carried it into the water while I held onto the swimsuit bottom. We laid crosswise with our chests on the board, our arms paddling, legs and feet dangling in the water and headed out into the cold salty Pacific. As we paddled, we were lifted up over incoming waves, the out-flowing tide gently carrying us beyond the breaking waves into the calm very deep water. I don't know if Esther could swim, but I knew she was blind as a bat without her coke bottle glasses, the lenses so thick it looked like she was wearing two magnifying glasses. She was not wearing her glasses as we drifted aimlessly. The blind leading the blind. She couldn't see. I couldn't swim. We were in very deep water.

Suddenly, I was aware of the danger we were in, terrified. My 12-year-old self shouted "head to shore." We were paddling with arms, kicking with legs, headed to the sand when suddenly, we were smacked, viciously, by a crashing wave and carried all the way to shore. I didn't know what happened. Where was I? I must be underwater because everything was pitch black. Was I sitting on the bottom of the ocean? I tried to stand but couldn't get my legs under me. I tried again and was pushed down, something was holding me down and pushing me down at the same time. Again, I tried to stand and again pushed down…by Esther, her hand on top of my head. Was she trying to drown me? She said "open your eyes." I did. Uh-oh!

Sitting in the sand at water's edge my chest was fully exposed to Esther and half of my eighth grade classmates, the top of Wanda's swimsuit around my neck. The bottom filled with sand. I quickly pulled the top down to cover my flat chest, but when I tried to stand up the weight of sand in the bottom half of Wanda's yellow two piece swimsuit pulled it down, way, way down. Embarrassingly south of my belly button. I could not pull it up. Each wave deposited more sand. I waited for a large wave to cover me so I could scoot into deeper water, stand up and wash sand out of the swimsuit, top and bottom. I held the bottom half to keep it from falling off my skinny body as I made my way back to shore.

Esther and friends had fun at the beach. They frolicked in the water, visited the snack bar, explored the rock jetty, played volleyball, built sandcastles. Wanda's yellow two piece swimsuit and I spent the day on my towel spread on the sand, watching. My pale skin had never been exposed to so much sun, sun reflecting off water or to salt water. This was years before sunscreen was a household item, before we became more knowledge about skin cancer and sun damaged skin. I should have found shade some place or stayed in the water. Live and learn.

It was dark when we left the beach. For me, the bus ride home was miserable. I was sick, shivering, burning with fever, burned to a crisp. When I got home and walked into the living room, Mother took one look at me and said "Oh, child!" shaking her head from side to side. I followed her into the kitchen where she opened the icebox, took out a crock of cold milk, the top covered with thick cream. She scooped up a handful of cream and slathered it on my lobster red body, cooling my body and moisturizing my skin. She had me drink a lot of water because I was dehydrated. My skin blistered and peeled, a miserable experience.

In spite of Wanda's swimsuit not fitting me, my chest being exposed to my classmates, and the sunburn, I enjoyed that summer day at the beach. Esther and I have stayed in touch over the past seventy-four years. I don't know what happen to Wanda or her yellow two-piece swimsuit. I imagine it went out of style when the bikini became popular in the sixty's, and more outdated with the current skimpy string bikini. Talk about designing women's swimwear to economize material!

Mom

by Judy Ginsberg

My mother made me eat mashed bananas, mushed up with cream or something, for breakfast every single morning. I hated it. Now I like the looks of bananas with their skins on, but I have never, ever been tempted to eat one.

However, she often served me baby lamb chops, and she seemed to love watching me devour them. It's a shame she's not with us today so I could ask her how she cooked them. If she's looking down now, she'll be instructing me, as long as she doesn't mention the health benefits of eating bananas.

And I won't mention the shot of scotch, so she won't be mad at my father. But it won't matter anyway because he's been gone a long time too.

Love to Mom and Dad!

Scotch

by Judy Ginsberg

When I was ten, my father took me to a family circle meeting at the home of a great-aunt. The living room was filled with relatives gabbing, while all the kids hung out at the back of the house.

Out of curiosity, I slipped into the living room to check it out. My father was sitting alone on a couch with a tiny glass of something in his hand, and I walked over to see what it was. He looked up at me with a grin on his face and said, "Wanna try some?"

The crowd was watching while I walked slowly to the far end of the room with the glass in my hand. When I saw my father watching, I swallowed the whole glass at once. The taste was shocking. But I slapped my forehead and said, "Oy, good!!!" Everyone laughed. It was scotch.

Many years later, I went to a local bar on a Friday night with my college friends and, trying to be cool, ordered a scotch and soda. "Oy!"

After that, I thankfully discovered wine.

Food Writing
by Judy Ginsberg

I have so much to do every morning but the thought of eating breakfast is the only thing that gets me out of bed. I run downstairs to the kitchen and start with a bowl of Cheerios with fresh blueberries and milk, munching it while I watch the morning news and weather.

But last week I found out that an important new medication tablet I had been taking along with my vitamins was not, under any circumstances, to be taken within four hours of swallowing anything else.

So now, I set my alarm clock to midnight every night, take the damn pill, which is on my night table, and continue watching *Perry Mason* on TV.

Every morning, I eat breakfast and take vitamins whenever the hell I want. In addition to the Cheerios, I've added toasted bagels with butter, sliced oranges, and a poached egg. Tomorrow I'll add a slice of bacon too. YUM YUM!

Spunky Little Ragi

by Ragini Goel

The child in me
Wants to go to the meadows
And pick wild flowers
When I come upon
A sign that says
Private Property
And no trespassers.

The child in me
Wants to chase butterflies
But as I look around
Those colorful winged beauties
Are nowhere to be found.

The child in me
Wants to run outside
And blow big bubbles
And run and catch them
But the bubbles elude me
And quickly fade away
Like a beautiful dream.

The child in me
Wants to go to the grove
And catapult ripe mangoes
When the gardener comes screaming

And I run quickly
To hide behind my favorite rock.

The child in me
Wants to go to the beach
And scare away
The seagulls on the seashore
But the stubborn seagulls
Don't care anymore.

The child in me
Wants to break the rules
Rebel to the hilt
And see the frowning look
On my mother's face
But Mom's gone away
To a land far away.

The child in me
Wants to dance in the rain
jump in the puddles
Mess up my clothes
Rain is so scarce in SoCal
There is no water
There are no puddles.

The child in me
Wants to go up tall trees
And climb all the way up
As high as the sky

There's a voice that I hear
you'll break your bones
Don't do this anymore.

The child in me
Wants to go to the park
and ride high up in swings
As high as the clouds
I'm denied that euphoria
As dizziness gets
the better of me.

The child in me
wants to fly a kite
But my kite flying mate
My beloved brother
Has gone far away
To a land where only angels can go.

The child in me
Wants to float paper boats
See them sail down the stream
When someone tells me
Don't pollute the water
You're old enough to know better.

The child in me
Wants to go on a binge
Eat chocolates and cookies
And candies all day

When the doctor calls
You better watch out
Too much sugar
Is not good for you.

The child in me
Wants to dance for hours
Like in a marathon
but the feet don't waltz
The same anymore
The desire is there
But the body is weak.

The child in me
Wants to be wild
have fun all the time
And never grow up
The wise man said
growing old is a must
Growing up is not!

Ragini Goel

Sterilized Muse

BY RAGINI GOEL

My door knobs are shining
    All locks sterilized
My bathrooms are sparkling
    My kitchen organized
Ive put away my perfumes
    I smell like Lysol wipes
Cleaning all day
    Im really sterilized
The Muse never knocks
    On my door anymore
Cooking and cleaning,
    Have become Mi Amor

I chat on the phone
    As I always can
I jog in the house
    Like I'm at the gym
I play bridge with the computer
    Instead of real people
I look in the mirror
    And powder my face
I go to my closet
    And try on some clothes
Then dress to the hilt
    But nowhere to go

I say to myself
> This cant be true

I'm sad and lonesome
> Not a creature around

Texting and what's app
> Doesn›t do it for me

I'm dying to hear
> A human sound

I long for the contact
> I crave very much

I yearn for the healing
> Of a grandchild's touch

Where is my family
> Where are my friends

Is this the same world
> Is this where I live

I wonder and wonder
> And ponder again

Confused perplexed
> I'm going insane

Scratching my head
> I start mopping the floor

When suddenly I see
> The Muse exit my door.

Guillermina "Minnie" Ayala Gonzales

BY MICHAEL A. GONZALES

The following Eulogy was read by Michael Gonzales at his Mom's Memorial service on January 12, 2013 at the Montebello Ward of the Church of Jesus Christ of Latter-day Saints Church.

Our mother, Guillermina "Minnie" Ayala Gonzales was born on March 26, 1914 in Santiago Conguripo, Michoacán, México to Adelaida "Mama Yaya" Zamora and Rosario "Papa Chayo" Ayala.

In September, 1917, Papa Chayo brought his family to the United States. Initially, they lived in Riverside, California until Papa Chayo purchased a piece of property on Railroad Street in Casa Blanca, a neighborhood of Riverside, California. He built the roof of the first room so they could move into the beginning of their home. Mom attended the Casa Blanca Elementary School beginning in the 2nd grade from 1923 to 1928.

As a young lady, Mom enjoyed participating in the various religious festivals. She played the guitar well enough to accompany herself while singing the songs of the time and also participated in a singing trio.

Mom wanted to earn some money for herself, so at age 17 she would hang around the Victoria Packing House. She so impressed the foreman that by age 18 she landed her first job, individually wrapping each orange, making sure to line up all of the Sunkist logos in the same manner.

During the Orange Festivals that were held, the packing house would pick her packed oranges to show. It was there that she met Francisco "Frank" Gonzales and they were married in 1935. In time Ralph, Michael, Rita and Alma were born to them. In 1948, the family was on the way to 1153 South Dacotah Street in East Los Angeles. It was there that the doors to Casa Blanca Market were opened and our youngest sister, Magdalena, was born.

Mom was a remarkable individual. Since Dad worked at another job, Mom operated the store six days a week from 7 AM 'til 7 PM with the help of each of the children. Gradually each of the children except Madge left home. Mom followed the example of her mother, Adelaida, by also becoming a naturalized citizen on January 6, 1961. Mom was proud to be an American citizen.

One day in the recent past, Rita asked her if she ever wanted to return to Mexico. She quickly shot back, "Heck no! I'm an American!"

Dacotah Street was no ordinary street; it was the neighborhood Familia. Everyone watched out for each other. We hold many memories of loving neighbors, kids having fun playing kick the can, Red Rover and baseball in the street — laughing and helping each other.

Many of the families who shopped at the Casa Blanca Market often expressed their love for our mother and were grateful for the kindnesses she showed them during the Dacotah Street years.

Madge remained with Mom through the closing of the store in February 1972. Shortly thereafter, Mom was able to fulfill a long time desire of her heart. She attended training at Buenaventura Convalescent Home as a Nurse's Aide. She worked there until she retired in about 1976 at age 62.

Following the birth of our sister's Triplets in 1981, Mom became a traveling Grandma, accompanying Alma's family on trips to Canada, Germany, Italy and other locations to help take care of the children.

Mom's energy and love seemed inexhaustible when it came to her family. All of our children were touched and nurtured by that love and energy as she visited each of us, blessing us with that something special that only she could give.

She always had a zest for life that was the envy of many people her age. Mom, never afraid to try something new, enrolled at East Los Angeles Junior College for the 1985 Spring semester at age 71 to take Music 412 — a singing course to enhance her musical talent. Mom had a wonderful alto voice and enjoyed singing in the St. Lucy Catholic Church choir for many years after she and Madge moved to Herbert Avenue.

She was never without the attention of her children. Her birthday celebrations hosted by Ralph, Alma, Rita and Madge were well-attended. Her friends and her cousins Chito, Glenn, and Chayo and their families rarely missed those celebrations.

Mom never really wanted for anything. She was blessed with good health and a loving family. Sadly, her long term memory gradually began to slip away. Amazingly, her musical memory was always there for her! She frequently burst into song at the slightest invitation. Among the many songs she liked to sing, her favorite was *Summertime*, the song that we heard prior to this service. Henry Mancini's music was also high on her list of favorites. Every time *Moon River* played she would quietly sing the words as she slipped into her afternoon naps.

She was indeed a wonderful person, ever willing to say a cheerful word to anyone who needed it. She had great hopes for all the children and truly loved us. She will always live in the memory of her family and be an inspiration to all who knew and loved her.

The greatest blessing for Mom was that she was never alone. Her constant companions, Anthony and her caregiver, Madge, were there to fulfill her every need and care for her during the later years of her life. It was not an easy journey for Madge but we are sure that she will cherish in her heart the privilege of having provided excellent care, concern and love for Mom.

Her descendants include: five children, 12 grandchildren, 35 great-grandchildren and 12 great-great-grandchildren, living in Arkansas, California, Florida, Hawaii, Idaho, Oregon, Texas, Nevada, and Utah.

'Til we meet again, Mom, have a great trip back home to the God who sent you to us!

Your Familia

Remembering My Grandfather — Rosario Ortiz Ayala

By Ralph A. Gonzales

My first recollection of my grandfather, Rosario Ortiz Ayala (my mother's father), was while living on Railroad Street in Casa Blanca, a neighborhood of Riverside, California.

At the time, in 1939, I was about two-years-old, I remember him as being lean and tall, wearing a full mustache, and with piercing green eyes. I remember that he walked with a noticeable limp, due to falling off a horse when he was younger and breaking his leg, leaving one leg shorter than the other. I remember calling him my "Papá Chayo". He used to take me for walks along the canal that ran behind our house, next to the orange orchards.

We used to walk for miles and then return back home walking on the railroad tracks that ran in front of our house. I remember the giant pepper trees along the tracks that provided shelter to the transient hobos that rode the rails. I remember the alfalfa fields and the wheat fields that we passed along the way and the walnut groves and orange groves we walked through, picking an occasional orange and eating it letting the juice run down my arms. He would break open the walnuts and share them with me. Sometimes my grandmother would pack us a lunch and we would sit on the edge of the canal and put our feet in the water, or sit in the cool shade of the orange trees.

I remember the house; it seemed large at the time. It had two bedrooms, a living room, a dining room and a kitchen. I remember the garage, the storage shed in the backyard, the chicken coop, the wash room, the walnut tree in the middle of the back yard, the pomegranate trees and my all time favorite apricot tree that was taller than the garage. Sometimes I would climb to the roof of the garage and lay in the shade of the branches, eating apricots to my heart's content. I remember catching the green June bugs that gathered on the apricot tree and tying a string to one of their legs and letting them fly around and around.

Only once, did I mistake a bumble bee for a June bug. They get mad and sting you. I never made that mistake again.

My grandfather worked as a citrus picker, picking oranges, lemons, grapefruit, whatever was in season. When I was four, he made me my own orange sack, downsizing a regular picking sack to fit me. He also modified the orange clippers to fit my hand and made a ladder that was small and light enough for me to carry. He would get me up very early in the morning around six so that we could be ready to be picked up by the truck that would take us out to the orchard that we were to pick that day.

I remember the smell of the hot coffee from the thermos that everyone was drinking on the way to work, and then warming myself by the fire that the workmen made to keep warm while waiting for the frost to thaw from the fruit. He would take me with him as his *rata*, which is what they called the kids that went with their parents to pick fruit.

I actually helped pick oranges, sometimes I could pick as many as 15 boxes in a day. He would let me get all of the fruit at ground level and inside the tree. The best part was when he would build a fire around eleven thirty, made with dried orange branches. By noon time all that was left of the fire were the white hot charcoal ashes.

On these ashes he would put the tacos (now called burritos) to warm up. They would crisp up and the beans and meat in salsa would heat up and be so delicious to eat. I remember nothing was better than having lunch in the open air with the aroma of all workers food heating up at the same time, and eating fresh oranges off the trees.

He had a dog named Prince, a short haired terrier, white with black markings, who would always be around my grandfather. I remember after work, grandpa would sit on the front porch, and prince would lay across his feet. He would call him his foot warmer. He would take me across the railroad tracks to Tiburcio's, a grocery store on Evans Street across from the big empty lot and buy me cream soda and candy bars.

We would walk to the depot and packing house and pick up orange crate wood. The wood was new, white and clean smelling and we used it to make all kinds of things. He made me my first sling shot, and with the railroad tracks running across the street I always had plenty of rocks for ammunition. I remember shooting at crows when we went on our walks, I could never hit any of them, but I sure made them scatter and fly away.

Next to our house was an empty lot that belonged to a relative of ours so grandpa would plow up the field and plant corn, chili plants, and all kinds of vegetables. When grandma made fresh tortillas I would grab one smear it with butter and run to chili plants and pick two or three of the young tender chilies and eat them with the tortillas. Boy they sure tasted good. I would play for hours in the corn field and eat fresh tomatoes off the vine.

I remember when the Japanese bombed Pearl Harbor; it even affected everyone in Casa Blanca (December 7, 1941). I remember the troop trains going by slowly in front of our house. We would give the soldiers bags of oranges as they went by and they would throw us money. There were many trains going by every day, troop trains loaded with soldiers and cargo trains loaded with war tanks, army trucks, jeeps, cannons, bombs and ammunition. I used to sit on the front porch and count how many railroad cars were on the train. Sometimes there were more than sixty cars going by.

My parents were the block wardens in case of an air raid. The sirens would blare and all the lights had to be turned off, they had to make sure everyone had their lights off. They also had to distribute emergency booklets and aircraft recognition pamphlets. I used to go through the boxes of stuff they had stored in the shed in back. I would spend hours reading/looking at the pictures of enemy planes, maps, and emergency supplies.

One evening as a train was going by, we heard a strange thumping sound that was not a common sound from a passing train, so we all went out to see what it was. Within seconds, we heard the screeching of metal and crunching of cars as they were being scattered on both sides of the tracks. A wheel had apparently broken from one of the cars and the train derailed.

Fortunately, the momentum of the train continued to push the derailed cars forward until it finally stopped. The last derailed car landed just 200 feet from the last house on our block. If the train had been going slower, none of us would know what had happened that evening. In all, about twenty box cars were split open scattering sacks of wheat, flour, huge cans of shortening, spam, butter and all kinds of food. The residents of Casa Blanca restocked their storerooms, as all through the night they were going back and forth picking up sacks of food scattered all over the place.

I remember my grandmother, Adelaida, I used to call her my Mama Yaya, probably because her full name was too hard for me to pronounce. She used to take me with her to the neighborhood grocery store to do the weekly shopping. It used to be a long walk to Don Francisco's Market. We had to walk towards the train depot, walk across the railroad tracks, and around the packing house, and up the street past Chano Soria's Bar, to the end of the block to Peter's Street. All in all, it was about seven city blocks in one direction. I looked forward to meeting Tranquilino, the ice cream vendor, pushing his ice cream cart with the big wagon wheels, along the way.

My grandmother would always buy me a cone of delicious home-made ice cream (for a nickel) and I would eat it all along the way. I know that the ice cream would give me the strength to carry the shopping bag full of groceries on the return trip back home. When we got back home we would unpack the bags of groceries and put the food away in the cupboards and in the icebox. In the afternoons I could smell the aroma of fresh tortillas being made in the kitchen and I would quickly make a bee line to the ice box for the butter and I would make myself a taco of hot freshly made tortillas smothered with butter, before grandma kicked me out of the kitchen.

We also used to take the bus to Riverside to go window shopping and sometimes go to the theater. The walk to the bus stop meant about a six block walk to Madison Street to get there in time before the bus left. Otherwise it meant another six blocks to Magnolia Avenue to catch that bus and then another twenty minute bus ride to Riverside. One of my fondest memories was when grandma took me to see a new Walt Disney film called *Fantasia*, this was I think back in 1943. To this day, I can still picture all of the scenes and the music of the *Nutcracker Suite*.

My grandfather would sometimes go out in the evening and not return until the very early hours of the morning. I thought that this was strange, because he would be very secretive about it.

Later he told us what he was doing. He would go and meet with a group of friends and they would go off to the hills of Corona and meet in one of the caves to have a séance and talk to the spirits of some ancient Indians that once lived in the area. He mentioned their names, but I can no longer remember them.

They would talk of buried treasure, gold, diamonds, rubies and the ways and means to discover it. However, as he described it, the treasures could be theirs only if greed would not rise among them.

The other stipulation was that once they were shown the location, all responsibility to find it would be theirs, and if they could not get it out their spirits would have to guard it forever. The reason this was a difficult proposition was that one of the spirits they contacted had been shown the location and could not extract the treasure. He was now the keeper and would remain so until he found someone else to take over the responsibility.

You see, just knowing where to dig was not enough, the revelation did not tell you how deep the treasure was or what obstacles were in the way. It could be under tons of solid rock or within a few feet of dirt.

Once you accepted the offer, you were committed and could not back out. There were many meetings and discussions among them and with other ancient spirits. He never revealed the outcome of these discussions with the group or if any accepted the offer. To my knowledge, my grandfather never accepted the offer; the price to pay was too great.

He was a kind and gentle person, but he was also a stern disciplinarian. I remember an incident that occurred only once, when I didn't do something I was supposed to do and was going to get spanked by him. And as he came to me, I ran and he couldn't catch me. I hid from him and after several hours the incident passed and all was forgotten.

Several days passed, and then I was in the backyard playing, he came up to me and showed me his knife. He asked me if I would take his knife and go cut a straight branch from the quince tree we had in the back yard. This was a treat for me to use his knife. I did and brought it to him.

He then said to use the knife and peel the bark off the branch until it was clean and white. After several minutes I showed him the branch and said that I had done a fine job. He then asked me to bring a rope we had in the garage because he was going to show me how to tie some knots. I went and got the rope.

First, he showed me how to tie the rope around the tree and secure it with a knot. Having done so, he then had me tie the rope around my feet and secure it correctly. I did this several times until I was sure I had done it right. He then grabbed the branch and told me "remember several days ago when you ran from me and I couldn't catch you, now run." I can still feel the welts from that clean quince branch that I worked so hard to peel. But, I never ran from him again.

One of the items he gave me that I kept for a long time were his pair of black boots that were a little bit big for me at the time, but I stuffed the toes with paper and I used them for a long time.

We lived in Casa Blanca until 1947, when my parents, Michael, Rita, Alma and I moved to Los Angeles. We came back to visit several times until 1952 when Papá Chayo passed away.

The Deputy Registrar of Voters
by Richard Gonzalez

It was 1960 when I first became involved with politics. I was excited about the possibility that John Kennedy could become the first Catholic to win the presidency of the United States. My father had raised me with the idea that a Catholic could never become president. I was eager to prove him wrong, so I volunteered that summer at the local Democratic Party headquarters in my hometown of San Bernardino, California.

One day as I was updating a card file from a prior election election against the new listing of registered voters from the County Registrar of Voters a man known as Doc Townsend barged into the headquarters and demanded to know what I was doing.

As I began to explain, he interrupted. "That's no way to win an election. Come with me and I'll show you how to win."

He informed me that he was a Deputy Registrar of Voters. Soon we were off in his car. We arrived at the first of several houses. There, he registered a husband and wife, repeating the process at several others'. At the last house he had me practice with another person.

"See how easy that is?" he asked me.

"Yes," I agreed. It seemed simple enough. Ask the person to swear to the truth; ask if they are a citizen of the United States; ask if they have ever been convicted of a felony; fill out the application for them and have them sign the form. Give them a receipt-strip from the form that confirms the new voter is registered. Presto!

We then drove to the San Bernardino County Registrar of Voters where he soon convinced someone to swear me in. Scarcely three hours had passed from the time I met Doc Townsend to my becoming an official Deputy Registrar of Voters.

Next, the persuasive Townsend convinced the manager of a busy Stater Brothers market on the west side of San Bernardino to let me have a choice spot at the store's exit. As I sat there with a card table and two chairs, I would offer to register customers as they left the store. Before leaving me, Townsend said, "Remember, you have to register every one, no matter their political party. I picked this spot for you because most the of the new voters here will register with the Democratic Party."

He also mentioned that I would receive 15 cents for every new voter. This was good news as it would help with gas money for my upcoming sophomore year at San Bernardino Valley College.

I did very well that summer. I registered a few Republicans, a couple of independents, but hundreds of Democrats. Doc clearly knew what he was doing when he set me up in this choice spot.

One afternoon as a customer was leaving the store, I asked him if he would like to register to vote.

"Can I?"

"Yes! It'll just take a minute."

As I began my interview, I asked him, "Have you ever been convicted of a felony?"

"Yes."

"Oh my. I'm sorry, sir, but I can't register you."

"Yea, that's what I thought," he said.

The man stood there for a moment as if in a daze.

I grew up in the Meadowbrook barrio where just about every fella had a record. This was my first encounter with a white male felon. For reasons I can't explain, I asked him, "What did you do?," as he seemed to be such a nice man.

"I married her," he stated matter-of-factly, as he pointed to a Negro lady who had been standing to my right all along. I was shocked.

"It's a felony to marry a Negro?," I asked.

"It is in Florida," he responded angrily.

I quickly determined by way of common sense that voter laws are a state matter, and I was sure it was not a felony in California to marry outside of one's "race." And I was not about to reify a peculiar and hateful law.

I looked at him and asked again, "Sir, may I register you to vote? Would you please take a seat."

When I finished registering him, I turned to his wife and asked, "How about you, m'am? Would you like to register to vote?"

What happened next is permanently imprinted on my memory.

The lady started to weep quietly and openly. Tears were streaming down her cheeks. I could barely talk when I asked her to take a seat and conduct the interview. After the couple left the store, I spent a few quiet minutes mulling over what had just happened.

I returned to school in September and stopped registering people. And I joined the campus Young Democrats. We were excited when we, as a club, viewed the Kennedy-Nixon debates. We were elated that Kennedy won, but disappointed that Nixon won California. It was a close race— a spread of a mere 7000 votes in this huge population. Even more disappointing was the realization that Kennedy lost San Bernardino County by 14,000 votes. In a word, we had let Kennedy lose to Nixon here in our own backyard. It seemed all of our hard work during the summer had been for naught.

But, for me, the most rewarding and meaningful act of the campaign in 1960 occurred when I registered that Negro woman while her proud husband smiled as he stood by with his grocery-laden shopping cart.

Cooking

by Mark Grinyer

When the band cooks the music rocks.

In the fall of night
    as a hot stove cooks
    green peppers halved
    deseeded, sliced — mixed
    with fresh red onions
    peeled, cut into halves
    then rings and chopped,
    sautéed with seasoned
    chicken breast strips —
    fajitas tonight
    that I cook now
    for myself and my wife
    reversing the roles
    of our years together.
We're making do
    as best we can.
    While autumn days
    grow shorter again.
    The music plays
    from our HomePod now
    instead of from dance
    or concert stands,
    or even in quiet
    social scenes,
    where diners share space
    and well-made meals
    in public rooms
    away from homes.

At home tonight
    where hummingbirds hover
    to feed from flowers
    on autumn vines
    the music comes
    from calling birds
    or from a cell-phone
    we have set
    on the table outside
    on our back porch
    away from friends
    and families,
    away from all
    that's become a threat
    to health and life
    to happiness,
    to lives once lived
    without these masks
    when bands still cooked
    and rocked the night.

Sunlight Sinking in the Sea

by Mark Grinyer

The sun climbed into bed with him
    and tried to wake the birds in his brain.
The birds said "No, I'll have none of this;
    it's much too wet and weird."
"But weird is good," the sleeping man said,
    "it softens the cage of your brain."
"A brain-cage, God," the bird brain said
    "I hardly know it's there, or if not there,
    not in your head, then somewhere out in the air."
"If dreams took flight, you'd know, I think,
    and you wouldn't spend so much time in bed."
    "Fie on sleep," he cried. "I like to soar the heights.
The nights that rock the souls of words,
    like birds that die when cats come by."
Mouths full of feathers are surreal things,
    they itch like peeling sunburn does.
It's a burning bed we leave, today
    with crispy critters where brains should be.
So fly away you pretty little bird,
    you don't want to mess with me, or
With sunlight sinking in the sea.

Dastardly Weather

by Mark Grinyer

Dastardly weather mistreated my day and gave me nothing but tea. Thanksgiving's coming, my friends all say, but I'm afraid to go out and see. I can't leave my house, to visit the ones I'd usually meet for a Thanksgiving feast or two. Two! You must be a pig, to feast so much, especially now, it seems, when so many people are all alone, out of work, and losing homes in pandemic storms that rain like pain on you and me. Such dastardly weather must be the worst, the pits from which we flee. Hopping like fleas on a hot tin plate, the plate off which wet weather bounced, laughing all the way. Mistreated days, like hopping fleas, foreshadow nothing to eat tonight and even less to say. The day has come; the weather's done — a dastard's legacy.

The Death of Cats

BY MARK GRINYER

Hiss last cat gave up on us. He died and went out to play. He played with his buddy, the cat we had before, who died too, and went away. They play together now, dancing with moonbeams beaming down from the harvest moon above. Its pale white light reflects so nice off fallen leaves and ice — ice on trees, ice on knees, ice on the edges of springs. Fresh water for cats, out in the freeze, making old paws cold on dancing feet at play. As cold as death, I say, as cold as today, when he's going away, away from you and me. The death of cats came home to us. This thought is sad to see.

So I sit outside for a while, admiring the ceiling above my head, where the rain fell through and onto you and me. It passed through dancing cats above and soaked the living room rug. This rug on which our old cats played, away from coyotes and hovering hawks, away from the threat of trees and freeze. I sit inside and wander around the great beyond today. Cat-less as the winter falls, I dream cold death away, I hope, but maybe not today. The hiss of his scythe is swinging near, the cats have gone to stay. We'll never see them home again, but on some winter day, we'll join them there, where icicles rule, and welcome their scrappy play.

Valiente

by Raquel Hernandez

He peered out of the window through a tiny crack, careful not to rustle the blinds, Miguel's dark round eyes widened. The police car was still sitting there. It had been over an hour now, and for Miguel the time stretched into an eternity. Miguel was raised to be cautious, to not draw attention. He knew what the price of doing so would be. His body trembled at the sight of the car parked directly across the street from the apartment that housed him, his mamá, papá, and abuelita. He was only ten, but his childlike innocence was fading quickly. This year he'd seen considerably more friends and neighbors rounded up and deported, and families torn apart.

"Qué haces hijito? Vente pa' ca." Miguel's mother beckoned with a voice that was barely above a whisper. She didn't want him to worry himself or arouse suspicion. He came into the tiny kitchen that smelled of freshly baked tortillas and jalapeños and took a deep breath. His mother wrapped him in a warm hug, and his stubby legs stopped trembling. Within the walls of their crowded two-bedroom apartment, there was a love and a warmth that melted away the tension of the outside world.

The world beyond their tiny apartment was unpredictable. Leaving their little apartment could mean never coming home, could mean being separated forever. It wasn't just the looming threat of deportation. In the past year, they had seen the country change. People changed. When they walked down the street, they were occasionally subject to looks of contempt. Miguelito heard the murmurs in the playground.

"Build a wall," chanted a small group of kids during recess. A phrase they'd no doubt heard from their parents, muttered at the nightly news or in conversations that occasionally took place between friends and neighbors. Miguel wondered if his classmates knew how hurtful it was, how alone it made him feel. What had he ever done for them to fear him, to think of him and his family as criminals, to want a wall between them? Miguelito couldn't understand. His padres used to tell him this was a land of opportunity.

"Porqué mama?" asked Miguel each time it happened. Innocence and tears gleaming in his round, dark, sad little eyes. His madre would stare back at him, eyes gleaming with tears, and lovingly reach out her callused hand to wipe the tears from his cheeks. So much had changed in the past year and she could not shield him from it.

"Sin razón, hijito. Seas valiente. Un día vas a lograr gran cosas. No importa lo que diga la gente," she would say before gently kissing his forehead.

All these thoughts raced through his mind as he waited, with bated breath, for the car to drive off into the hot Dallas summer night. As he helped his mother set the table, the comfort of her presence eased his worry. This was their little cielito. Their home was full of love, laughter, the scent of spices, and at night the sound of music as they sang along to banda. Here there was no wall, no snide comments telling them to speak English, no one to hurl insults. Remembering his mother's words, Miguel knew he could be brave. He took a deep breath and let his thoughts of the police car melt away.

"Te amó mamá.", he said hugging his mother tight. They ate together as a family. His abuela told stories of Mexico. His father recounted his day. Though they had little to eat, but it was what they had was made with love. The love filled them, and every corner of their tiny home.

Before heading off to bed, Miguel peered out of the window once more. The police car was gone, and, for the moment, all the people that he loved were safe. Tomorrow would be a new day. For now, they were together, and that was enough.

"Seas valiente!" As he drifted off to sleep, Miguel heard his mother's words again in his mind and his heart. Her words would keep away the nightmares. He could be brave like her, brave for her. He was so proud of her and his hardworking family, that had sacrificed so much for him. No one, and certainly no wall, could ever change that.

Hope Deteriorates in the Air
by Raquel Hernandez

What started as a year of hope turned quickly
New love faded fast
And turned suffocating
And toxic
So did the air the around us
It hung above us
The looming threat
Shutting up people
Shutting down countries
Shutting the window on hope
I saw them through the cloud of thick, sick air
And I saw them for who they really were
Pretense laid bare
No longer pretending to pretend
They were themselves
He was himself
And I didn't love the him that I saw
The people I loved
Like the air around us
turned toxic
Or maybe they always were
And in the cloud of sickness
In the quiet stillness of the new world
I could finally see it

Desert Disappearance
by Raquel Hernandez

The faded green 2004 Kia screeched beneath the hood, and she knew she had run her POS car into the ground. The timing could not have been more inconvenient. She veered to the side of a two-lane road out in nowhere Nevada. Far from the glitz and glamour of the Vegas strip, lay vast empty stretches of desert. It was 105 degrees, and the sun hung high in the sky promising several more hours of scorching heat. The summer sun beat down, burning the top of her shoulders slightly as she leaned in under the hood of her rust bucket Kia.

She checked her phone, but there was no reception out on this empty stretch of road. Beads of sweat dripped down her olive skin. She had seen a lone gas station a few miles back and she thought walking it would be better than slowly baking to death in the desert heat. She hiked along the desert road for about a mile before she stopped beneath an overpass. The sweltering heat was unbearable. She was lightheaded, and in an instant she slipped out of consciousness alone beneath the underpass.

When she awoke, she felt as though she was in a giant coffin. She wasn't sure where she was, but the small wooden shed smelled of death. The chains that binder her wrist looked well worn. She knew if she didn't think quickly that she would suffer the same fate as their last wearer. She heard the sound of heavy steel toed boots on the ground approaching. She feigned an unconscious state, as the wooden door creaked open on its rusty hinges.

Going Up The Hill

by Richard Hess

This year I have been looking at my genealogy and I have had "chance encounters" with many of my ancestors. In 1730, Jeremiah Hess sailed across the Atlantic Ocean to America with his wife Anna Maria and their four children. His 15-year-old son, Johann Conrad Hess, is my direct ancestor. I imagine traveling with you, Jeremiah, on your long, perilous journey crossing the Atlantic. I feel your excitement for a new beginning, but also your anxiety, bringing your family to the New World, with so many unknown perils. You and your sons fought in the Revolutionary War — what was that like? And later I see my ancestor Henry Hester — Henry, you fought for the Union in the Civil War. I am proud of you for volunteering, and I see your picture as a distinguished older gentleman. You made it through the War with all your limbs still intact. Good job, Henry! I would love to hear about your experiences!

As I think of my ancestors, I see a long line of people going up a steep hill. One by one they reach the top of the hill, and then disappear down the other side. First Jeremiah and Anna Maria pass over the hill. Then Johann Conrad and his family. Then, five generations later, my grandparents pass over the hill, and then my mother and father. Today I am near the top of the hill and I reflect on the journey that we all take. As children, we are at the bottom of the hill, playing, enjoying the moment, not thinking about the hill we are about to climb. Then, as teenagers, we realize that we must start to climb the hill ourselves. Decisions must be made. Do I take this path or that one? At times this gets scary — we realize that our actions now will have big consequences later. Then, farther up the hill, we are now married and have children. More responsibility. We are going steadily up the hill, with great determination, and as fast as we can. Not much time to look back and enjoy our accomplishments. Because we must keep climbing up the hill. There is still a long way to go and the going is getting tougher.

Finally, we near the top and our pace gets slower. Our days of frantic striving to accomplish more and more — are over. We are getting weary. Our steady, confident march has gotten slower. Now we are plodding along — one foot in front of the other. We need to take frequent breaks to catch our breath and work up the strength and the will to take another step. We are near the top of the hill – and we can feel it.

I can imagine our ancestors as they reach the top of the hill. They each pause, then disappear down the other side of the hill. There is a time to start walking up the hill – and a time to reach the top and reflect on the journey. A time to start our climb up the mountain and a time to finish it. We should pause and give thanks to God that He has given us this journey. We shall see what awaits us on the other side of the hill.

Good Advice

by Richard Hess

Today we ponder a seeming paradox, that some people who have gone through difficult times can offer simple, helpful advice and encouragement. By facing their tough challenges, they figure out what is important in life, and what things are just passing annoyances. And they share their insights with us. We get stronger muscles by lifting heavy weights. This makes our muscles work harder and they get stronger. Would not the same principle apply to our minds and wills? A popular song says, "What doesn't kill you makes you stronger." And perhaps wiser.

Life gets complicated when we focus on our problems. When we were young, we could run and have fun. Now, sometimes just getting up out of a chair rates a high five. In Fairbanks I had a patient, an elderly woman, who had severe rheumatoid arthritis. The joints in her hands were horribly swollen and misshapen. That looked very painful and I asked her how severe her pain was — I assumed 8 or 9 out of 10. But she said, "Oh, maybe 1 or 2, I try not to think about it. Then she had a great big smile and said, "Let me show you pictures of my grandchildren. I am going to see them today. Aren't they beautiful?" Yes, we can see a beautiful sunset. Or we can focus our attention on the weeds. It is our choice.

Recently, we mourned the passing of Chadwick Boseman, an exceptionally talented black actor who starred in several movies, including his portrayal of the Black Panther. For the past 4 years he had terminal colon cancer and endured many surgeries and rounds of chemo. He did not complain about it. In fact, the actors who worked with him did not even know he was sick. But his messages about life were simple and positive.

Another interesting person is Socrates. He had a hard life –

he fought in the Peloponnesian War in the 5th century BC. He fought on the side of Athens, which ended up losing this war. Final score – Sparta 1, Athens 0. He was critical of the government (what else is new). He was arrested and charged with corrupting the youth of Athens and not respecting the Roman gods. He drank some hemlock, and that was the end of the story. A difficult life, but here is some of his simple wise advice which is as relevant today as it was back then.

"The unexamined life is not worth living.

Wonder is the beginning of wisdom.

Be kind, for everyone you meet is fighting a hard battle.

Strong minds discuss ideas, average minds discuss events, weak minds discuss people."

That is still wise advice.

Show Me the Money

by Richard Hess

Last year seems oh so long ago, yeah, we sure had it good
We all got out to see our friends as often as we could.
A monster out of China came, and COVID 19 was his name.
Our governor said stay home, and we all knew we should.

We ended up in quite a mess
Those money woes can sure depress
But no need to muddle through, we knew just what to do.
We found the answer happily – a good old printing press!

We used to think "We spend too much; these deficits are bad."
Someday our kids will pay for this, and that just made us sad.
Seems deficits don't matter. Yeah, that was silly chatter.
Who would think green paper would make us feel so glad!

Oh, happy days will sure arrive
With George on the one and Abe on the five.
Now we can be so bold – cause our money's not backed by gold
So let's put this press on overdrive!

Abe took us through our worst time – the Civil War a bitter pill
And his picture really looks the best – On a good old five-dollar bill.
The prettiest sight we've seen – cause our favorite color is green
So let's just print out lots of dough – cause we have big pockets to fill.

Some say having money is bad, and loving it is a vice.

But we need it to buy our food – and stuff that is kind of nice.
So please don't sit around and cry – and yearn for days gone by.
They give us money we take it, because we are men not mice.

So, folks are really struggling, COVID put us to the test
But we all know we will come through – because of our printing press!
Oh, George and Abe were great – such wonderful heads of state
Ben Franklin's on the hundred bucks. That's why I like him the best!

Bouquets

BY CONNIE JAMESON

Bouquets of Flowers
Given for recognition, celebration, love
Providing a message from giver to recipient
Chosen for beauty, color, details
Individual flowers complimenting each other

We can give Bouquets of Flowers to our Land
Planting them in the soil
Flower gardens, orchards of blossoming trees
Enhancing the beauty seen as we walk or drive by Land

Now, let's go higher, viewing more of Land
Up and up, by hot air balloon or airplane
Look, we see more bouquets — Big Bouquets!
Groves of trees with their spring blossoms
Woods ablaze in autumn colors
Vineyards and fields of produce
Beautiful in the precision of their rows

Wait! There are more bouquets
But not bouquets of flowers or plants
Bouquets of colorful beach umbrellas
Rooftops of buildings
Sports team uniforms, festival crowds and tents
Layouts of cities, parks, roadways
All these, and more, give Land its color, design, variety
Bouquets to be enjoyed

The Very Best Bouquet to give our Land
Would be a Beautiful "People Bouquet"
A mixed bouquet of People as Flowers
A wild, wonderful mixture of our colors, shapes, sizes
With so many differing, interesting details
The beauty of each individual Flower enhanced
By being held closely together with all others

Oh, that we could provide this Bouquet Gift to our Land!

Wrong Victim

BY CONNIE JAMESON

The trap was set!
A newly-purchased wire box contraption
Some sort of food bait placed inside
Strategically placed
Now, we could just wait for the desired results
Capturing one of those rats lurking near our house

I took a quick glance at that empty trap
Ready in its location
I certainly did not want to see it *with* the victim
A trapped rat, inside
But, I feared that my husband, the "Great White Hunter"
Would be eager to show me
Oh, please, just tell me about it — No "Show and Tell!"

Next day, sounds of a captured critter caught our attention
However, he was not the intended victim
Certainly not!
It was just a little bird in the trap
Was he a hungry bird, an inquisitive bird, a foolish bird?
Probably all three!
We released the poor little fellow uninjured
(Except for his frightening ordeal)
I was so happy that our little "unintended victim" escaped safely

(I don't recall *ever* catching an *actual* rat in that newfangled
   trap!)

"His rage has borrowed legs"
by Connie Jameson

He used us
We *let* him use us

We all knew how he could be
So easily angered
Spouting off without thinking or checking
Just letting his emotions run wild

But this time — Oh, boy!
He really came unglued
Screaming, ranting, accusing
His face — bright red, contorted in anger

His behavior hit a new extreme level
It was so embarrassing and really scary

And look what we did!
We talked about the scene he'd made
The hateful content of his screaming tirade
Then, not only did we talk amongst ourselves,
We shared with others

I know I did. I bet you did, too
So, admit it, we actually assisted him
In spreading the effects of his horrible actions

His rage borrowed legs — *ours!*

Yes, *yours and mine*
Spreading his toxic message far and wide

Shame on us!
Let's determine, here and now, to *never* allow this to happen again
We'll use our legs — to just walk away

Mrs. Potts' Sad Iron

BY ANN KANTER

It was a gift from Helen Gropen, one of my parents' friends, at my high school graduation party in 1966, in Riverside, California. Helen was petite, had jet black hair and a memorable New York accent. Her husband, Joe, was my father's colleague, a dermatologist. Helen's gift to me was a small antique iron which has traveled with me ever since that party, as she intended. It became a reminder of ancestors, a placeholder for my great-grandmother's brass Shabbat candlesticks. I knew nothing about the candlesticks, and very little about Shabbat, until my grandmother gave them to me thirty years after high school because, she said, I was the granddaughter who would use them.

On her graduation card, Helen said that she remembered women in her family using these irons, that it was hard work, that I had accomplished a lot but there would be more hard work ahead for me. She noted that the iron was missing a handle and that someday I might find one for it. She probably pictured fun excursions to thrift stores in L.A. knowing that my mom liked to take me along.

In those days, I couldn't think past the next Friday night. I was 17, preoccupied with who might ask me out to see what movie, being responsible for taking paste-ups of the school paper out to the printer in West Riverside, and writing cologne-doused letters on pink onionskin paper to a boy in Claremont who I hoped to join at college in the Fall. I can't remember anyone my age at the graduation party — only my parents, their friends, and my younger sister and grandmother.

I took the iron with me to Pomona College, where it sat on an old dresser in my dorm room. At 23, returning home after living back East for a year, I found the iron in my trunk and then packed it in the Rambler when I drove to the Bay Area. There I searched the help wanted section of the Oakland Tribune, applied for work at a preschool and wasn't called for a second interview, and eventually got a job as a typist at the Alameda County Bar Association. The iron sat on my desk in the first furnished apartment where I lived alone near Lake Merritt. I would walk through a morning gathering of winter geese on my way to work in the old Tribune Tower building, where Hal Norton, a portly, retired lawyer who always wore a gold pocket watch and vest, encouraged me to apply to law school.

After that, the iron stayed on or near my desk for almost fifty years, through law school in San Francisco and eight different offices in Sacramento. Eventually it joined the shelves of small gifts from my immigration law clients and colleagues: a brass elephant from India, a crystal turtle from Hong Kong, a small papyrus scroll from Egypt. In all that time, only one person commented on the iron, that she had seen her grandmother use one.

The heft of the iron when you hold it is what's notable. I never understood the use of paperweights, and I had better doorstops, so the iron remained useless except as a reminder of the long-ago day when I received it. It looked rusty and somewhat dirty even though it was regularly dusted. And its small size — size 1 — was perplexing. Possibly it was used for ironing collars, or children's clothes, or maybe to train small girls.

I read that a young girl from a Southern California tribe learned to march and to iron at Sherman Institute in Riverside during the First World War. She later said, in words translated from the Luiseno: "The children ironed their clothes. And we could not [do] nonsense. We weren't supposed to stretch things when we ironed. We ironed them properly. We'd have to show it to the director first. And the director would look at it carefully. And then it was all right. Then we would put it away. If we didn't do it right, then we'd do it again. We would do it (again). It was pretty difficult at first. But we learned. We knew what to do. And we did it right."[1]

I imagine my grandmother as a teenager using a Mrs. Potts sad iron during World War I in Brooklyn. This would have been shortly before her arranged marriage to the wealthy owner of the belt factory where she worked, a man in his forties who did not become my grandfather. Mrs. Potts' irons had been on the market since the 1870's, and there were few changes in the models. There is no room to put coal in this iron — maybe they poured boiling water into the double hole in the top. But after some research I learn that women would keep three irons of increasing size going on their coal-burning stoves, changing them out as they cooled. The detachable handle worked for all three irons. And you could buy the whole assembly for 65 cents in the 1890's. The wooden handle was an innovation — the earlier handles were also iron, forcing women to iron using a potholder. And "sad iron" didn't mean that customers were unhappy. In the 19th century, "sad" meant "heavy."

On retiring about six months ago, I brought the iron home, and sometimes I have it with me on the card table in my living room where I sit by the fire on rainy evenings. Mostly it sits upstairs on my small California Mission desk where I write, filling notebooks before selecting which paragraphs to make digital on the computer downstairs.

I found a trivet for it on Ebay, and I negotiated a handle. I took a photo of it sitting next to a ruler — the iron measures six inches point to point — showing its rusty blonde color. Melissa, the Ebay seller, was quite sure that her handle would fit.

Outfitting my iron is part of a sifting process. What I am choosing to bring with me now I want to be repaired, identifiable, even usable. I am thinking about the objects I will pass on to

---

[1] Villiana Hyde and Eric Elliott, from "Going to Sherman." Reprinted in *Inlandia, A Literary Journey through California's Inland Empire*, 2006

sons and daughters-in-law, grandchildren, younger friends. I have new regard for simplicity — and integration.

The handle to the sad iron came in a small cardboard box on my doorstep. Melissa was right – it had a trigger-like mechanism that attached with a satisfying click, though the handle overlaps the pointed edges of the iron by about half an inch. I thanked Melissa, who was herself grateful that I hadn't delayed in buying it.

One of my four great-grandmothers, the Episcopal one from Upstate New York, remained a lady in her mind and her community's, even though she had divorced, raising three children with the help of her sister who had also divorced after a brief marriage to a concert violinist. It was great-granny who first taught me how to iron when I was about six and she had been staying with us for several weeks. She was tall, white-haired, somewhat stern, and she did not allow me to use steam in the first lesson. We started with easy items like my father's handkerchiefs, and she showed me how to fold them in quarters before the final pressing. Later I was allowed to try a blouse. "Always do the collar first, then the sleeves," she said. And she rewarded me by reciting a poem she had written and had published, called "My Heart Garden."

If great-granny and her sister had had maids as children and early in their marriages, they no longer had help by the time they retired to the village where they had once summered in Upstate New York, after working at a nearby private high school. My mother spent the winter of 1941 with them in their cold house with the antiques, the piano and the vegetable garden. She remembers that great-granny used a sad iron. So did one of my mother's girlfriends who came from a poor Catholic family and lived in a house with no electricity.

My grandmother had already taught my mother to iron using

an electric iron, leaving her the handkerchiefs and pillowcases to iron each week. My mother did her own ironing all through my childhood, especially if she could watch one or more Million Dollar Movies on the black and white TV. She had "mothers' helpers" but she didn't trust them with the ironing.

For my grandmother and great-grandmother, as for many in their generation, the point was to remain (or become) a lady and leave the ironing behind. Much easier said than done. Standards for ladyhood changed constantly, and the bar was higher for divorced women, recognizably Jewish women, women who read to much, and scribblers. All of which most of them were, and all of which I became.

Snapping the handle onto the iron gave me a feeling of completion, and so did setting the iron on its lacy wrought iron trivet for the first time. There was a feeling of something being off kilter before these two additions arrived. I possessed an old-fashioned iron that I would never actually use, yet it was figuratively burning a hole in my bookshelf all those years. I seem to remember a nightmare — sometime after the California earthquake of 1987 when the brick wall of my fourth story office shook hard — that the earthquake had upended my bookcase of client mementos, starting a fire and flinging my heated iron through the window.

The iron reminds me of earlier mindsets, from law school through motherhood, that life is hard. And yet it smooths itself, sometimes with little effort. These long days at home, I like to do a half hour of ironing, maybe twice a month. And carrying a warm stack of freshly-ironed placemats or T-shirts, putting them back on their recently-organized shelves, brings its own unique peace.

Dreaming

by Naresh Kaushal

Everyday I look at the sky
and I know it isn't there.
My tiny human mind tries
to hold itself together
as the universe comes to sit in my head.

There is no sky.
Just the cosmos and it's ominous hello.
I put a frame on it cos they told me to.
You told me to.
You're even telling me to now.

But it's just dreaming.
Cos nothing scares you like unending space.
We construct great cities in our minds
giant gleaming towers of importance
sleek shiny buildings that glow with vanity

But they are sticks in the wind.
Brittle huts as refuge for the delusional.
The Something is the raft you build
to save you from the nothing.
But the lost river will drag you away anyway.

So dream your dreams if you must
with your fantasist architecture
and your blind truths.
Just remember: the river will come for you in the end
And the void will not be denied.

I Never Told Anyone

by Naresh Kaushal

But I told you. I peeled off my layers
And you laughed.
Machine gunned air rubbing salt in my wounds.
Your indifference bit me
with its broken glass smile
and I withered in the shade
of your midday sun.

We blinked in that harsh light
skin sweating as coarse heat eroded it.
How much space there is between us
I thought as I melted into a swamp,
all burnt skin and molten bone.
A puddle of regret.
Hidden in plain sight.

I did tell one person

God help me she said.
Fat chance I said.
Slumped at the back
And disheveled at the front

I don't know if it even registered
Not the faintest of flickers
The gentlest of gestures
The smallest of signs

I gave my pain as a present,
all wrapped up and pretty,
eyes wet and pleading.
Like a dog desperate to talk

She tossed it to the side.
Probably gave it away
in a Secret Santa
or left it sobbing quietly on the shelf.

I never told anyone

But I'll tell you he said.
My heart sank as he
put his weight on me,
hung it around my neck like a giant chain.
Then threw away the key

I didn't want his dreams
Or his box
I felt like he grabbed my wrists
and crapped in my hands.
Leaving me there. Stranded.

Public Relations. Specialist.
by Naresh Kaushal

The wind meets the wall
and we laugh a bit longer than usual.
Then the tears.

Sadness sits inside of us
Like a giant throbbing tongue.
Salivating.

We talk more.

There is ice cream and sunshine
And effort-laden smiles;
weaved between us like tangled hair

Powerful silences batter their way in.
And we fall.
A constant crumbling.

Why do Elephants in cartoons
Stand on such small stools?
They're massive.

It's all I can think to say.

Weirdo musings on the mundane
Falling into my head
like insistent hail

A cloud passes the sun
The seafront darkens then brightens.
Such a fine line between restarting and stuttering

Previous happy visits
Sit around us like tutting relatives.
Why did we come here again?

To save the marriage?
I thought
Or to save myself?

You laughed here once
As you teased me about my job.
Public Relations. You said

Eyebrows arched as we
Snuck around in front of everyone.
The only way we could meet.

Specialist. I smiled back.
Long hair blowing into my mouth
Tickling my happiness into delight.

Now wind soaked dreams
Grasp our feet like concrete boots
And we can neither stay nor leave

Squashed up close;
We cower before the sea
Drowning in our distance.

You will find me

by Naresh Kaushal

striding down the tow path
all metronomic and lazy.
Like a messy arrow.

Gritty soil will crunch my feet.
Plateaus of sound will float
through my ears like windy kisses.

Hot dry air
will rub my face.
Like mischievous sandpaper.

And of course the river,
forever rolling, will drag my soul
through my eyes

and once more
I will taste the cosmos.
We will meet again.

I will find you.

The Bus Driver

by Naresh Kaushal

I cleaned the bath last night,
all shined and gleaming.
She'll never know. Drunk again.
I'll have to hold her hair
as she vomits in the bowl.
Of the toilet.

It's ok susan I will say
As she wretches
You will beat this.
More wretching
A rub of the back
Still hesitant after all these times

You can do it
A gurgle of thanks
And a large string of spit
Yo-yos tantalizingly into the bowl

I can never do enough for you
But it's too late
I'm already thinking
where now to hide the vodka?

Coffee Pleasures

by Cleone Knopfle

After 19 hours of driving from my college campus, I'm home at last to the anticipated smells and joyful traditional 10 am coffee shared with any family member available.

I see children running, playing, and laughing in the warm summer morning sunshine in the grassy yard near the growing garden. Then that oh, so distinct smell coming from the open kitchen window of freshly brewing coffee, to be served in the big white enamel pot with thin red trim accents. It holds enough for whoever is nearby to stop for a shared cup, along with telling of the morning's follies for all to enjoy before heading back to their tasks.

Coffee can be a habit or a comforting taste while taking time for yourself, or a time for contemplation. Sometimes a caffeine lift will zoom you over the next hurdle. In any situation that life might be presenting to you, the aroma and taste of coffee can help. Never miss a chance to partake in its complexities. Coffee is a treat to appreciate and savor.

And when traveling, with questions to be answered or discovering the local flavor of a new landscape, find and follow the smell of the area's coffee shops, and your answers will be found.

I recommend "History of Coffee in America: from Colonial Days to Your Cup," by Laura Minton Gonzalez, December 20, 2019, Public Goods.

The Wrightwood Post Office
April 16, 2020

BY DR. MJ (JOAN) KOERPER

Properly distanced six feet apart, due to the COVID-19 outbreak, only two customers are currently allowed to wait in the service lobby of the small Wrightwood California Post Office, in addition to any patron at the counter. Four package pick-up slips in hand, I am lucky to be one of them.

I'm fetching mail for myself, the Art Center, and neighbors who are more medically compromised than I. Two days prior, I retrieved mail from the boxes in the outer lobby, but refused to wait in the long line for the packages.

"I passed the bank on the way here and couldn't help thinking about the robbery," I muse aloud, breaking the silence.

"That was the first time a bank in Wrightwood was ever robbed, wasn't it?" queries the second customer, wearing a flowered face covering.

"Indeed, it was," I respond, chuckling. "Remember how we'd all go to the bank in our hats, sunglasses, and scarves, before the robbery? Then, after the robbery, the sign on the door demanded we remove our hats, sunglasses, and bandanas, or we'd be denied entry."

We scan each other, appropriately garbed for the pandemic in facial coverings, large glasses, and baseball caps, with our long hair tied back out of the way. Laughter erupts.

"They even hired that security guard!" chortles the gloved man at the service window. "Isn't the bank closed now? Due to the virus?" he asks.

"Yup," I quip. "The teller machine is still there, but for face-to-face service, we have to drive the ten miles to the Phelan branch."

That location has drive-up windows."

"Sure hope they re-open this here branch after Covid has passed," the man says on his way out the door.

"I hope the Post Office is still here," I mutter softly. "It's the heart and pulse of our village. What will we do if it's defunded?"

"Can't even imagine," retorts Mike, a neighbor, stepping into the lobby. "Whoever wants to close down the USPS has no clue about its history. Founded in 1775. Benjamin Franklin was appointed the first Postmaster, no less. It's critical to this country, and rural communities like ours especially. Essential."

Heavy plastic sheeting hangs from the ceiling to below the service counter obscuring, among other things, the samples of stamps available. Holes are cut in the appropriate places for mail, packages, and purchases to pass through, and credit card machine access.

Behind the counter, Becky, our postal worker, garbed in mask and gloves, is sweating. Despite the fifty-degree temps at 6,000 feet elevation in the San Gabriel Mountains, the lobby seems stifling. Becky describes my stamp choices, takes the blue slips, and returns with my parcels.

Hoisting a filled canvas bag over my left shoulder, I extend my right arm and make a one hundred and eighty degree sweep of the post offices' interior. "Look at us now," I say, voice dropping, glancing around the once friendly and familiar, surreal surroundings. Our heads lower, nodding slightly back and forth.

"Who would have ever thought…" utters the woman in the flowered mask, her eyes tearing as her gaze falls to the floor.

Perspective: Empty Shelves, Riots, & Chaos

by Dr. MJ (Joan) Koerper

"Really, Eddie," I said to my brother into the phone. "With our COVID-19 restrictions, I've only been to two grocery stores, each a few times. But I was starting to freak out seeing the empty bread shelves. I couldn't understand why."

"We're having a hard time finding bread here too," he replied. "I'm ordering all I can from my favorite bagel shop right here in downtown Salem, Oregon. Fresh every day."

I redirected the conversation to avoid a familiar tangent on bagels. "Back to the empty shelves. I was really having a hard time in the stores. It wasn't just the fact that the shelves were stripped bare. By my third trip to the grocery store I realized I was having flashbacks. Part of something larger. At first, I couldn't figure out why. Then my mind's eye saw it all as clear as day: where I lived through it before, and why it is so profound."

"Mary Joan, we've never lived through this before. There's never been a time like this in my life, especially in the stores," he said sternly with his "I worked in retail all my life and I know what I'm talking about," voice.

"*Don't* tell me what *I* remember or *know*, Eddie," I retorted in an equally firm voice.

Suddenly it occurred to me why he might not remember. Eddie, my only sibling, half-sibling actually, is seven years older than I.

"Eddie, when were you in the Army?"

He thought a moment. "1967 to 1969."

"Then you weren't home, in Michigan, when it all happened. You were out of the country."

"When what happened?" he queried.

"The Detroit Race Riots were in July of 1967. In addition to so much destruction downtown, city and suburban grocery stores, among others, in the whole region were practically cleared. People panicked.

"The same thing happened in 1968. People were frantic. In April, Martin Luther King, Jr. was assassinated. Then in June, 1968, Robert F. Kennedy met the same fate. Two of our top Civil Rights leaders murdered. All hell broke loose. People were terrified that tyranny was at the Country's door.

"In 1968, I saw the panic up close and personal. Remember Awrey Bakery?" I asked. "It was one of the two top bakeries in Detroit. In fact, it's still in existence."

"Yes, I remember Awrey's," he said.

"I was working for Awrey Bakery as a 'flyer,'" I started.

I didn't even have to close my eyes to see me at eighteen, on the job. Tall, thin, athletic, shoulder length hair, parted on the left side in a flip, wearing my uniform, a gold, shirtwaist waitress-style dress, with a short apron, nylons, and penny loafers.

"It was one of my part time jobs in undergraduate school," I continued. "At that time, I was delivering flowers to mortuaries, churches, and other customers for Burrell Flowers owned by, as you know, our dear Uncle Gordon. After my duties at the flower shop, I'd drive my little 1965 seafoam green, VW Bug, to five area grocery stores in the afternoon, 'flying' for Awrey Bakery.

"My job was to make sure the bread and baked goods shelves were neat and fully stocked. I'd re-arrange the goods, then go in the back to get the baked goods rack delivered that morning, bring it out, and re-stock the shelves. Remember how the bread shelves were fairly near the front door of each store, usually on the right-hand side?" I asked.

"I remember. They still are in most grocery stores," Eddie replied.

"Well, walking into the stores after the assassinations was shocking. The emptiness of the shelves and the commotion. People were stocking up, hoarding, rushing, crushing, and yelling, pushing overloaded carts.

"At first, I was unprepared to be in the middle of it. When customers saw my uniform, and realized there would be more baked goods out in a few minutes, they'd surround me. I was given a hero's welcome. I didn't even have time to put the items on the shelves. I'd just stand by the rack and hand out the goods. I was polite, but didn't let them push me over, or be rude. It was chaotic.

"I spent extra time at different stores to help out, unofficially, because they needed me. We were stocking and working as fast as we could. I have great empathy with how hard the grocery workers are toiling right now during COVID-19. To get what they need and keep the stores stocked.

"To top it all off, in 1968, I was deeply grieving the loss of two of my heroes, MLK, Jr. and Bobby Kennedy. I saw Bobby killed in real time, via television, just like I saw his brother, JFK assassinated when I was 14, in real time, via TV. You know, John F. Kennedy was the first politician I campaigned for."

"I don't remember that," Eddie said.

"Long story short, I've always honored that I worked in the grocery store environment. I learned a lot about it, even though it wasn't a long stint, and I wasn't part of the full-time staff. It was intense, demanding and required crisis intervention skills. But, until I walked into the grocery stores during this COVID-19 crisis, I'd buried most of the emptiness and bedlam of that experience. It's understandable, really, compared to all the roles and experiences I've had in my adult life. But, when I think about it, what a powerful time. So, there I was at my local grocers, Stater's or Jensen's, having Post Traumatic Stress symptoms and didn't know why until those memories surfaced."

"Huh. I didn't know that," Eddie said.

We went on to talk about how the rest of his family was doing and caught up. Everyone was managing as well as possible, despite COVID-19. Good news.

"Love you," I said.

"Love you too," he replied. We hung up.

The conversation was enlightening. It helped me articulate the source of those unsettling PTSD symptoms. Once again, the sight of swaths of empty shelves came flooding back, carrying with them memories and sensations of perilous, terrifying times. The hangings and beatings of Black people. The Cuban Missile Crisis. Freedom and Civil Rights marches. The Women's marches. The death of a classmate in the Vietnam War. Seeing "highlights" from the war aired nightly on the news and the protests against it. The Kent State massacre. The serial murders by the Co-Ed Killer, John Normal Collins, in Michigan, when I was in undergrad. And those were just the start. One sensation triggers another.

It reminded me how critical perception and perspective is. Not having gone through two major community and national events, as they were unleashed, and the aftermath they brought, Eddie felt his memory was correct. To him, the nation had not been through anything like COVID-19 generated before. But, it has.

I was lucky on another front. Our mother, an avid baker when I was a child, freely shared her life stories with me. As I sat on the kitchen table snitching dough, she explained the do's and don'ts of living. Some of those stories had to do with her being a child, ages 4 to 6, during the Flu Pandemic of 1918. She watched while neighbors who died during the night were carried out to, and laid by, the curb for the Red Cross wagon to pick up the remains.

Her strict habits were logically explained, including why to always carry a hankie. She scorned men who spat on the sidewalk leaving possibly infectious spittle for others to walk in. And, she would not use public "unclean" bathrooms, among others practices.

Her actions were best attempts to keep one's health and not catch, or spread, disease. When internalized, our mother's stories become part of us, part of our DNA. I learned.

Eddie didn't hear those stories. His, shared by a grieving widow, centered around keeping his father alive in his heart. William Edward Asman was killed in WWII when Eddie was two.

As a scholar, I also heavily researched the Flu Pandemic, and others, for a story I was writing. I wasn't surprised to hear that COVID-19 erupted. It was time. A hundred-year pandemic.

Writing this, another layer of my perspective on the empty store shelves, and the feelings that visual generates, surfaced.

In lieu of going on my high school senior trip to Washington, D.C. in 1967, since I'd already been there, I hit the road alone. My destination? The Adirondacks in Northern New York State to visit my best friend who was attending summer reading camp. En route, through a quirk of fate, I ended up standing on the streets of Newark, New Jersey, at a point in time toward the end of the Newark Riots that raged from July 12-July 17, 1967. Bearing witness.

Lining the streets, directly in front of me, a combined police force was fully deployed: local, state, and National Guard. Rifles in hands. Poised. Ready. Tanks rumbled down the middle of the quaking street. Sights, sounds, and sensations that have been buried deep in my cellular/visceral being ever since.

Both sides of the street held, what had been, inner city businesses. The baked goods shelves of corner stores were not simply empty, they were destroyed.

Returning home, I found my city engulfed in one of the most destructive and violent conflagrations during the "long hot summer of 1967." The Detroit Race Riot began on July 23. When it ended, July 28, 1967, 43 people were dead.

That fall, I started college. Major? Sociology and Social Work: Social Justice. I had to be part of trying to make the world a better place, even if it is just an infinitesimal breath of the solution. I still do.

The Scale

by Jessica Lea

If I step gingerly, daintily on
would it take off pounds?
How about I quickly jump on and off
stand on one leg
try the other leg
take off glasses
take off watch
hell, take off everything

contemplate a haircut
toenail clip
shave legs moonlighting as faux fur rug
give it the stink eye

try again

breathe out completely
air could weigh something
WAIT
maybe if I breathe in fully
maybe imagine floating like a balloon
maybe that would make a difference

light off
candle on
could romance work?

a little sweet talk
maybe dirty talk

clean it off
dust could be a half-ounce, right?

same as yesterday

I flip it the bird
step off
start my day
contemplating the extra steps
I would gain
by walking out to the garage
grabbing the rock hammer
and showing it who's boss.

I AM

by Jessica Lea

I am a sputtering solar fountain
spraying water droplets onto cracked cement.

I am shimmering reflections
dancing on water.

I am dampness seeping into bones
before the first glimmer of sun.

I am the pause between coos
of the mourning dove.

I am the scent of mown grass
with a hint of gasoline.

I am subtle shades of green blending into one dimension
pressing the world flat.

I am the space between letters on unturned pages
in your dusty book.

I am cracked tile that feels like a nail
crucifying the bottom of your foot.

I am the last purple flare of color on clouds
before the sun escapes.

I am your gasps of pleasure
and pain
which are sometimes the same.

I am
your unspoken desires.

Standing Outside
by Jessica Lea

in the backyard
moon
covered by
atmospheric lace

woven feathers
hang around stars
dreamcatchers
constellations consumed
by growing eastern light

Great Horned Owl
flies overhead
in breathless wonder
in a moment of grace

Windy Day

BY JESSICA LEA

Anna's hummingbird
fighting gusts
feathers ruffling like a child's flight simulation suit
clings to branch of plum tree
while crispy brown magnolia leaves
soar past.

If it weren't for
distant palms bending in for a kiss
the rhythmic movement
of swings
without riders
would feel haunted.

Drawing energy from the Santa Anas
hoping to stay rooted
that anything dead inside
shakes loose
blows away
becomes
a bird's nest
or lizard hidey hole
or nourishment for the trees.

Smudge

by Nina Lewis

He came to me
in a dream,
smudged at first, fleeting.

Before long he moved closer
opened himself up. Like daylight
he became clear.
Face of youth.

I hoped to see
some part of him I knew.

Like all dreams, this wasn't real.
I'd wake up feeling lost again,
knew I sought sense
even when pieces didn't fit.

After a while I'd look forward
to the smudge of a man
loitering
in my dreams.

Casually propping himself into scenes
knowing we were strangers,
echo and rotate,
image after image,

none of them

grown from places I knew,
countries I'd travelled.
A new territory unfurled –

nights brought me closer,
drew truth lightly
in a circle, encompassed
my deeper me.

Homing Birds

by Nina Lewis

There is pleasure in admiring birds,
a lot to learn of trust.

She yearns for the freedom
to spread her own wings, escape this city.

She wants to prove to her son there is no need
to be afraid, labels come from fear.

Like xenophobia and the slow acceptance
of foreigners to these cobbled squares.

She wants to teach him how to belong to place.
That it's okay to be different, to be surrounded by flight.

No Network Connection
by Nina Lewis

You are inoperable,
I click the link of you
and get Error 404.

You no longer exist –
except, I know you do.
It's me who's blocked.
Locked out. Shunned.

You are outdated,
haven't bothered
with your upgrade
Truth 2.0.

If you had, you
would know your view
of all this, is skewed.

But we're both screwed
on this connection,
because the server's down.

These are ghost pages,
little fictions I'm creating
to fill in the gaps
your carnage left behind.

That lingering reminder

of what happens when
someone gets it so wrong.

The lines of communication
    – broken.

Alkaline

by Nina Lewis

A promise written
                on water
will simply
         float away,

invisible words

           without record,
no echo
         of your swirling hand.

Traceless,
      the water has
                  moved on.

     Wild swimmers
          are on their second drafts.

                    T r e s p a s s i n g
through water,
    one   word   at   a   time.

Kite
by Nina Lewis

She floats along the deck
the boat has no sails,
holds no superstition.

She takes thermals
upwards and glides
into cloud wisps of air,

doesn't look down,
she's never liked heights.
She wonders how to descend.

Wriggles out of her parachute
skirt, turns head down, arms
dart steady. Expects to plunge.

Finds she has plume power,
is rocking backwards –
forwards.

She knows they'll wait
with ropes to bind her,
like some village giant,

misunderstood.
The choice is air-sky
or people-land, the place

of family wins every time.
She lets them reach up,
grab her, feet and hands.

Time, Out of Mind

by Robin Longfield

No-one who knows me would ever argue the fact that my relationship with time is complicated. Or, simply, non-existent. If I were to have my own personalized timepiece, I am certain it would feature wings, hands that moved backwards, and numbers of different sizes, arranged in a non-orderly fashion.

"Pokey," as in the children's book "The Pokey Little Puppy" may be the kindest word people have used when recounting going to museums or other points of interest with me. Everything I see must not just be seen, but experienced, processed, felt, and known. In his essay "On Nature," Ralph Waldo Emerson much more eloquently stated this way of being when he wrote " … I become a transparent eyeball. I am nothing. I see all…" I am certain my two daughters have their own terminology for what it was like to go anywhere with me. I am grateful that their own special words for me have been consigned to the secretive, sacrosanct, language of sisters.

Within my family I was called "The Snailette." This name was coined by my Aunt Carole, who had nicknamed my father "The Snail" for his ability to enjoy a meal and coffee (any meal, not just dinner) for at least an hour. I have inherited that tendency. Often, I am engrossed in conversations around me and forget to eat. Other times, I think of it as being firmly engaged in the moment. With zero thoughts being given to whatever moments are planned for the near future.

These tendencies are complicated by the other side of my time challenge: the amount of time it takes for me to either get out of the house to go anywhere, or, start on things at home that are important to me, such as reading or writing. To say it can take hours, is not an exaggeration. Being a "morning person" might be helpful. However, I appear to have been blessed with the circadian rhythm of a vampire. Not so bad when I was in my twenties; not so great now that I am teetering on the precipice of Medicare eligibility.

My dear, long suffering husband, Mr. Sunshine, is my opposite in all the above respects. One of his many special talents is his ability to begin his day emerging from a death-like sleep and to the fast food restaurant of this choice with the urgency of a volunteer fireman responding to an alarm. He appears to have been born with a set of invisible "blinkers" that ensure nothing gets between him and his goal. I, on the other hand, appear to be the one in need of such an accessory.

As he runs out the front door, I want to ask him things such as "What do you think is going to happen now? Is the car in front of you going to get the last of the hash browns? Is there a shortage of eggs?" As he has explained to me, countless times over the years "I know how to prioritize." Uh huh ….

A typical day in our home, especially in these days of quarantine and sheltering in place, proceeds in what has become a pattern, a rhythm, a film score that vacillates between the Keystone Kops and Dr. Zhivago, depending on who is doing the "doing". For example, much of the time, I have been awake long before Mr Sunshine. Unlike him, I have been up at least once during the night with a dog or a cat who needs to go outside. This will have been either to investigate some real or imagined goings on, or, attend to business of one sort or another. There may be a cat who managed to evade our attempts to bring it inside earlier, and has now decided that 3:00 a.m. is a good time to come indoors. Or maybe someone just wants a treat. Maybe I just want a treat. Never the same thing two nights in a row. Sometimes it is all of those events in one night. Mr. Sunshine is quite hard of hearing these days, and is aware of none of these happenings. I think this is the real reason why he can be so darned cheery and efficient in the morning.

After dislodging a cat or two from my head and our dog, Snickers, from on top of my feet, I lumber past the doggy stairs at the side of the bed, and make my way to the sliding glass door. If it's a good morning, I have remembered to turn off the alarm and open the door before either the cats, dogs or I crash into it. By this time, Mr. Sunshine has already been to the drive thru window for breakfast, and is in line for an oil change or dropping off yard sale items at the church. Or any number of other destinations so methodically plotted out on his daily "to do" list. He is a habitual "Lister." He will also have made at least three Facebook posts about his experiences crossing items off that list. When he returns, there will be a quiz for me about his account of the morning's adventures. There will have been adventures. The man can hardly walk to the mailbox without a reportable incident.

As for me, I am listless, in more ways than one. Still in the backyard, I notice the empty bird feeders, plants in need of water, and empty dog dishes. Unfortunately, I also notice a large airplane taking off, quickly gaining altitude. After over six months in quarantine, it does not take much in the way of visual prompts to transport me totally off track. At this point, my own internal rails are more like "Sherman's Knots," neatly upended and completely useless for getting me from one task to another. Before I realize what I have done, I have messaged my daughter, my best friend, and my sister in law. I've also registered to four Zoom events, spent $150.00 at an online Pampered Chef party, and signed 3 online petitions.

Somehow, in the midst of all those activities, I have also managed to fill the bird feeders, water the plants, and sweep the patio. All of it accomplished with the mindlessness of the all too familiar situation of having driven miles on a long stretch of road, getting to the destination, and realizing I don't know quite how I got there. Now I can go inside. Snickers follows me back into the house and stops where the doggie treats are kept. "Mommy loves her good girl," I say to her, while tossing her the first of many treats she will catch mid-air. Mind you, I have no idea what she actually did to be a good girl. I was too busy staring at airplanes or into my phone to notice. She's cute; that's enough.

I start a coffee in our Keurig. My favorite mug, an 18 ounce, turquoise, Fiestaware beauty is in place, and ready to catch the dark, magic, liquid inspiration that will soon warm both it and me. This does not always happen — sometimes the countertop and the floor get the coffee before I do.

There are other dogs pleading to be let outside now. Snickers and Stella (another Chihuahua) are mortal enemies. Therefore, they live in a perpetual state of quarantine from each other. Stella has two companions — Mackie, another chihuahua, who is afraid of everything, and Mary-Babes, who is afraid of nothing. Mary-Babes (Babes for short) has the sort of ancestry that could only be determined by a DNA test. No-one here is that curious — at least for now. A few more months under quarantine may change our minds and give more urgency to that question. But for now, we're good…

After grabbing a handful of doggie treats, I open the sliding glass door to the patio, then the door to their crate (which is right next to the sliding glass door). These doggies always get treats when they go outside. A marrow treat for Miss Babes; soft treats for Mackie and Stella. The soft treats are new to their routine. Last month, Stella developed a terrible cough, which, we learned, was not an illness, but rather, her attempts to cough up a piece of gravel she ingested, thinking it was dog food. The x-ray of her stomach revealed the presence of the gravel, which looked like a jagged pearl at the bottom of her stomach. The gravel has since been "re-homed." Mr. Sunshine and I are still recovering from the trans-wallet resection surgery we underwent to pay for that little event.

I must make sure that the door to the crate is positioned exactly in a way that will not allow Mary-Babes to escape into the house. For her, entry into the house is a means to an end — her eventual escape to the great, unfenced outdoors. Much of the time, Mr. Sunshine and I question the logic in going to retrieve her. But, fortunately for her, someone's cooler head always prevails.

If the doughnut shop is still open, Mr. Sunshine is probably there now. Or has stopped and ordered cookies or candies via Amazon, and made a shopping list for me, detailing his Instacart wish list. My phone is pinging and pinging with Facebook notifications. Many of these notifications are from him, detailing his experiences with the people he has encountered while slashing through his "to do" list with the deftness of a modern day D'Artagnan. Chris O'Donnell, Gene Kelly, or even Douglas Fairbanks have nothing on him in this particular role. Woe to the person or institution that stands in his way.

Meanwhile, I must now go into the garage and attend to the 4 cats who live here, as well as the ever changing amount of those who know, via the Kitty Information Network, that this house is a good place to stop by for treats and vittles. I open the garage door, and most of the cats who actually live here, run outside as though they are involved in a prison break. The ones who do not live here, rush into the garage like it's Walmart or Best Buy on Black Friday.

While in the garage, I remember there are towels in the dryer. I open the door, and all four of the softball sized dryer balls fall out and roll in four different directions. The cats think they are toys, and bat them about until they are now invisible to me. My motto about this being "There's plenty more where those came from." Mr. Sunshine does not use them anyway, and will notice neither their presence nor their absence. An immense, gray cat called Frankie, has bedded down in the laundry basket. A handful of treats thrown some distance from him provide motivation for him to move. I lug the now overflowing laundry basket back into the house, and deposit it onto the sofa. Someday, I'll get around to folding it. The Marie Kondo method of folding laundry has become the closest thing I have to a meditation practice. You should see my linen closet.

I remember the coffee at the Keurig machine, which by now is ice cold. I put it in the microwave for 30 seconds, hoping that none of it spills over. While this is happening, I notice dishes in the sink. Then, I start the process of unloading the clean dishes from the dishwasher, put them away, and begin loading up the dirty dishes.

Looking down at the floor, I notice that once again, it looks dirty. The vaguely beige-ish color of the tile, coupled with its rustic faux-Italian marble pattern, render it impossible for me to tell if it is or is not in need of cleaning. Mr. Sunshine sees this as a positive, but I am of the opposite opinion. So then, I am off to the garage again to get the fancy mop. If I am lucky, there will be several clean microfiber pads nearby. This mop cost more than most of my wardrobe items. The cool, smooth, sensation of its handle in my hands does not elicit the same sensation as putting on a fancy dress and accessories.

I am immediately distracted by the NPR program on the kitchen radio. It is an author interview. The Amazon app on my phone appears to open of its own volition, as if it knows precisely what I am thinking. An order confirmation quickly appears on my screen. In a few days, the book; a small, black Christmas Tree; 6 new ornaments; and 3 bags of coffee will be mine. There will also be 4 bags of cookies for Mr. Sunshine.

That task done, I am now ready to finish cleaning the kitchen floor. According to the young, energetic, consultant who sold me this mop, it should take no more than 8 minutes to transform my floor from dingy to dazzling. It has taken me at least 45 minutes.

Instead of young and energetic, by now, I look more like Penny Marshall's character in *Hocus Pocus*.

The coffee (remember the coffee?) did not spill over in the microwave, but is once again ice cold. Now it's unsalvageable, only fit for fertilizing the potted plants on the front porch. As I open the door, I am confronted by a box bearing the Amazon smile. This box is roughly the size of a 4-year-old child. Having no idea of what it may contain, I just leave it there. After all, it may be some sort of trick, Pandora's Box. So — I gingerly walk backwards into the house, pretending that the box was just something I may have imagined for a future story. I must face forward in the event Mr. Sunshine gets home before I am safely in the house. To successfully play dumb, one must think smart at the same time. But what would the plan be if he actually did come back now? Best option would likely be a sudden case of the vapors.

After making yet another coffee, finally, with a mug in hand, I head toward the bathroom. Now, it's time to get, "Put Together." During the time of the Great Pandemic, with its apparently eternal "stay at home order," the concept of "Put Together" has become increasingly loosely defined. It may mean the pajama pieces match, or at least, were not worn the day before. It may mean making my formerly short and stylish hair look just slightly removed from appearing to have been styled with an egg beater — or by one or more of the cats. Maybe I'll just throw on a hat and draw on some eyebrows. I, at least, can do that most days.

Just as I am about to begin with the eyebrow powder, my dog Snickers, begins barking and runs to the front door. It's Mr. Sunshine, with chocolate chip cookies, and a chocolate infused diet coke. My favorite fast food combo. However, he has also brought the Amazon package into the entryway and opened it. "What the $%#$?" He says. There are at least 10 items in it for which I evidently have subscriptions. And also received last month. And now I do not need any of it. Someone is going to have to find a home for all that dog & Cat food, paper towels, laundry items and cannellini beans. My protestations that "They cost less this way" are quickly overruled by Mr. Sunshine's impeccable mathematical and economics based logic. "Not if you get them every month!"

Maybe Mr Sunshine can rearrange the toilet paper in the garage and find room for all of that stuff. Being the master of efficiency and engineering that he is, he is much better suited for this type of job. My own brand of methodology falls more into the category of " If it doesn't injure someone when it falls out, it's good enough for me". But no such work is going on today. It is lunchtime and then nap-time for him. After that, since every item on his to-do list has been completed, it will be TV time for him. If there is ever a TV gameshow based on the trivia of Dick Wolf"s television shows, my Mr. Sunshine will be the James Holzhauer, Ken Jennings, and Brad Rutter of that show. Only sports, and I mean ANY type of sports, will deter him from that mission. To him, the television set is not so much an object, as a holy shrine to pursuits of passion performed by other people. He has transformed the act of spectatorship and mastery of the remote into its own Olympic-worthy sport. I can barely manage the remote. This has become a great source of amusement to him. I do what I can, when I can, for the cause of his happiness, no matter how fleeting the moment.

Meanwhile, it may be reading or writing time for me, provided I don't remember a load of laundry that needs to go into the washer right away, or a Zoom class or lecture. Or a person or animal who needs attending to. If I look out the window and see a butterfly in the front yard, it could be dinnertime before I know it. Hopefully, there are no phone calls to the Midwest or east coast that need to be made or returned. Other time zones are a whole different dimension to me. How DID I handle Skype a decade ago, when our daughter was on a study abroad program in Sweden? How do I ever accomplish anything or get out of the house at all? It could never have been my own sense of time at work. I'll never know. Maybe I should ask Mr. Sunshine.

Rising Sea Level

BY MERRILL LYEW

Shawnette strolled a few feet away from her doorsteps to the salty foam rolling up the beach, the warm tiny waves caressing her toes, as her reddish toenails vanished in the sand. Ripe almonds dropping down from the trees with large leaves. Miles on the horizon, majestic whales spewing colorful rainbows above the sea surface. A gray bearded fisherman rowing his loaded boat ashore, same as other villagers returning with their nightly catch. Vocal seagulls feasting behind the boats. Each morning one step less for Shawnette's foamy encounter, until one sunny morning the almonds were floating in her living room.

A Night at the Amphitheater
by Merrill Lyew

Pelias was cruising in his gray BMW SUV on the Redlands Boulevard, when the yellow traffic light turned red and he stopped at the corner of the Sixth Street. He first gazed randomly in the rear mirror to glimpse at the huge red ball sinking in the horizon, then his sight wandered to the control panel and he sighed as he noticed the fuel needle hitting zero, and thought,

"What a coincidence, two gas stations right there waving at me." As he pulled into the Shell gas station, his cell phone rang.

"Supper is ready, Pelias honey," whispered Sineidin on the other end, as he pressed the green icon on his iPhone.

"I'll be right home, dear, I just noticed that I am driving on an empty tank."

"Okay, but hurry up, we need to be there by 7:00 o'clock, the presentation starts at 7:30."

"Need to be where?"

"At the amphitheater in the Prospect Park, have you forgotten as always?"

"Yes, I am so sorry, I totally forgot, and I bought tickets for the Harkins Theater tonight."

"Well, you can forget the Harkins, we are going to Prospect Park tonight," countered Sineidin in her usual calm but commanding tone, as if she were still deployed in Iraq.

The couple drove in Sineidin's black Pontiac Firebird from their home on Wabash over to the Prospect Park, where they found a parking lot two blocks away from the corner of Highland Avenue and Cajon Street.

"If we had left home earlier, we would had found a closer parking lot," was Sineidin's remark as she stared reproachfully at

Pelias, while they walked back to the park.

"Yes, but maybe we should had compromised and stayed home tonight," he replied.

"Pelias, honey, how long have we been planning to see this presentation?"

"Yes, yes, over a year, you're right as usual. Let us stop arguing, we are approaching the amphitheater now," said Pelias waving his right hand at a colleague from work.

At around 9:30, halfway in the park, heading back to their car, Sineidin felt an urge.

"Honey, I need to go to the toilet right now."

"But Sineidin darling, we are just five minutes away from home."

"There is no way I can hold it in that long."

The couple was quite familiar with the facilities in the eleven acres of their favorite park.

"Okay, I'll wait for you here," said Pelias, stopping under a dim light pole to check his phone as Sineidin was rushing away in the darkness. After twenty minutes, he started to wonder why she was taking so long. Pelias went over to the toilets, he knocked at the door, shouting "Sineidin, Sineidin, Sineidin."

He tried opening the toilet door, it was not locked from inside.

Had he gone with her; he would had known what happened. Is she suddenly playing hide-and-seek? This was not the right moment. Did she get angry at him for leaving her wonder in the darkness and she then drove home alone?

"Who will ever understand these women …? "

Pelias was getting angry, puzzled, curious, clueless about what to do next. He walked to the parking lot; the black Firebird was still there. He walked back to the lonely park, hoping to find Sineidin or anybody he could ask, if they had seen a blond female in her thirties, around five feet seven inches tall. There was nobody else in the park but Pelias. For an instant, he remembered reading about haunted parks in the Inland Empire, and the girl murdered in the fifties in that park. But his focus now was Sineidin and nothing else but Sineidin. He called her cell phone so many times, went back and forth many times to the spot where they separated.

At around one o'clock in the morning, he decided to request the help of the Redlands police department.

"Sir, people wander off for no reason all the time. You need to wait more than 24 hours before filing an official report of a missing person".

On the second day at the police station, Pelias is introduced to Detective Chevell Jipson, who will investigate his case. At the introduction, both men stared petrified at each other. It was as if they were looking into the mirror. Tears and a smile of joy and fear in both faces, both scratching their heads at the same time. Clearly, they were twin brothers from their identical resemblance, but how come they did not know anything about each other before? How come their parents did not let them know they were adopted? Not knowing what to say to each other, Detective Jipson stuttered "If, if, if we are what I am sus-sus-suspecting we, we, we are, I, I, I shou-should not investigate you, you, your case…I, I, I nor-normally do, do not stutter, don't, don't know what's happening to me."

Pelias tried to respond, but also stuttered, "This, this is the biggest shock I have ever had in my, my entire life."

As later that day Pelias and Detective Jipson were going over the circumstances of Sineidin's disappearance, a call came in for Jipson, who did not report anything to his superior about his potential twin brother in the case he was assigned. They told him that a 911-call came in, reporting a person found in a well in the Prospect Park. Both men rushed to the Community Hospital where the patient was taken.

They entered the room where a smelly and awfully swollen Sineidin explained that while she was trying to find the toilet in the darkness, an owl chasing a rat flew awfully close behind her and she was so frightened, that she ran and accidentally fell into the uncovered well on a nest of scorpions. She was severely bitten in such a way, that she passed out for two days, and miraculously survived the large amount of scorpion venom.

Puzzled by their identical resemblance Chevell Jipson and Pelias Knetzgauer investigated their own records and discovered that they were born ten minutes apart from the same mother, who gave them in adoption to different loving couples.

Thoughts

BY Pamylla Marsh

Thanksgiving now one day past
myriad thoughts filtering down…
Thoughts of gratitude
Thoughts of reflection
Thoughts of concern for humanity.

Hope is a bottle, a buzzword, a balm
Yet what other product is there
to give solace that we'll make it
personally, globally,
and spiritually?

We've always had our sanctums;
they are nothing new.
Now perhaps wistful lighthouses,
beacons, and a placecard
of tomorrow's tenuous promise.

Flash Flood Casualties

by Terry Lee Marzell

I took a step back and regarded my reflection in the mirror. The royal blue sundress with green and white trim fit me well, and the light white sweater I threw over the top was a nice touch. I'd twisted my long, blonde hair into a flattering French twist and accessorized with a barrette featuring a yellow silk orchid. But the coup de gras was the pair of newly-purchased matching heels I'd bought to coordinate with the ensemble. These were the first color-coordinated shoes I'd ever had the money to buy, and this was the inaugural wearing.

I was looking forward to this evening. The three of us, my roommate Kristin, her mother Pat, and I, were planning to spend an evening with our friend Cindy. Since she'd accepted a job as an interior designer at that Palm Springs firm, we seldom got to spend time with her. "I'll drive," Kristin offered.

Kristin had discovered a back road that cut the drive to Cindy's place by half an hour. Today's weather forecast for the desert communities mentioned rain, with a slim possibility of flash floods. Not a problem for well-maintained roads, though. The three of us chattered gayly as we flew through the desert. Halfway to Palm Springs, a light sprinkle made windshield wipers necessary, but this wasn't the cloudburst that had been predicted, we commented as we sped along the peripheral road that dipped through usually dry washes. Tonight, that road featured only trickles of water easily traversed by car.

Once we arrived at Cindy's, the four of us enjoyed a great meal and convivial conversation. Cindy praised my chic outfit, especially the color-coordinated shoes and the hair decoration. Then she regaled us with stories about her new boss, who evidently was quite thorny to work with. "In fact," she finally got around to admitting, "I have a presentation tomorrow in Costa Mesa, and I should probably call it a night, since it will be a long drive in the morning. I'll have to get up early to be there on time."

Kristin suggested that Cindy come back with us and spend the night at our place. The drive from our Tustin apartment would be much easier than the long drive from Palm Springs. And she could extend her visit through the weekend, which would be fun for all of us. Cindy readily agreed. She quickly packed a small travel bag as the rest of us swiftly cleaned up our dinner party dishes. It was decided that we would caravan back to Orange County in two cars. I would ride back with Kristin in her Toyota, and Pat would ride with Cindy in her Buick. When we all set out on the road about an hour later, the rain was heavier, but, we all thought, still safe to drive in. Kristin and I were in the front car; Cindy and Pat were behind us.

Negotiating the road was harder and took longer than expected. About an hour later we were still in the desert, driving along that peripheral road we'd traveled earlier. Only now, what previously had been trickles of water were now discernibly deeper. Kristin slowed her speed, especially when we reached a rivulet of undecipherable depth. Cars had halted on the other side, but she decided to venture ahead anyway. Behind us, Cindy had stopped at the rivulet's edge, idling there. Clearly she was undecided about whether or not to attempt a crossing.

Kristin and I were about halfway to the other side when the car engine quit. Just quit. And it wouldn't restart. The two of us sat in the dark, listening to the intensifying rain pelting the windshield, hoping that if we sat it out for a while, by some miracle the engine would decide to cooperate. Again and again and again my friend tried to revive the engine, but after many minutes she was forced to admit defeat. We were stuck there, in the middle of what was now a rushing stream.

We waited like that for perhaps half an hour, and then, suddenly, two highway patrolmen dressed in yellow slickers embellished with silver reflective tape appeared at the windows, one on each side of the car. One of the officers tapped on the glass on the driver's side, and Kristin rolled her window down.

"Don't you think it's time we go now, girls?" he said.

Kristin shook her head and raised her hands in a gesture of futility. "I can't make the car go anywhere," she said.

The man looked askance. "I mean, get out and swim, because this car is going to wash away any minute now." Later we learned that it only takes 18 inches of rushing water to sweep away a full-sized automobile. No wonder the patrolmen insisted we get out of there immediately.

Kristin turned to look at me, and our eyes locked. I took a deep breath. "I don't think I'm in the right shoes for this," I remarked. My friend gave a short, sardonic laugh. "I don't think there **are** the right shoes for a flood," she philosophized. But I was determined to save my heels. I slipped them off my feet and grabbed my purse. Holding both above my head, I nervously announced, "I'm ready."

Simultaneously we each took a deep breath and opened our car doors. In a split second, the flood rushed through my car door. And out through Kristin's. I rolled my body out of the Toyota and, with the policeman's help, waded through the murky waters, clinging to a safety line that had been secured to a telephone pole on higher ground. Which was difficult to do with just one hand. I was prepared for the wet, the cold, and the current, but I was surprised by the chunks of rock and sharp twigs that swirled around me. Despite my bare feet, though, I managed to get to the higher portion of the road that, by now, was more like a shore than a street.

I took a moment to survey the personal damage. My lower legs and feet were scraped and battered. The rushing water was only knee deep, but because I'd been seated when I opened the car door, I was soaked and muddy up to the waist. Why had I chosen to wear a sundress when the weather forecast said rain? The yellow silk orchid in my hair was ruined, but my royal blue heels were still safe.

By then a tow truck had arrived, summoned by the highway patrolmen. Despite the pelting rain, the driver was able to hook up Kristin's disabled vehicle and pull it out of the torrent and muck. But by the time the car was rescued, another gulch road not far away also washed out, leaving the four of us, the policemen, and the tow truck driver stranded on a piece of high road between the two ruined sections of highway. And it appeared that we would all be there all night.

"Can't you arrange a helicopter rescue?" Cindy all but shrieked.

"No helicopter," one of the policemen responded. "Our lives are not in imminent danger."

"That's easy for you to say," she returned, dropping her head into her hands. "But my boss is going to skin me alive if I miss that meeting with the client in the morning."

The best he could do, said the officer, was use his police radio to contact the station, where a call could be patched through to her boss so she could let him know her situation. A solution Cindy reluctantly accepted, since she really had no other choice. All of us crowded around the patrol car, window rolled down, the better to hear the exchange between the boss and Cindy as she described the circumstances.

Now, either that man was completely lacking in empathy or he flat-out didn't believe her story.

"So," he spat out crossly, "Does this mean you will **not** be able to make the meeting with the client in the morning?"

Every jaw dropped.

Then one of the policemen seized the microphone. "Sir, this is Officer Shannon of the California Highway Patrol. Your employee, myself, and five others are stranded on a two-mile stretch of highway between two washed-out desert roads," he said. He provided very specific detail about where we were located, just in case it mattered. "And we'll be stuck here until the flood recedes. My guess is late tomorrow morning, at least," he grimly explained, not entirely patiently. "So, no, your employee will not be able to make her meeting with the client in the morning."

"Fine," the boss snapped. And then he hung up. For several long seconds we all stared at each other in silent disbelief.

We'd all been standing in the lashing rain, and so we ladies piled into Cindy's Buick. There we all settled in to wait for dawn. I dozed fitfully, still clutching my rescued heels. An hour later, however, Officer Shannon once again knocked on the window, and when I opened my eyes, I saw that the deluge had, for the most part, subsided.

"We're going to try to drive out of here," the policeman declared. To Cindy he said, "If you want me to drive your vehicle for you," he offered, "I can do that. Two of you ladies can ride in the police cruiser with my partner."

"Sure. You can drive my car," said Cindy, who frankly never passed up an opportunity to play the damsel in distress.

As Kristin and I clambered out of Cindy's auto and into the police cruiser, Officer Shannon slid behind the wheel. Our new caravan proceeded in an excruciatingly slow crawl across a stretch of unpaved road on high ground parallel to the washed-out gully. First the police cruiser, followed by Cindy's car driven by the officer. The tow truck driver, alas, was left alone to wait for the waters to recede before he could make his escape with Kristin's Toyota.

At last, even though it was still dark, we found asphalt. I think we all sighed with relief. Even Officer Shannon. Once we were on civilized ground, the officer pulled over to the shoulder, climbed out of Cindy's car, accepted a round of hearty thanks, made his goodbyes, and rejoined his partner in the police cruiser. We girls set out again, and for a while the cruiser followed behind at a safe distance.

We'd all made it safely through that flash flood. But there were two casualties. One was Kristin's car, which her insurance company declared a total loss. Once mud gets under the hood, her agent explained, it's nearly impossible to clean it out well enough for the engine to function again. That was no surprise. The second was Cindy's job. Her boss never did believe her story about being stranded in the desert, and he fired her for missing the meeting with the client. Cindy didn't argue with him. She simply declared she was grateful she didn't have to put up with an abusive supervisor anymore.

The real survivor was my pair of royal blue shoes, which lived on to form chic new outfits for years to follow.

The Beauty in a Hundred Mundane Moments

BY TERRY LEE MARZELL

Marian arrives 15 minutes late, but that's OK. There is plenty of time to get the job done. I've already loaded the donations I've collected into the back of my car. My little dog Kurby greets her with furious barking. "I don't know you," he tells her, "and I must protect my family." I hand her a dog biscuit which she promptly gives to him. He takes the biscuit in his mouth and trots away, satisfied that she is friend, not foe.

"You're going to need socks for those bare feet," she tells me. "Your sandals are not enough. It's cold out there." I grab a clean pair from the laundry room and ask my husband if he would please give me sock service. He kneels before me and wrestles a sock onto my left foot, and then my right foot. He gives each foot a three-second massage and a pat, smiles, and then gets up and goes back into the kitchen.

Outside, Marian and I take a quick assessment of each other's pile of donations. We decide it would be best to transfer my pile into her van, so we do that. Then we climb into her vehicle. We're going to a food bank that we haven't donated to before, and I've already done a MapQuest search. I was surprised to learn it's only a mile away.

As Marian follows my driving directions, we compare our lists of who donated this month. In addition to my own contributions, I received donations from Rod and Lee, I tell her. She says in addition to her own, she received donations from Cathy, Stephanie, Mary Anne, and Nadine. We comment that it's amazing that Nadine can find the time to participate, in spite of her own physical limitations and the fact that her husband has been hospitalized and is very ill. "I'll send him a get-well card later," I tell her. I mention that I think it might be nice if, for our community service project in November, we collect cash to give to an organization that provides service dogs for wounded veterans. "That's a great idea," she responds.

When we pull up in front of the food bank, I'm surprised. It's not the commercial facility with an office and neatly-labeled shelving that we usually encounter. It's actually just some pop-ups set up in the driveway of a private home.

Marian parks, and we clamber out. We walk up the driveway, encountering two ladies who work there that neither of us knows. The ladies are busy sorting boxes of produce. I'm surprised to see boxes of salads, vegetables, and fresh bread. Usually we see canned nonperishables, diapers, and paper products such as toilet paper and paper towels. Meanwhile, Jim arrives, and he introduces us to Ned, the organizer of the food bank. I think maybe he's also the homeowner.

We ask to borrow a cart on which to load our donations, and Ned rewards us with a large wagon with high sides. I think this will work well. We roll the wagon over to Marian's car and Marian, Jim, and I begin to load up our donations. Jim grabs two sacks of canned goods from his own car and throws them in the wagon. We open Marian's van and pile the wagon as high as we can. Right away we realize it's not all going to fit in one trip, but we pile it as high as we dare anyway. But as we roll the wagon across the street to the sorting area, a wheel falls off the darn thing, and there is Jim in the middle of the street, struggling to re-attach the wheel. The two nameless ladies rush over to help. So does a third woman. This third lady, who has been hovering on the curb across the street, is apparently homeless. Eventually we abandon the effort to re-attach the wheel, and each of us, including the homeless lady, grabs as much as we can carry and haul it over to the sorting area. The two nameless food bank helpers give each of us a rose to thank us for our donations. Frankly, these roses have seen better days, but we accept the gifts with sincere smiles and thank-you's.

We're still waiting for Lou to show up. Jim, Marian, and I huddle in a group at the end of the driveway and exchange pleasantries while we wait. A few minutes later, Lou pulls up in his pick-up truck, which is loaded to the gills with donated foods he picked up from the local grocery store. Again, I'm surprised. He's got gallons of milk, dozens of eggs, and packaged trays of cooked meats. Marian and I set down our roses so we can help him unload his truck.

When we're done unloading, Marian whispers to me that we must be sure to pick up our flowers, or the lady who gave them to us will have hurt feelings. So we reclaim our dilapidated roses. The four of us say our goodbyes, and Marian and I stroll toward her van. Then the homeless lady stops Jim to ask him if he would give her a lift to the community center, which he agrees to do. "I gave her a ride a couple of months ago," he explains, "when I saw her walking down the street lugging a huge turkey. She really looked like she needed help." He grins. "She remembers me."

We all get in our cars, and drive away. Our community service project for this month is done. I smile at the loveliness of the crisp, clear morning, but also about a hundred small — almost mundane — kindnesses that can take place in the space of just an hour. These moments are the beauty of the world.

May 9, 2018

by Phyllis Maynard

Our assignment in class was to write something as if we had a special "power" to make a change (or changes) to a situation (or person).

This was an opportunity to write about a horrendous experience of just two weeks earlier.

(Maybe this piece can help me get closure.)

I was in the intersection with my dog, "Lovie" (my 15-pound "Min-Pin").

I was trying to snap her leash's clasp back onto her collar. She wiggled away from me and was no farther than three feet away from me. I wasn't concerned — it was in a quiet neighborhood, with no traffic observed, and there were stop signs at the intersection. I did see a car coming (east) very slowly, approaching the stop sign…which gave me no worry since I could see the car was stopping a few feet from me, and could obviously see me and my dog.

The car began slowly moving from the full stop, and KEPT ON COMING! The car was approaching Lovie and I could see the front end of the car lift slightly, and then I heard a soft "thud."

She was gone — crushed and bleeding. I think she heard me — or saw me.

She wagged her tail, and then nothing.

The car was older — the color had been a metallic gold hue, but age turned it into a faded "mustard" color. The driver stopped the car and backed up a few feet — to see what happened — and then began moving forward still very slowly. If the driver were unaware (or didn't care) what had happened to my dog, he (or she) DID hear me scream to stop for help.

No, I didn't get a license ID — nor could I even identify the driver. All this time, I was watching Lovie. I could not believe this was happening in front of me, in slow motion.

This was a terrible ordeal, to witness a deliberate act done by someone who actually stopped to see what they did and then left the grief that's been mine ever since.

(With my "power" I simply want to "punish" this driver.)

Scene 1 - neighborhood intersection 8:30 - Ms. Kreman with her two children in their car going east on Rubidoux Avenue. Ms. Kreman (impatiently) talking on her cell phone.

"But, you'll HAVE to pick up the children after school. I have a 3 o'clock appointment, and what do you mean, it's my problem — I'll have to handle it?"

Suddenly, Camie Kreman, yelling from the back seat, "Stop, Mom — there's a dog — STOP!!!"

(A loud thump, and screech of tires)

"Oh, Mom — you hit that dog, you hit 'em!"

"That lady is screaming — it was her dog. Stop, Mom — she's yelling for you to stop…she wants you to help her!"

Ms. Kreman, on the cell phone, "Oh, my God — I hit a dog, what'll I do?"

5-year-old Kathy Kreman begins crying, screaming at her mother, "Stop and get the doggie!"

(voice on the cell phone) "You did what? Just drive! Get the hell out of there. Don't stop…go, go, go!"

Ms. Kreman, momentarily stopping the car — looking at the small dog agonizing terribly with obviously fatal injuries.

(voice on cell phone) "Are you driving? Keep going. Drop the kids off at school — you couldn't help that dog — just keep going!"

(loud crying from the back seat from 5-year-old Kathy and 7-year-old Camie) Camie tells his mom, "You did it. You ran over that dog!"

Scene 2 - Ms Kreman returned home - called to cancel her morning appointments - shaken from the episode that morning. A hot cup of tea, the morning paper and a comforting cuddle from her kitty-kat. That's all she needed to get things back in perspective. But, wait — what happened to kitty's calming purr? No sounds come from her but threatening snarls and hissing! What's wrong with her? She wants to go outside, away from something inside the house that appears to be very menacing.

And the dog — what is happening with the dog? His incessant barking is unnerving! Ms. Kreman went outside to calm poor old Cosmo and upon approaching him, he circled the yard until he found a small space under the fence where he could escape and take off! He ran out of the yard and down the street like the devil himself were tailing him.

Scene 3 - The Kreman family approaching the animal shelter to retrieve Cosmo after being picked up by the "catcher."

"Yep, Mr. Kreman. Your dog there was running like the wind and not about to stop. Something sure spooked him, but he'll quiet down now that his family is here!"

Cosmo began wagging his tail when he saw the two Kreman children, but he suddenly began growling and slunk back into a corner, hackles raising, ears laid back. What was wrong with this guy?

Mr. Kreman wrestled Cosmo to the car where he whined on the way back home.

Scene 4 - Two days later, Ms. Kreman and her children were at the local mall and approached the pet shop. The trauma of two days ago was wearing off slowly but not until a fuzzy, baby rabbit was promised to Kathy Kreman, to help erase the tragic scene she had witnessed.

What was happening? All the animals in the pet shop suddenly became antsy. They began pacing, whining, anxious to get away. Camie and Kathy were looking for the rabbits, while Ms. Kreman was looking at the puppies. All of a sudden, a scream came from Kathy, when one of the baby rabbits had scratched her — All of the rabbits huddled in a corner of the cage, making small growling noises when Ms. Kreman picked up one of the baby rabbits, gently holding it so Kathy could see it didn't really mean to scratch her. The rabbit was immediately subdued, and lay very quietly...too quietly. It was dead! What was happening? The shop owner told his customers he would need to close the shop, due to the animals unruliness that afternoon. No rabbit for Kathy.

Scene 5 - It was Saturday, and the yearly "Blessing Of The Animals" event was about to take place outside the church near the park. This was a happening that everyone enjoyed — especially the animals. It was a time when all animals seemed compatible with each other. There was romping, chasing, lots of good fellowship between the canine and the human animals. The Kreman family got out of their car and were walking toward the area where the priest was giving the blessings, when suddenly there was chaos! The dogs began howling eerily, the puppies were straining at their leashes, whimpering and trying to hide behind their owners' legs. It was obvious that the animal blessing event was momentarily over, at least until the animals could be quieted down. And they did quiet down and resumed the happy environment that was earlier — but it was only when Ms. Kreman retreated to their car, because Cosmo was just too much for her to handle, so she handed the leash to Mr. Kreman.

Scene 6 - Later that day, the Kreman children were due for a lesson at the horse stables. Both children were assigned smaller horses since they were both just beginners. Mr. Fetlock, the stable master had gotten the children seated, cinched up and ready for trotting. When Ms. Kreman left the car where she had enjoyed a second cup of thermos coffee, the horses began prancing and twisting around as if impatient to be sheltered in their stalls.

As Ms. Kreman began walking toward her children, their horses began nervously pawing the ground and trying to rear their small charges off their backs.

Mr. Fetlock, noticeably edgy over the horses' behavior, advised Ms. Kreman, "It'd be best, Ma'am, if the children dismount, and we cancel the session for today."

Scene 7 - Another two days had passed with the Kreman household in an endless state of agitation with a constantly barking dog and the cat missing for the past couple of days. Mr. Kreman had resigned himself to being "Mr. Mom" to the kids, with Ms. Kreman spending more and more time in the bedroom with a sick headache. The unsettling events of the week began with a visit from a representative of the Children's Protective Services. It appears Kathy Kreman's kindergarten teacher requested the involvement with CPS because little Kathy had told her teacher, "And my mom killed a little dog, and she killed a baby rabbit, and my kitty ran away from her, and I think I'm kinda afraid of her!"

It didn't help matters when Mr. Kreman explained to the CPS rep that "Their mother is impatient and becomes short tempered when the kids and mutts get noisy."

Some counseling sessions were advised.

Scene 8 - The psychiatrist's office, a beautifully decorated setting — the gentle-green walls with urns of plants and flowers tastefully placed around an aquarium holding a multitude of exotic fish.

You can imagine the next scene — The slight rumbling followed by water splashing everywhere! The fish forming a solid wall of agitation, created a crack in one of the tanks. Each of the fish tanks, one after the other began swirling with water, causing them to move and crack as if their occupants were trying to escape their watery enclosure.

Final scene - After a very wet Mr. and Ms. Kreman returned home, the doctor was called (since the migraines had become almost a daily occurrence). He advised Ms. Kreman to stay home, alone — no kids, no animals, no outside activities, no driving. Just medication and rest and quiet.

Mr. Kreman to the kids: "You heard the doctor, kids. No noise, and nothing upsetting to mom…and, just to make sure her bedroom has a pleasant, peaceful atmosphere, I have a surprise for mom — I bought a small aviary with a family of tiny finches to sing to her all day…"

Lovie

by Phyllis Maynard

I remember the day
    When droplets of dew
Kissed the clover leaves
    That blanketed you
'Neath the warming sun
    And gentle breeze.
I'll miss you friend —
    Now, hear me, please
We'll meet again
    We'll laugh and talk
And, sweet little friend
    We'll finish our walk!

Food With My Family

by Thomas McCabe

I'm not naive enough to think my family was special in the way we ate our meals together, or that our culinary skills set us apart. Just the opposite in fact. Our family meals were a cause for celebration, but what set us apart was the number of people that took part in our "celebration" and the way my parents, okay, my Mom, pulled it off.

Because of the extraordinary number of brothers and sisters that enjoyed our meals each evening, the preparation was a real undertaking. Just the logistics of seating a lot of children of varying ages and personalities was tricky. My parents were aware of our age differences (you know, they had each and every one of us!) so, to keep us close and connected, we were seated with an older sibling on each side of us: younger, older, younger, older. This arrangement helped us talk to and have an opportunity to get "to know" each of our siblings, not just the ones closest to us in birth order. To achieve the seating arrangements, we had two meals each evening, early and late. One luxury in our family was being able to say what meal you wanted to eat, early because we were "starving" or later because we were not starving. Just because we could state our preferences didn't always mean they were honored, however. And the reason for the denial could have been a long, involved explanation or as easy as the ever popular "Because I said so" answer that everyone loved so much. One more thing about the seating that I would like to share. During times when my dear parents thought we should all sit together, like holidays, especially Thanksgiving and birthdays, they would bring a plank of wood and place it on the seats of the separated chairs, thereby ingeniously creating "bench seating" on both sides of the table to make room for the entire group.

A fond memory I have of food preparation when I was growing

up involved coming home from school and meeting my brothers and sisters in the kitchen and helping with the task of peeling potatoes for dinner. This undertaking always involved ten pounds of potatoes and all of us helping. As terrible as it sounds, it was the one time during the day that we all visited and told stories of school and shared what was going on in our lives. It's remarkable to me that others wanted to take part in this daily ritual, and we were often joined by friends.

My mother would put the vast quantity of potatoes in an enormous pot and boil them unmercifully until she determined they were "done." And in an effort to protect her loving brood, she cooked all food to be consumed until it was DONE! There was no chance that any of our family would ever suffer from food poisoning from undercooked anything! She was determined in this area and it wasn't until much later that I learned that steak didn't break in half when coaxed. To be fair, my Mother became a much better cook later, when she was blessed with more time as our family grew up and left for school or marriage.

Growing up with 9 sisters and 6 brothers was a gift that I am really grateful for. We all made it to adulthood and no one ever suffered from food poisoning. We are aware of the little things and we are grateful in life and knowing we all have enough food to eat.

The Best Time in My Life Was About Who-With Not What-Had

BY BARBARA MEYER

I grew up with a Mom who had to work in order to pay the rent on the place where we lived. So, I decided that, when I get married, I am not going to work away from home, if I have any kids. When I met my husband, Marvin, that is one of the things we talked about before I agreed to marry him!!! Marvin is a very good man and a hard worker so I was able to follow this plan!!!

Marvin and I were married in 1959 and we have followed that plan. Our three children were born in 1961, 1963 and 1967.

Even though their father worked a lot of different jobs, and schedules were not always convenient, he always found time to spend special time with each of our children, as they grew up.

Beauty
by Marvin Meyer

When I think of visual beauty, nothing comes close to God's creations: the stars on a dark night, the telescope images from outer space, this earth and His paintings in our sky! When man finishes a drawing or paints a picture, it remains the same or begins to deteriorate. However, God's beautiful paintings in the sky are constantly changing. He has white, grey, black, yellow, red, orange and pink in His pallet when doing sky painting. If one could find or take the time, he could just sit or lay and watch a part of the sky and witness the work of this fantastic artist!

Barbara and I used to attend some of the Gates Cactus and Succulent Society meetings. Those people go all over the world searching for the plants that they love. They put up with terrible heat and often much danger because the plants and especially their flowers are so beautiful.

I am so thankful to have my eyesight in order to enjoy these views.

The Mask Dilemma

BY ROSE Y. MONGE

After my last shopping trip to Stater Bros., I'm annoyed. Before my next visit, I need a face covering to do my grocery shopping. Another requisite of the COVID-19 health crisis! I'm not a happy camper.

My first option is to wear a bandana. I've collected many of them over the years to use as fashion accessories. Questions swirl. Do I wear one while driving? Will I be able to breathe through the fabric? Will the bandana become damp from my breathing? What will I do if I sneeze unexpectedly? Will the fabric muffle my voice?

As I stew over my predicament, Facebook is abound with "do-it-yourself" videos about face coverings. The no-sewing option calls my name for I have zero sewing skills. All I need is a bandana and two elastic hair bands. The video instructs me to fold the bandana four times towards the middle and then attach one hair band on each side to wrap around the ear. What could be simpler? Epic failure!

Then, as mana from heaven, my brother Rudy texts me. Good news, he writes. Sally is making masks for us! My sister Sally lives in San Francisco and is an accomplished seamstress. How thoughtful of her, I reply. She's mailing them next week. I'll call you to make arrangements, he adds. I'm giddy with anticipation. I know each of the masks will be one-of-a-kind.

The following week, Rudy tells me he has the masks and is coming over my house to drop some off. When he arrives, his face and head are completely concealed. He resembles a Ninja warrior. His eyes are barely visible. We speak briefly through the screen door but he remains standing underneath my carport. His next stop is Moreno Valley to deliver masks for my brother Ralph and his family. It's good to see him but I regret not able to hug him or get close to him. We say our goodbyes and as he drives away, I retrieve the masks wrapped in a plastic bag.

I open the bag and as expected, I'm delighted. The cotton masks are colorful and unique bearing illustrations related to Mexico. My favorite has the iconic images of the Mexican card game-Lotería. I text Sally immediately to thank her. Send me a photo with your mask, she texts. Seriously? All you're going to see is my forehead and eyes peering through the mask, I respond. Just humor me, she writes. I'll consider it, I tell her. I have yet to respond to her request.

The following afternoon, I test-drive my brand new Lotería face mask when I pick up my carne asada combination plate from Alberto's drive-thru. Sweet success! Stater Bros., here I come!

(April 2020)

In Praise of the Flour Tortilla
by Rose Y. Monge

Did you know that flour tortillas originated in the northern states of Mexico such as Sonora, Chihuahua, Durango and Sinaloa? I certainly didn't and find this cultural food fact quite fascinating. I just take it for granted that everyone in Mexico enjoys the tasty morsel as part of the daily cuisine. I later learn that the soil in these states is better suited for growing wheat rather than corn. Mom probably finds it easier to make the flour tortillas than the corn, which requires special skills to prepare.

When the family immigrates from Agua Prieta, Sonora, to California in the late 1950s, I discover that some of our Mexican relatives consider the flour tortillas as "inauthentic." When they come over for dinner, they ask for corn tortillas and skip the flour — a staple at all our meals. I love tearing portions of the tortilla to scoop up my frijoles, chili sauces or anything that's in my plate. Who needs a fork or spoon? All Mom can do is apologize but makes sure to have plenty of corn tortillas for future invitations.

Gustavo Arellano, author of *Taco USA: How Mexican Food Conquered America*, made these comments on an article by Francis Lam in "The Opposite of Locavore," April 19, 2018.

"In Mexico, most Mexicans don't even have an opinion about flour tortillas because they're historically situated in The Borderlands of Northern Mexico – right on the U.S./Mexico border. As a result, historically, Northern Mexico has always been considered a land apart - *la tierra de los salvajes,* or 'the land of the savages.' That's in Mexico. Then, of course, in the United States, the great Mexican food evangelists see flour tortillas as a *gabacho* or a white appropriation of Mexican food, which is totally not the case."

Why is there such a controversy? Arellano continues his praise in the following essay, *In Praise of Flour Tortillas, An Unsung Jewel of the U.S.-Mexico Borderlands.* (January 13, 2018).

"The corn tortilla is an easy symbol of pride, an elemental food that connects Mexicans to our indigenous past and ancestral homeland. Those made *de harina* (of flour), by contrast, are bastard children of the U.S.-Mexico borderlands, a hybrid of the corn flatbread that has existed in Mexico for thousands of years and the wheat that the Spanish conquistadors brought over. Recent Mexican immigrants deride flour tortillas as a gringo quirk. (My own mother had never even tasted one until she arrived in Southern California from central Mexico, during the late nineteen-sixties.)"

Food fusion inevitably occurs near geographical proximity. Is Arizona to blame for promoting the "bastardized" Sonoran version of a culinary icon? Yes and no. Arellano considers the state as the American capital of the flour tortilla. The tortillas in Arizona "are prepared in a manner virtually identical to that of the ones across the border in Sonora. In Arizona, you can find versions as small as a palm or wider than a basketball hoop. No matter the size, they're surprisingly sturdy and versatile in ways that their U.S. peers aren't. Fold one up, and you get what Arizonans call a burro and the rest of the world calls a burrito; dunk a burro in the fryer, and it becomes a chimichanga. Bake the bigger tortillas with cheese and meat, and they transform into what's known as a cheese crisp."

Many of us will never experience the culinary joy of a great handmade flour tortilla. Arellano blames that on tortillas from brands like Calidad, Mission and others, which taste "metallic, rushed, with no soul." These brands find their way to American restaurants like Chipotle, Taco Bell and most national and international markets.

As a child in Agua Prieta, I remember that Mom makes her tortillas with magical ingredients: flour, salt, baking powder, lard and warm water. She mixes the ingredients with her fingertips, adding water in small increments. After blending, she kneads the dough, forming it into a ball and letting it rest for a while. Afterwards, she divides the dough into smaller circular portions or balls and covers it with a damp cloth to let it rest some more.

She flattens each ball on a floured surface with a rolling pin. Her tortillas are round, thin, almost transparent. A final step is to pat them with both hands before placing them on the hot comal to cook. In Mexico, we only have a wood-burning stove. Imagine my delight when Mom hands me a small portion of dough to make my own. Of course, mine are never round or thin but the woodsy aroma and the warm chewy texture is just as delicious, transporting me to tortilla heaven.

Memories of tortillas continue when the family enters the United States. We are poor and to supplement Dad's income, the family joins the summer migrant circuit for ten years. In Fresno, we live in abandoned barns, tents or railroad boxcars. Mom cooks our meals on the portable two-burner Coleman propane camper stove. Making tortillas is an outdoor affair. One of the fondest memories I have during this time is seeing Mom in the coolness of the summer evening standing next to the outdoor makeshift comal patting her tortillas into shape. The aroma is exquisite as it permeates throughout the campsite and unlike any other I have ever experienced.

In all fairness, we also eat corn tortillas. You can't make savory enchiladas, tostadas or tacos without them. On occasion, Mom makes "gorditas" which are small but thick corn cakes that she fries on a skillet and later tops with meat and vegetables. Delicious! It goes without saying that I enjoy both corn and flour. However, when a server at a Mexican restaurant asks me if I want flour or corn tortillas, there is no hesitation. I smile and proudly say: "Tortillas de harina, por favor."

Maybe Dreams Aren't Merciless

BY MARY-LYNNE MONROE

Dreams may not be merciless.
They may catch us unawares,
teetering on the precipice,
watching backs turned on us.

These times are clear as glass
left for the taking.
Broken and mended and
rebroken all again.

Wandering in desert sun,
blinded yet somehow unafraid,
following the pathless flight
of hawk and eagle and vulture.

Perhaps it's not so cruel
a time for epiphanies.
Perhaps they are necessary.

Warriors Like Us

by Mary-Lynne Monroe

Slipping across the sky,
swords flashing bright,
flaring into brilliance.

We march onward.
Knowing, moment by moment,
we face overpowering odds.

We fight a bitter
battle on another field
and lose ourselves there.

Hatred, fury-fierce
revenge slamming through our arms--
injury possessed.

Yet again we rise
to find ourselves alone. The
battlefield gone cold--

remorse for what's done
sinks deep into our souls.
Salvation lies in death.

Until the Fires Die
by Mary-Lynne Monroe

Swirling through an orange sky
warily waiting for water.
Charred, chapped and crisped,
ash floats on waves of wind.

Even now, remnants live
buried in hard wood and packed earth
banked by stone surroundings
where water cannot flow.

Until it all burns out
with winter rain and cold,
Until the fires die--
the embers live on bold.

Within the human breast,
there sits a razor edge of fear
unsure what may be hidden--
or, more precisely, where.

Wavering in the Wind

by Mary-Lynne Monroe

It was the most amazing thing,
to see the light winking,
growing larger by the moment
as it flittered closer.
Excitement expanded exponentially.
What was this dancing light?
Standing frozen in place
on the hill, next to the tallest oak,
watching with warm wariness
as the light took form.
No flickering flying candle,
this was definite. Wild
heart beating within my chest,
my eyes beheld the shape
while my mind whistled tunelessly.
A Dragon?!

Redefined

by Mary-Lynne Monroe

In what world
are we separate
from definition?
I have yet to find one.

The BLM movement
is - at its core -
a definition,
not only of the effects of racism
but of the strength
and diversity
and power
of Black lives and voices.
"Mama."
One word that's changed
our world,
our perception,
our definition
of ourselves,
the other and our relationships.

So in the midst of this
moment - movement -
of redefinition,
I am in the midst
of being redefined -

as a cancer survivor,
as a racist,
as an emerging antiracist
with surprisingly in-bred
antiracist roots
and a body
that got tangled
in forgetfulness,
white privilege
and ignorance.
Yet - like the
Himalayan blackberry
in Oregon fields -
continues to grow
wild, tangled, and
bearing sweet fruit.

En la Sombra Del Águila
by Roberto Murillo

Dicen que vinieron del sur. Que eran una gente perdida — gente ignorante, sin ambición, sin respeto, sin orgullo. Dicen que eran extranjeros, mojados — que eran ilegales en su querido AZTLAN.

Dicen que cruzaron EL RIO GRANDE sin permiso. Que vinieron de una tierra llamada México.

They endured discrimination. They were hated, scorned and treated with malice by the power structure. Les aplicaron presión to make them despise su cultura y sus costumbres — and their language.

Los forzaron to live among rodents y insects in tents and open fields. They were forced to live in hidden, selected areas. They were forced to create their own boundaries, their own Barrios and to defend themselves against intruders, and their own Raza.

They were induced and inducted into their armies. They were impelled to fight y morir por las guerras de sus opresores. They were compelled to become the MIGHTIEST SOLDADOS of the land. En las wars, they have repeatedly exhibited to the world sus corazones, sus bravuras, sus determinación. They displayed sus ancestor's fighting spirit, sus inborn **royal majestuosa SANGRE**.

As a reward for their sacrificio por sus vidas — for their patriotism — they were bestowed with labels: *beaner, wetback, greaser, spic*, among others. They returned to their sanctuary, to their beloved Barrios wounded, proud, and humble. They reunited con su querida raza, con sus queridos padres, hermanos, hermanas, tíos, tías, primos, amigos, y con sus santos abuelitos — esos viejitos quienes sabían toda la historia. Esos viejitos quienes no pedian nada a nadie, nomás **respeto y dignidad**.

For a chance, for a hope of acceptance, they were shamed into adding labels to themselves: Mexican-American, Latino, Latin-American. Hispanic, Brown-American, and more recently Latinx and Chicanx. Thus, creating even more disunity.

Pero disen por ahí que sus venas son highways por donde corre puro ROYAL BLOOD. SANGRE NOBLE. Dicen por ahí that Cortéz was not the ONE they were waiting for. When will he arrive?

¿Estan listos? Many attempts have been made and failed to forget that they are of Royal Blood.

Nunca jamás! Never will they forget que son

HIJOS DE
KINGS
HIJOS DE REYES
Somos
¡Chicanos!

Nuestro Pastor
By Roberto Murillo

Ya no sé en cual religión rezar.
todas me quieren reclutar
todas me prometen la Gloria
todas me ofrecen perdón
todas me piden ofertas
todas me piden dinero.

¡Ay! Diosito Bendito,
tantas religiones
y un solo Sagrado Corazón.

Tantas promesas
tantos engaños
tantas mentiras.
¡Tanta hipocresía!

Mientras que yo rece y rece
en está gran iglesia,
que es mi sufrida Casa Blanca.

Rezando por mis vicios
rezando por mis pecados
rezando por mis errores
rezando por mis muertos
rezando por mi hipocresía
rezando por perdón.

Tantos vicios
tanta enfermedad
tantas balas perdidas
tantos sepultorios
tanta falta de respeto
tanto desperdicio
tanto dinero perdido

Tan poquito dinero ganaron
mis santos viejitos
por sus grandes labores
tantos impuestos
tanta pobreza
tantos viejitos tristes.

Tan poquita educación
reciben mis niños, después de
tantas protestas
tantas marchas
tantos gritos
tantas juntas
tanto dinero robado.

Tantos niños sin ejemplos
tantos niños cuidando niños
tantos niños teniendo niños
tantas lineas para mantener
los niños
tantas madres buscando padres.

Tan poquitas organizaciones
tan poquita gente en las juntas
tantas juntas
tantas discusiones
tantos argumentos
cuantos líderes pretendientes,
que hablan sin la voz del pueblo
destruyendo lo que el pueblo,
con su gran labor logró.

Tantas mentiras
tanta diversión
tanta sabiduría
tanto talento
tanta bravura
tanto orgullo
tanto sufrimiento
tanta gente rece y rece.

¿En donde está nuestro
PASTOR?

California Jam

by Cindi Neisinger

"What are you lookin at!?" I yelled at my boyfriend, Michael. A tanned blonde girl had taken her top off.

She was on her boyfriend's shoulders, whipping her long hair to the beat. Deep Purple had burst onto the stage at dusk, with the song, Highway Star. "Nobody gonna take my car, I'm gonna race it to the groouund!" It was April 6th, 1974, at Ontario Motor Speedway, in California. California Jam was a rock festival, our version of Woodstock. I was pissed at my boyfriend, but I felt the energy of being one with the crowd of 250,000 young people. I would go to many more concerts in my life. Still, the spiritedness of this event would never be replicated or forgotten.

My boyfriend Michael, his brother Donny, and his girlfriend Maggie — who was saturated in Loves Baby Soft Cologne — had brought us a lid of marijuana. Four fingers of it. We didn't have scales yet; that's how it was measured in a baggy. Am I betting some of you know that? I met Michael in high school. He was one year older than me, at 17. He had long blond hair, green eyes, and always wore a men's suit jacket over his T-shirt, which labeled him as cool. He played in a rock band. Double cool. I was exotic looking with long shiny black hair, a tiny waist, and a petite body. He was a contrast to me. My skin was mocha brown and even darker in the Summer.

This was the day I found out about racism. No, seriously. It never came up till this day.

I grew up in a white suburban neighborhood. It felt colorless; nobody ever mentioned I was brown. I never said they were white. My mom was never home, always working two jobs because her goal was to buy a house. Which she did accomplish. I roamed the block and was usually in my girlfriend's living room watching *The Monkees* or just riding around the neighborhood on our banana seat bikes. When invited for dinners, which was quite often, there was usually white bread in the middle of the table, instead of tortillas. That should have been a clue, right? I went to a private Catholic Elementary School and then to a public high school where there were only three Mexicans, counting me. And that's where I met my first love, Michael.

Michael and his brother, Donny, decided we should leave the concert early. Little did I know, it would involve some acrobatic maneuvers. While strobe lights filled the sky and Emerson Lake and Palmer sang, "Welcome back my friends, to the show that never ends!" We moved through a sea of Bic Lighters, waving in the smoky air. Onward we trudged, trying to get past the crowd to the parking lot. We finally got to a wall of chain link fence. We were all so high, everyone yelled, "Bitchin!" and just laughed hysterically, at the challenge ahead of us.

The guys went; first, a tall chain-link fence about two stories high, it wasn't too scary, but when we looked to the very top, we thought, bummer, it had a top layer of barbed wire. Everyone in the back of the crowd turned to watch. The guys straddled the fence at the top, strong, young men in their youth, and us, damsels in distress, saved by our trendy two-inch leather belts, on our low hip-hugger pants. They lifted us over by grabbing our belts. The crowd went wild, cheering us on. Well, maybe not, I was still buzzed; it was good weed.

So, on the way home…we had to go through a bad part of town and someone pissed Donny off; it was a low rider with a few Mexican cholos. They cut us off as we were getting on the 60 freeway. Donny looked back at me while driving, and angrily, almost blaming me, said, "Why don't they just go back to their country? Fucking Mexicans!" I said, "Whoa! Whoa! Wait! Am *I* a fucking Mexican? Fuck you, Donny!" I always knew I was Mexican, but I had never felt racism.

Michael and I broke up that summer. My family moved to our new home in a "culturally diverse" neighborhood later that year. And soon, I started hanging out with some Mexican American friends for the first time. I'm not gonna lie, that kind of made me nervous. I don't speak Spanish. A colossal taboo if your Mexican. Unless you like to be called a pocha!

Lucky for me, disco was the new thing — "Lady Marmalade sang, "Gichi, Gichi, Ya, Ya, Da, Da!" and well, I had to fit in — I started wearing high waisted pants and riding in badass low rider cars. Even married a handsome Cuban-Mexican American.

Since starting my writing journey and talking to many great Latinx writers and champions of our culture, I have fully embraced my Mexican heritage. One of my Latina friends is a creative writing professor at a university. She said, "Fluency of Spanish is not a measure of your cultural heritage." I'm a third-generation American Citizen born in Montebello, California. My children grew up on Rock n Roll and oldies. But, ya! I'm a proud Mexican American. Not a Fucking Mexican! Adelante! Peace out!

A Tipsy Business Plan

by Cindi Neisinger

I grew up in a beauty shop called Dorita's Hair Fashions on Beverly Blvd in Montebello, California.

My mother, Dorita, had a business plan ahead of its time. I say that because up until recently, I saw an advertisement for a shop in Rancho Cucamonga that copied her idea — kidding, but she did it first.

When I was a kid, my mom would take me to her beauty shop to work. My job was to sweep the floors in-between haircuts. I was not too fond of it. She always wore her clean white uniform top and a black skirt with black heels. To save money, she used that black skirt for many years. Washing it and reworking it for social occasions too.

Looking back, she's inspired me with her determination and thinking outside the box. My mother, Dorita, was raised by immigrant parents that dreamed big, worked double hard, and owned a market and a home in Los Angeles. In 1945, World War II had just ended, and prosperity was around the corner for all.

In the 1960s, the trickle-down of generational wealth continued and provided the money for her schooling, in a trade that she would excel in Cosmetology School, through the gift of her inheritance. My mother forged through with the same plan for her children. My siblings and I will do the same for our children. It may stop there. Because owning a home to provide an inheritance for your children, after you pay it off, is almost impossible nowadays.

Mom worked hard in her beauty shop, coordinating haircuts and rolling perms on pin-straight hair that pinged out of white tissues everywhere. Dorita's Hair Fashions in the 1970s was successful and ahead of its time. A business plan uniquely for the gals who worked 9 to 5.

She advertised in local papers: Working ladies I'm open after 5 pm, and Saturdays, for you. I specialize in the newest styles and up-do's, too.

Her phone rang off the hook, back to back appointments, booked months in advance. Working hard was easy for her. She loved her job of coiffing hair.

So the timing was perfect, and it brought lots of business, but here is the secret of her success. At 5 pm, she would lock the doors; no walk-in's allowed by appointment only. Mom would walk to the backroom, emerging with a platter of refreshing cocktails to serve her clientele.

Her customers would smile from ear to ear, under hot, hooded dryers, magazines would disappear. Soon you heard the clinking of glasses and laughter. An ambiance of womanhood — Mom, would ask them, "Who wants another drinky-poo?"

Her hands and bobby-pins flew everywhere, cutting and trimming bangs, perms, frosting hair in a cap, bleached, tinted, and some wore a tiny wiglet on top. They all walked out, back-combed to the max. All glammed up, and they couldn't wait to go back. She was booked solid.

Mom bought us a home in an up and coming place, with all the money she saved. It was her goal and motivation, a better life for her children and future generations. To this day, when I step into a beauty salon for a service, the smell of the chemicals used to color and perm hair takes me back in time to my hardworking young mother.

One client at a time and a drinky-poo, a tipsy business plan, and she made her dream come true of owning and paying off our family home and providing prosperity and generational wealth for future generations: Mamá, a chingona of her time.

MAGA

After Percy Bysshe Shelley

by S. J. Perry

"What the hell have you got to lose?"
— Donald J. Trump

I met a poet from America
who said, "Steel beams of a once-shining
tower remain among the ruins of a once-great
city. On Fifth Avenue nearby rusts the burned-
out hulk of an armored limousine — no tires,
no window glass. Tattered skeletons
stoke fires in blackened fossil fuel drums
or tourniquet scarred arms with ragged belts
and search for veins. Nobody gives a shit.
Hanging aslant across the twisted beams
huge, once-golden letters: 'UM,' and below,
on crumbling, cluttered sidewalk, 'TR.'
No gilded gauds remaining anywhere.
Echoing through the concrete canyons,
a dog's haunted, hungry howl."

Soapy Dishwater

BY CHRISTINE PETZAR

Soapy dishwater. Looking out the window and wishing I were anywhere else, on an adventure instead of at this sink full of water and a jumbled stack of dishes and glasses and pots and pans to my right.

And yet, a sense of satisfaction as I move each item into the sink, the slippery soap cleaning my hands as well as the dishes. Dirty dishes from the right, coming out clean on my left, stacked neatly in the dish drain, ready for their next use. No adventure, maybe, but a calming restoration of order.

There are miracles here — traces of a good meal and the miracle of clean, hot, running water coming out of a faucet — the everydayness of it that I take for granted when millions do not have either luxury.

And the view from my kitchen window a miracle, too. Cars, joggers, people walking dogs, children on scooters and skateboards, the mail truck and the street sweeper. A parade of people passing by my window in their own moments of drudgery or adventure.

* * *

Maybe the thoughts that go parading through our heads are like dishwashing.

I visualize my thoughts approaching in waves, by my right ear. From there, they spend some time in my brain, and exit on the left. The trick — so I've been told — is to give each thought its proper space. Not all thoughts need the same amount of attention.

Just like dishes. Some dishes just need a bit of soap and a quick rinse. Deal with them quickly and stack on the left. Some thoughts are like that, too. Make a note of them — "oh, there you are" — and let them go. Other thoughts — like deep grief or sadness — require more effort and time, like scrubbing a pot or a pan. They merit more attention.

Then there are the dishes and thoughts that have been ignored too long — pushed away or avoided. The ones you don't want to deal with. They will require even more work now that the dirt is hardened and baked on, and might even require some extra soaking time to loosen things up. They could have been dealt with more easily if I hadn't spent so much time avoiding them. But even those don't deserve to be whipped up into a tidal wave — that just creates more chaos.

Give each dish its proper attention, each thought its proper space — no more, no less. Take the dishes out of the sink, stack them on the left, order restored until tomorrow. Set the thoughts aside, too — for now. Look up and focus on the view where you are. There's a whole other parade out there.

A Memorable Holiday, Christmas Eve 2019

by Christine Petzar

My sister says that every woman dreams of having her "Camelot moment" at the holidays — one perfect moment when the house is clean, there are no cooking disasters, the family isn't bickering, the gifts are just right, and all the work needed to "make the magic happen" pays off. But let's face it, we rarely (if ever) get that moment. Someone has the flu, there's a power outage, the sink gets clogged and a plumber has to be called. Every one of those things has happened to me. (Note: Carrot and potato peelings don't go down the garbage disposal — you know who you are.) No doubt you have your own list of minor misfortunes, but one thing you can say for them, they do make a holiday memorable!

The closest I got to a Camelot moment was in 2013 when my husband, Doug, and I hosted the annual holiday dinner for his book group (The Geezer Readers) and their wives. An uncle had died that year as well as my brother-in-law — the first family death of my generation. It was a stark reminder to seize the day and say yes to life while you have the chance. I said yes to hosting the dinner, channeled my inner Martha Stewart and thoroughly enjoyed it all — really! And after everyone left, there was that "good tired" feeling as Doug and I cleaned up the dishes and chatted idly about the evening — pleased that we had accomplished something together and that a good time was had by all.

2018 would turn out to be Doug's last Christmas, but of course we didn't know that at the time. He had a bad cold and we had to postpone Christmas Eve dinner and settle for FaceTime with family on Christmas Day. The silver lining was a wonderful dinner and fun family game night later in the week — perhaps more enjoyable with the Christmas rush behind us. And after years of trying to make the perfect apple pie (his favorite) I finally achieved it that year — it only took until age 69 to get it right! Everything worked out in the end, just not the way we had originally planned.

2019 was definitely not a Camelot year. It was my first year After Doug (A.D.) and the year Before COVID (B.C.) but the virus wasn't quite on our radar yet. The first Christmas without him felt like going through the motions. Life does go on, but it's muted. My daughter's family all pitched in to help with the preparations and support me. The grandkids helped put up the tree. My son-in-law put up the outside Christmas lights and helped get things down from the upper closets, grabbing the step stool and cheerfully announcing, "rickety since 1984!" as he headed down the hall. That step stool never quite locked into place right — you'd be on it and suddenly it would go ka-chunk and drop an inch, throwing you off balance. It was a running family joke.

The plan for Christmas Eve was to have dinner at my house, and I made the perfect apple pie once again, in honor of Doug. We were then going to open just a few gifts, watch a movie, and go to the 11:00 p.m. church service, filing out to the courtyard at midnight to light candles and sing "Silent Night" together in a circle in the cold night air.

After dinner, with Blaze (their Boston terrier) happily feasting on table scraps, we proceeded with the plan, settling in for the movie. For some inexplicable reason, I had never seen *National Lampoon's Christmas Vacation* with Chevy Chase. In the interest of broadening my cultural horizons, that was the movie of the evening. Its madcap craziness was a good thing, to lighten our mood.

There is a scene towards the end of the movie where a dog chases a squirrel through the house. As the two animals crash through the door into a messy and jumbled garage, what do I see on the left of the screen but a familiar-looking object. "Stop the movie, go back!" I shouted. Sure enough, it was my "rickety since 1984" step stool — the step stool of family legend. With the movie paused on that frame, I got the step stool from the kitchen to prove my point. It was exact, right down to the bolts underneath (we counted them).

We were laughing uncontrollably at this coincidence when it happened. Someone sniffed and went "ew"…the unmistakable odor of a neighborhood skunk was seeping in, even with all the windows and doors closed. Then, in slow-moving horror, I realized that I had just let Blaze out the back kitchen door.

It was like that scene in the movie *A Christmas Story* when the Bumpuses' dog knocks the turkey off the table — chaos and shouting as everyone jumped up to deal with the situation. My son-in-law went out, grabbed the dog, ran down the hall with him (at arm's length), threw him in the bathtub and started the water. My daughter ran for detergent and baking soda. One of the kids grabbed a towel from the hall closet. I started opening windows. In the midst of all the activity swirling around him, Blaze himself was as calm as could be — serene, even. This was not his first rodeo when it came to skunk encounters, so I guess he knew the drill.

Needless to say, we did not make the 11:00 p.m. church service. Although we certainly would have had a pew to ourselves, we decided to spare the other church-goers. Once we got Blaze more-or-less decent, we put him by an open window and finished watching the end of the movie. Then, to keep the stench out of the car, my son-in-law walked the dog home. Blaze was in seventh heaven to get a walk out of the deal, and the rest of the family drove home in the car.

It took at least a week for the smell to finally dissipate from the house, so the memory of that night stuck around for awhile. For the record, I did finally buy a sturdier step stool (the better part of wisdom), but the old one is in the garage — just like in the National Lampoon movie. What can I say? It makes me laugh.

So, no — 2019 was definitely far from a Camelot moment, except for the perfect apple pie. But in a somber year as we all grieved Doug, it was the comic relief we needed. For a moment, life — in all its unpredictable glory and chaos — was good. And he would have loved that.

My Beef With World War II

by Raymond Price

December 7, 1941 was "A day that will live in infamy," our president, Franklin D. Roosevelt, said. The Japanese had attacked Pearl Harbor. We would soon be at war.

My father announced, "We must make sure that the family has what we need to survive during this war. We're moving to a farm!" Dad found a farm to rent that was close to our home in Great Falls, Montana. We would not even have to change schools. Our seven-member family moved to the farm in early 1942. I was 14, Bill 12, Patty 10, Richard 8 and Jacqueline 6. Dad said, "This is a way for all of us to be patriotic and help with the war effort." None of us wanted to be unpatriotic and besides, living on a farm could be fun. None of us knew anything about farming, but we were ready, we thought, to learn. Oh, how innocent we were!

Americans received their first ration cards on May 4, 1942. The first card, War Ration Card Number One, became known as the "Sugar Book" for the most popular commodity that was rationed. Each family member was allowed one half pound of sugar per week. When you went to apply for your ration card, you were asked how much sugar you owned on that date. If you had sugar, you were allowed to keep it, but your allotment was reduced accordingly. An example of reducing sugar use is the attached recipe that originated during that time.

This was the first experience Americans had with rationing. Since it was seen as a patriotic duty, it was enthusiastically adopted. Everyone wanted to be patriotic. During WW1, conservation was not mandatory, but Americans complied in order to save vital food resources for the military and for our allies.

Meat was rationed beginning in December, 1942. Each family member was allowed 28 ounces of meat per week. On May 3,

1944, thanks to a good supply, all meats except steak and choice cuts of beef were removed from rationing — temporarily. For Thanksgiving in 1944 the supply of turkeys was short and all meats were returned to rationing. Things improved after V-Day in Europe and meat rationing finally came to an end.

Rationing certainly affected the way Americans would eat for a number of years. I was almost fourteen and had a sweet tooth, but my favorite food was a juicy T-bone steak. Both meat and sugar were rationed. Our farm produced milk, eggs and vegetables but no sugar or T-bone steaks. Rationing really affected me.

Dad's skills were needed back at Electrical Products, so he scheduled a business trip for mid-July, 1943. He invited me to go along with him, saying, "You can have as many T-bone steaks as you want while we're on this trip." 14-year-old Raymond II jumped at the chance.

We arrived late in the evening and were met by the local manager. He suggested that we could stop by the Mint, a famous local steak house, for a snack. When we got there, he asked me, "What would you like?"

"A medium rare T-bone steak, please." He looked at Dad and shrugged.

Dad said, "Let's give the boy a steak."

It was the first of the thirteen steaks I had on that four-day trip. Dad kept his promise.

That meat binge may have cured me of T-bone mania, or perhaps it's the fabulous food that I have at home. Now though, I may eat beef as seldom as once every two or three years, I never crave it. But I cherish the fond memories of my business trip with Dad.

APPLE BROWN BETTY

Adapted from the "Sweets Without Sugar" pamphlet distributed by the Federal Food Board of New York in 1918.

Start to finish: Approximately 1 hour

Servings: 10

- 5 medium apples
- 1 ¼ cups bread crumbs
- 4 tablespoons of melted butter or cooking fat
- ¼ cup hot water
- 1 ½ tablespoons lemon juice
- 5 tablespoons dark corn syrup
- ½ teaspoon salt
- ½ teaspoon cinnamon

Grease a glass or ceramic baking dish and preheat oven to 350° F.

Pare the apples and cut them into thin slices. Toss the breadcrumbs with the melted fat in a small bowl. In a separate bowl, mix the hot water, lemon juice, corn syrup, salt and cinnamon together.

Distribute a third of the bread crumb mixture into the bottom of the greased dish and top with half of the sliced apples and half of the liquid. Repeat with another layer of breadcrumbs, apples and liquid and top with the remaining breadcrumbs.

Bake in the oven for 45 minutes.

Sea Dance

by Cindi Pringle

slowly, gently
    bobbing gracefully
        to waltz melodies
            she weaves among
                the waves
                    of couples
casts flirtatious
    side glances
        to unattached men
            she searches
                for a bowed
                    welcoming elbow
                      to clasp
gossamer ruffles
    flapping at the small
        of her back
            her dress changes
                colors under
                    ballroom lights
petite, she cuts
    a curvy silhouette
        in a sea of darkness
            with a shy nod
                she pivots
                    grasps a gentleman's
                        outstretched arm

    entwined they
        float together
            circling, swaying
                a glint of
                    romantic attraction
                        in her eyes
rapt in his aura
    imagining
        lifelong companionship
            dainty as a seahorse
                swooning
                    in the ancient ritual
                      of dance

Haiku

by Cindi Pringle

Flight Home

    skirmish in the sky
    six sparrows orbit red hawk
    baseman slides home safe

Blaze Trail

    skeletal charred trees
    sky backlights black outstretched limbs
    flames' triumphant scourge

Music of the Spheres

    rainbow's chorus shouts
    arias across the sky
    listen to the moon

The Hole in My Life

by Randolph Quiroz

My wife and I had a problem. We kept too many things. As our household clutter grew, I wondered, *Are we hoarders?*

Deb and I had lots of rules for cleaning up when our kids lived at home, so we'd set a good example. But after they moved away, we got lazy. We'd leave things out and go to bed. We'd make a mess and decide to pick it up… later. When they moved out, clutter moved in.

Deb's mom and my dad, the last of our parents, died around the same time, leaving us two houses we had to sell due to our financial situation. It also meant figuring out which of their possessions we'd haul away and which we'd keep. Deb was too busy at the pawnshop, working extra hours to keep us afloat. As the unemployed one, I had to sort through all our precious junk.

I procrastinated. Sure, I knew to keep certain things like photographs and family heirlooms. But I risked angering Deb if I made a poor choice. No matter how often she said, "I trust you," I never felt at ease.

I didn't want to throw away anything we might need. We couldn't afford a new one, whatever it might be. I moved most of it to our backyard, even emptying the pool to create more storage space.

Then the seasonal rains arrived.

I used tarps from my dad's garage to cover everything. When winds tore them off, I used duct tape to hold them in place. But the rain and the wind were relentless. Eventually, I had to quickly cram things into every available spot inside the house.

"What do others do in this situation?" asked Deb. "We can't be the first."

"Online, they recommend a storage space or moving everything to a large basement." She frowned. "We might be able to afford a storage space if you got a job."

She was right. I sighed. "Our basement is so full, it's hazardous to walk down there. I just don't know where to put all of it. I'm trying to throw out as much as I can, but it's slow-going, Deb. Could we maybe have a yard sale this weekend? That way, you could be there to help."

"I'm sorry, sweetheart. I gotta say no. I don't want the entire neighborhood to see our throwaways. It's so cheap-looking — the kind of thing that screams 'low-class neighbor.'" Deb came from money so her reaction wasn't completely unexpected.

As time passed, our problem grew worse, and we stopped letting anyone inside. Stacks of this and piles of that formed in every room and still we added more. Still, we never left food or anything odorous around. Maybe we were messy, but neither of us tolerated filth.

Among our treasures, we had boxes we might one day need for gift wrapping, plastic bags filled with clothing we'd never wear, paperwork and unread mail, tools and kitchenware, magazines with that one article we wanted, artwork from our kids in grade school, letters from friends and relatives, that table and bookshelf we might someday need, newspapers with headlines that might interest future grandkids, unfinished crafts and art projects, and all our books from college classes we'd attended over twenty years ago. We had it all.

Eventually, the stacks grew so high and crowded that we could only get from room to room, following tight, treacherous pathways that often left us bruised as we wound our way through them. The stacks grew taller until we could no longer use the ceiling fans, and much of the house fell into darkness, making it mandatory that we keep flashlights regularly interspersed throughout. Falling debris became a constant danger, so we had to move slowly through the increasingly confined routes weaving through our house, or risk an avalanche.

Then, after narrowly being crushed by a box full of stuffed animals I should have thrown out, I got an idea. I cleared a space in the center of the basement and found my old sledge hammer. As I held it, I thought, *Is this crazy?* But I had to do something, so I swung at the basement floor. Maybe the concrete was extra solid, or maybe I was just not as strong as I was in my youth, but I couldn't make a crack in it. I barely even chipped it.

Renting a jackhammer made all the difference. I broke through the foundation and cleared away enough space for excavation. The digging was difficult, but I developed a routine. Each day when Deb left for work, I'd be ready to go. I'd dig and shuttle dirt. At first, I spread it around the yard and put some in the bottom of our garbage cans, figuring the pickup crew wouldn't notice. They didn't, and that worked for a while; but, eventually, I had to make dump runs. Fortunately, we'd figured landfill visits into our decluttering budget.

At the end of each day, I'd run the backyard hose through the washroom window and down into the basement. I'd water down the area I planned to dig next and move a workbench over the breach in the foundation. I'd covered that with power tools, full five-gallon paint buckets, and a large tarp; certain no one would find the entrance to what I'd come to call The Hole.

When I could no longer climb down to my digging level, I lowered a ladder for easier access. At ten feet below our basement floor, I was more than deep enough to safely avoid power, water, gas and sewage lines, but I feared if I tried to dig further down, the chances of collapse would be greater. So, I branched out to one side.

After only a month, I'd excavated the equivalent of a medium-sized room and, though it seemed pretty solid, the possibility of collapse worried me. Online, I researched how professionals shored up mines. I couldn't afford proper oversized lumber, so I made do with less, emptying my stockpile of unused and leftover wood, supplementing that with whatever I could get from friends. I'd say I was building a fence or doghouse or whatever it took to accumulate the lumber to make the space as safe as possible. At one point, I even destroyed some inherited furniture for the wood it would provide.

After tamping down and flattening the earth beneath my first underground room, and leaving enough space to dig more, I ran wiring to provide power for lights and whatever else. I plastered the walls and floor with split open garbage bags to provide a moisture barrier. Then I threw rug remnants down and moved things in.

First, I cleared the room that had once belonged to our daughter but had since become Deb's sewing room, emptying all the clutter into The Hole. My wife had grown increasingly snippy with me, but having access to her sewing room once more made her happy and kept her from asking questions. When she said, "I don't want to know what you've done with everything," I smiled, feeling much better about keeping the big secret from her.

Every day, I added to my subterranean estate, carefully avoiding the pool area. I would have hired someone to help, but I couldn't afford to have anyone know what I was doing, what I'd done. Too risky. Also, too expensive. Our financial situation hadn't improved. I was still unemployed.

I added room after room, trimming our trees to provide more lumber. I added space further back on our lot and also to the sides. When I ran out of area below our yard, instead of digging deeper, I moved sideways, below our neighbors' yards. At ten feet below our basement floor, I was roughly twenty-four feet underground.

I figured that kept me safe from detection, but I often wondered what they were doing above me. I considered digging upward to give myself an escape route, in case of cave-in, but I never did it, fearful I'd be caught emerging somewhere. All it would take was one kid spotting me. My entire network would be discovered.

When Deb asked after a pair of her mother's shoes, praying I hadn't thrown them away, I spent the next day searching for them amongst the many chambers within The Hole. Thank God I found them before she got home the next day.

I continued my project for over two years, moving everything in until finally I cleared enough clutter to make our house look perfect, if not a bit empty. I left our basement crowded to suggest I'd gotten rid of nearly everything. By the end, I moved much more than we'd received from our parents. I even moved my beloved baseball card collection into The Hole. I'd created something I was proud of and I considered showing Deb, but resisted. I'd be crushed if she made me shut it all down. At night in bed, I'd fantasize that I'd never have to stop digging, that I'd create an area spacious enough to rival the catacombs of Rome.

My storage solution worked perfectly, enduring like a champ… for roughly seven more months. Unfortunately, an especially heavy rain season collapsed my 'catacombs,' burying all our possessions within.

Portions of my neighbors' backyards fell into deep earth depressions, ruining them. Consumed with guilt, I prepared myself for prosecution at their hands for all the damage I'd caused. Fortunately, police explained it away as merely a giant sinkhole. Such things happened in our region of the state, and homeowner's insurance covered every one of us.

The Hole was gone. I guess I'd been lucky. A cave-in could have happened much sooner and trapped or killed me. At least, my subterranean estate had been a temporary success.

Thankfully, we still had our family photographs, and a few treasured items kept in the basement. The Earth swallowed the rest. At first, it depressed me. Then I got angry. I'd lost both my great creation *and* my treasured baseball card collection. I considered digging it out but had second thoughts. It could be risky. After the collapse, any digging could raise suspicions. Someone might figure out what I'd done and hold me responsible.

At least we no longer had so many possessions. I'd have to explain all the missing items to my wife, somehow, but it was still a great relief. To own something, really is to have it own *you*.

I was no longer *The Moleman,* tunneling everywhere. I'd lost my underground kingdom. Now I'd have to quit digging and *really* search for a job. Who knows? Maybe that was for the best. Now, Deb and I would just have to watch our bad habits in the future. If we were careful, we'd have the whole of our lives to enjoy a neater home.

Maybe I could get a job digging somewhere.

On Writing

by Kristine Ann Shell

You've paper to write,
and a pen full of ink.
You've something to say.
So, write what you think.

Just be who you are,
and write what is real.
Share what you know,
and write what you feel.

You won't need a map
if you just use your mind,
and head for the places
your heart wants to find.

Where life winds its way,
upstream and down.
Where hearts can be mended,
and lost can be found.

So, write where you're headed,
and share where you've been.
And let your life flow
from the tip of your pen.

Social Distancing

by Stevie Taken

Cautious and curious, Kathy scans the neighborhood from her front door as she reaches into the letterbox which is fixed on the wall. She spots her neighbor from across the street stepping out of her BMW. Janice? Janet? Janice, it's Janice. Janice and her husband...Rob(?) have had a 'For Sale' sign posted in their front yard since before the quarantine... Janice sees Kathy, they wave hello, like so many times before over the past 20 plus years, with rarely a word exchanged. Kathy takes a step in Janice's direction,

"You're moving!?" asks, or, rather, declares Kathy at a volume and pitch that will carry the distance.

Still from across the street and in her driveway, "Yeah! Tonight's our last night!", shouts Janice.

Janice continues speaking as she crosses the street moving towards Kathy, stepping onto her lawn, maintaining the distance between them; only Kathy is wearing a mask.

"After 28 years we are moving to Arizona, can't believe it. Ron and I raised both boys here. It's the only home Sean ever knew before he moved out last year..."

Ron, not Rob.

"...Seany's been driving out from Arizona every weekend to help us move load by load to our storage unit before the new house is ready. Since both boys moved out, we've been waiting for the right time. They're just too far away, and now we're ready."

"Oh. Wow! So, it's already sold then? That's great! You just put that up right, uh right...before...before everything..." Kathy trails off.

"Well, it still hasn't closed; any day now. Our agent says the buyers are as eager for it to close as we are, which is good...

their lender still hasn't signed off, I guess. So, we're all waiting on that…Anyway, how is, how is everyone? How's, uh…your family doing?" diverged Janice.

"We're good. Jim and I are doing well. Well, as well as…well, you know. Grandkids are good, just hard being apart from them, without knowing when…Mainly just staying busy, you know um, gardening and making bad art. I started painting flowers onto my bedroom door, I'm not a painter. So, I've been watching instructional YouTube videos, at least I can always just paint back over it if I hate the final results, which I think I'm going to do tomorrow. Oh, but I have a friend…her husband, he passed away last night. He was…"

"Oh, no. I'm so sorry, is your…"

"He had a lung disease, not the virus, he's been sick now for a couple of years. He was admitted to Kaiser in Riverside last month, and she wasn't able to see him. Couldn't go to see him. Had to keep her distance. So sad, he died alone. My poor friend. That's the worst part. She feels so guilty about not being there next to him, holding his hand. It's just so sad. I can't imagine the pain of…it's terrifying, and I am so…"

"I know, it's ridiculous, they won't let anyone go anywhere. People are suffering! My niece, she's a single mom. A hairstylist. If she and her client want to make a choice to make an appointment, what business is it of anyone, if they want to do that…"

Kathy had her suspicions in the past, now she was certain, Janice is an idiot. Kathy felt better about the 20 plus years' worth of not receiving, nor extending invitations to each other's cocktail hours, pool parties and Bunco holiday ornament exchanges.

Kathy had tuned Janice out.

"…right? So, yeah, if you want to stay home, stay home. I want a haircut!"

Although Janice could not see Kathy's mouth behind her mask, the blankness in her eyes revealed enough.

"So, we should have you over to the new house for a glass of wine when, you know, when this all blows over…" said Janice.

"In Arizona?" asked Kathy.

"Right. Well, you know, if you're in town, look me up."

"Yes, that would be nice. Thanks, Janice, we'll do that."

Kathy smiled behind her mask at Janice, Janice smiled widely back at her, both maintaining the polite and comfortable distance between them.

What the Builders Knew
by Elizabeth Uter

First the sands
and then the dust
deviling up a storm,
surrounding a pre-dawn dream
of man's achievement.
A world of beginnings and ends,
Here we are, entering one
of the many Cities of the Dead,
it conjures up lives well-lived,
steps taken at every turn in sync
with some sign,
some pattern in the heavens,
auguries, omens.

Who could not notice
this huge fact, the detail
shooting towards the sky, marking it
like a note in time with the beats of the sun.
It's a journey through time.
A great pyramid
signalling equinoxes,
the architect's choice -
its coordinates.
A puzzling plum in a desert lush with
academic letters trailing its fame or is it frame?

We change the way we look at the planet
when we view this wonder.
The how of its construction.
Why doesn't anyone ever think of the means
of its building - exotic belly-dancing around our senses,
an enticing choreography under our noses,
a music of masonry sinewing about us?

The builders: Gods? Aliens?
Slaves? Masons?
We couldn't do it today, no one could.
Three chambers - descending passages,
sloping angles, impossible feats.
Two million stones of different sizes,
each as heavy as a sedan.
Master stoneworkers
building with breath-taking precision.
Accurate and intact, surviving earthquakes,
pointing true north,
we have only just reached this level of measuring.
Eight sides, instead of four, slightly bent -
are the bends intentional?
No two blocks alike.
Made by a madman's mind -
'Health and Safety' today would never allow it.
Twenty years in the making, they say.
Every two and a half minutes, a block slotted in.
Some system of measurement to make it stand

as it does and not by happenstance.

While the rest of the world wore animal skins,
this was in the making.
One house, this roof, the walls -
all the data streaming in -
over several millennia - is confusing.
Let's go back to square one - off the block:

It's the only one, a once in a life time act,
never done again.
A will to order, reshaping blocks -
a razor blade can't squeeze between each rock.
Hewn with simple, tempered tools.
No crack lines and
still around for us to muse on.

Techniques used
that are not understood,
not even whispered about
amongst the experts these days,
forty-five foot stones…
what the builders knew remains
with them -
like mummies in their tombs
- encased in the heads of the long dead.
Forgotten, frozen.
Last thoughts.

Young Girl Meets Boy King

by Elizabeth Uter

It has travelled from countless countries,
this wonder of the world and I am all smiles
and sighs as we move up, in an endless awe of
a queue we have stood in for hours.
My feet are sore, head heavy, we have driven
forever and a hundred miles to be here.
The glory of kings still manifesting their mastery over
us, lesser mortals - a sway of three thousand years or more
- he hasn't lost his touch - holding subjects captive.

We enter the hush of a room like a church
in the dark - my child hands reach towards
the encased mummy in tomb,
fingers are stopped by thick glass.
My eyes, dazzled-wide by the treasure -
the golden, glittering return of a king
to the world of the living,
from sands riddled with the dead.

Gold is an undying x that marks the spot
as far as the eye can see, exhibited.
Antiquities.
Records that crumble to dust
but not the precious yellow.
Crafted, reproduced in books, magazines, TV.
The boy king's fragile masked head

beyond the price that a pen can fix.
A voice circles like a hawk over dunes
above us and in ever decreasing circles
until it's gone:
"The exhibition will open
with the beautiful painted-wooden
torso of a young king, 18th dynasty..."

Curses entomb him, faithful priests have wrapped
him tight, smothered him in blessings and praises.
I peer at his glowing, deathly face - he, like me,
seems tired at the end of a long day,
I think his blue eyeliner is running at the sides
- the deep blue glass -
I see his sad, tranquil, gemstone eyes,
liquid as if ready to cry.

Steal Away
by Elizabeth Uter

This particular truth has an evil eye,
it causes bad luck, illness, or death.
The curse of Pharaohs is a truth
that stings and shivers to the very marrow
of imaginings.
Only touching those who disturb
the ancient ones - who know no difference
between archaeologists or thieves.
If you disturb these bones
they will rattle in your life
an eternity or maybe less, if you
have earned merit of sorts in your life
- a feather might weigh as much as you,
come your judgement day, but raiding
a grave cancels it out I think.

Once upon a time, no one could imagine
desecrating the tomb of a man, a woman, a child's
final resting place. A cultural taboo, feared in
every tongue by peoples the world over.
An abomination, which today is done
with profile empty: eyes unblinking,
not even facial muscles twitch.
Does the ticking of the clock
count down the hours of the defilers?

Ancient curses can appear inside
the tomb or on the face of it, your fingers
might unwittingly have slid or rubbed against them.
Who would risk being haunted
by old-time mummies in their dreams?
Particularly not the irate, child variety.
You know how vicious a knowing, or
unknowing, youth can be when thwarted.
Who would be haunted by children in their dreams?
Who would bear that heaviness of mind?
A mysterious death to come? The bite of a mosquito
- the fever poisoning? Would you wish to risk it?

Windows by Souls
by Elizabeth Uter

First her eyes burning the face she catches to a crisp
- yours - sweat, the first sign you are on fire,
unredeemable, living the last of your breath.
Solar, she cannot be gazed on by the naked eye,
a medusa with basilisk hair to draw you in,
pin you down, keep you entertained, she sings
- for at least three days. Legend has it - hers is
a body that wraps around its prey. No one would dare to say,
you are a lover, that implies choice, you have none, sorry, mate.
Fingers hooking into tender skin of first chest then back,
slowly pulling each hair until they scream and curl away,
she straightens them and pulls again and again.

You, the hapless victim feel the heaviness
of hope seeping away, overcoming you as you sleep the deepest
you have ever known, lost in the floating weirdness
beyond R.E.M, in the fastness of the deep sleep dimension.
Your muscle tone is low throughout your body
and what you see inside you, hits you vividly,
you wish it didn't.
You beg your mind to wake up, wake up,
let the dreaming end.
Your spirit has wandered for days,
weeks, years, you have become a vacuum
for things of the night to catch and suck you in.
These are the tales of the succubae who will catch a man

when windows are open, nights long with balm.
Drenched with your troubles, she crawls in, grinning at her luck.

And for the woman? Do not feel left out,
you, too, are blessed with the unwanted companion.
He is incubus, you, too, lady, must have a care
where you let your thoughts drift and lie down
during the day. Fantasies, daydreams, longings
are grist to this pairs' eternal mills.
Still unyielding, ever on the prowl,
these folk, a lot like leaches, waiting to couple
with you until you, the host, are a husk.
Parasitic eyes move on to the next in line.

No Place To Be

by Elizabeth Uter

The bus rattles away and is lost in the dark mumble
of a place that isn't anywhere I know.
"Wait-a-bit."
Tree frogs warble their joyous chant.
There is slithering sin in the night grass
to each side of the road
and the buzz of the bulb hanging before the static police station.
The rustle of clothes as I turn to look at my brother and he at me,
deep breaths, the exhaling hijacked by mosquitoes
squeezing, sneezing, breezing by.
The stiff swish of two nodding heads:
the middle of nowhere in a foreign land past sundown,
has the staccato beat of a movie soundtrack when foolish folk
are entering a vampire's lair.
We hold hands - warmth swarms out from our hands
and becomes one with the stifling heat.
We walk up creaking stairs, feet dragging against
chipped wood, then, on the floorboards of the porch.
There is a single body in the shade,
silent, and still as a gun on a table.
He shifts forward and up from his squishy chair,
the light halos him a moment and it chitters
like burning flames, we see him in his uniform
that is screaming out *authority's name.*
I open my mouth that has lost words in a dry throat

bleaker than an endless desert, swallowing once, twice, until
wet smack of spittle allows me to say, "we are lost,
we took the wrong bus, my family's waiting for us."
The long, watching face of the cop, lasts the length of
a scratch of nails across a blackboard.
He jerks his head for us to follow
and with it there is a scrape of
belted buckle and buttons that back him up.
We drift likes shadows into a ghostlike realm
of bulletproof vests, knives, sprays, walkie-talkies.
But no message home as of yet.
He stands behind a grand desk and offers us two stools before him
A king in a court of complete control as his jaw twitches,
vein throbbing loud.
We scuttle forward like mice cornered between a cat and a trap.
He unholsters his gun - leather stretches - he levels it at us.
We gasp.

The Stay

by Elizabeth Uter

It was a darker day than night,
trees knitted together in tight coils,
legs thick, an upright army
that would not let us pass or so it seemed.
We had to squeeze by as they creaked to catch at us
with their twig-sharp, gnarling fingers.
The leaves, avenging scavengers swooping
down, sticking to our eyes.
Roots like sly feet ready to trip us up
- the bark scritch-scratching at us as we passed.
We soldiered on, who knew a forest could
be so full of malevolence and for what?
The ground, too, offered resistance diving us into sinking sand,
stinking swamps, hellish with sulphur.
Mosquitoes swung by with all their drinking buddies,
to sip from us, we were nipped, shredded
as if the tips of knives were at our throats.

We arrived at a cottage, tumbled down roof, caved in walls.
Cracked door on the floor and the dark beat of feet
that had threaded through fire - when dampened - leaving their mark,
smears of ash to tell of a burning. We waited,
warring with our instincts that said move on, keep alert, it's a trap.
We paused. The shattered domicile, foreboding as a ghost-filled
graveyard, whistled, no wind coming through,
whining as if haggish beggars had come to town.

Mysterious as a Baba Yaga's hut on a single chicken's leg
- capturing us, stopping us dead within its burnt offerings.
Consuming us.

Empty Town
by Gudelia Vaden

Riverside, like many towns screams of loneliness

Masked people are the new norm

More staying home

Parks closed to children's dismay

I see despair and emptiness in people's eyes

Store shelves empty

Where has all the toilet paper gone?

Commodities and food are scarce

Even the birds have left

Resembles ghost town

When will this pandemic end?

Fears

by Gudelia Vaden

Every time I hear someone cough, I want to run and hide
These are scary times and I wish they would go away

Every time I hear the word pandemic, I want to run and hide
Washing hands for 20 seconds with warm water and soap is better than hand sanitizer

Every time I switch on the news and people are dying, I want to run and hide
Masks are now required when going out

Every time I see a person in a supermarket getting close to me, I want to run and hide
Disinfecting supplies are hard to come by these days

Every time I hear of a commercial cruise ship that was highly infected, I want to run and hide
I am doing my part to flatten the curve by staying home as much as possible

These fears belong to me

Silver Dollar Summer

by Gudelia Vaden

When I had just graduated from eighth grade, I was almost thirteen and looked for something to do during the summer. Something that would be interesting and bring in a little cash. Over a soda at the malt shop, my friends, Janice and Jeannette, told me about the job at Hadley's Farms, which was just off the 99 freeway in Planada, CA. It was 1957 and no work permit was necessary if an adult supervised you. I ran home as fast as I could and asked my parents for permission to work in the packing shed at Hadley's Farms.

When I got home, practically out of breath from running, I asked my papá if I could go work as an apricot cutter. He said, "No, you stand a chance of cutting your hands." Dad was stubborn and when he said no, he meant it. I must have inherited my stubborn streak from my father, as I was just as stubborn as he was. I was not going to take no for an answer and convinced him I knew how to use a paring knife. He finally gave his consent and that put a big smile on my face.

On that first morning of work, Mom and my siblings, Elisa, Eliseo and Vince, were up early. The rooster did not have to wake us up, though it was nice to hear the rooster crowing. It was cool and pleasant in the early hours. We packed our chicken sandwiches, potato chips, bananas and sodas in a cooler. Sometimes, Mom would pack bean and potato burritos to vary the menu. We each brought our own knives and placed them in a bag. We were all excited and ready to work. Socorro, my older sister, was 16 and usually dropped us off, then headed for the cannery where she got a job working with my Aunt Lupe. I missed her, as we usually did everything together.

The atmosphere of the packing shed was filled with loud blasting music from the supervisor's radio. I especially liked listening to Elvis and other rock and roll artists while I worked. Music made the day brighter and the time go faster. I recognized some familiar faces, kids from my school and other young people from my neighborhood. It was a big place and some adults were not known to me.

I practiced at home cutting with the sharp wide blade of the paring knife. At work, Mom taught me to cut the apricots around the middle, drop the seed in the pan and lay the apricots onto a big 3 feet by 6 feet wooden tray. Mom also helped my younger brothers, Vince and Eliseo, who were 7 and 8 catch up on their work. Vince, the youngest, stood on a box to cut fruit. Eliseo was tall and did not need to stand on a box. The pay was 50 cents a box, but I do not recall how many trays we could fill in a day.

The apricots were jumbo size and had such a tantalizing aroma. During my break I would pop a few apricots into my mouth, savoring the juicy fruit. Even now, my mouth waters as I recall munching on those plump and juicy apricots. The work was hard, the sulfur was sometimes too much to bear with its foul odor and, at the end of the day, I often felt hot and sticky with orange stains all over my shirt and jeans.

I felt a sense of pride and accomplishment, as my family worked and had fun together. But the best part was that our boss paid us with clean and shiny silver dollars. They were mine and I could spend them however I wanted. I thank my parents for instilling the work ethic in me. Even though, we worked other summers, this summer was special because it was my first. Oh, how I miss that silver dollar summer.

The Outhouse

BY GUDELIA VADEN

In the 1950's, my parents purchased their white wooden home on Stanford Street on a one-acre lot in Planada, California. Among an assortment of apricot, cherry, almond and walnut trees and a corn patch was an outhouse way in the back. It was seven or eight feet high and four feet by four feet wide. There was a large hole for adults and a smaller one for children. It had a half-moon carving, just enough to look out, like a peep hole. There was also a metal latch inside for privacy.

My family was very artistic and I suspected my older brother Paul was the artist that drew designs of a colorful sun, some sunflowers and wispy lines of grass. I never asked who the artist was. The one thing that stands out in my mind is that Hollyhocks grew abundantly and thrived around the outhouse. The flowers were brilliant with red, purple, yellow and white hues.

At six years of age, it was my job to help with spring cleaning. I was in charge of sweeping out the floor with a broom and knocking out the spider webs. My dad replaced our kitchen linoleum floor and used the left-over pieces to cover the floor of the outhouse. He also would put some sort of lime powder to keep down odors since there was no way to flush. Mother would bring a large bucket with lye water and wash it down from top to bottom and let it set for a day or two. After it was dry, she painted the seats on the inside. After being told, "It may be wet," I went to relieve myself and got paint all over my bottom. A downside was that if we had to urinate in the middle of the night, I was scared. My sister's hand must have hurt when I squeezed her hand so tight it turned white. In the winter, it was so cold that we would almost freeze our bottoms off.

In the summer, my siblings, the neighborhood kids and I would love to play Hide-and-Seek. Sometimes I would enjoy hiding in the outhouse, as no one wanted to look for me there. And, it was better than hiding in the chicken coup.

Dad had had enough of the rainy weather and muddy trips to the outhouse. The hems of his pant legs and shoes were often caked in mud. I am not sure what was the last straw that broke the camel's back, but every Halloween some prankster would climb the redwood fence and knock down the outhouse. Father was a good sport for taking up the task of reassembling the outhouse.

One day, my father decided to install indoor plumbing with the help of his brother. It was pure heaven to use a toilet that was in our home and easy to get to. There was only one toilet for our large family of nine, but we were all so happy with the arrangement. Most homes did not have more than one bathroom, like now. Today, I have two full bathrooms and that is probably the norm.

The generations of today and future ones have never heard of an outhouse, much less used one. They will never know of the childhood dilemma of having to use an outhouse. I have tried to grow Hollyhocks in my garden, but to no avail.

The Sock Doll

BY GUDELIA VADEN

My sock doll was unique and homemade, unlike the dolls of today. She was beautiful and the softest doll ever. Today, most people who want a doll can go to the store to buy one or order one online at the touch of their cell phones. Rarely do moms take time to make dolls for their family like back in the days of my childhood.

My petite but strong mother could accomplish many things. In Mexico, she learned to embroider at the young age of four. She taught herself to sew and make dolls. Her light olive complexion was filled with sweetness, like the Capirotada she made for us on special occasions. When she was not in the kitchen or her rose garden, she would retreat to the casita. The casita was a small brown rectangular shaped room that was separated from our house by a few cobblestones creating a path. It was her sanctuary, where she could find her solitude. But most of all it was a place to create.

On this particular dark and gloomy stormy day, as a small child of four, I wanted to go out and play with my friends, Janice and Jeannette. It was not only a rainy day, but one with thunder and lightning. No mother would let their little ones out on a day when the torrential rains were coming down in sheets, knocking down telephone poles and flooding the streets.

How I longed for the warm sunny days when the twins would spread a blanket on their lawn and share their dolls with me. We were the best of friends; we not only shared toys, but food as well. I would trade my jelly sandwiches for their sugar sandwiches.

Cookie, their older sister, had an electric stove and would make fried potatoes. How we loved her special potatoes!

My siblings were ignoring me and I felt left out. They were all having fun and engaged in some form of play. The older ones were pushing the younger ones in a toy car. Most of the time, we played well together but the rain had dampened my spirits.

I was practically in tears and told Mom that my doll is getting old and falling apart. Her arm is dangling loosely off her shoulder. Soon, I will not be able to play with her. Mom placed her arm around me and dried my tears. She knew just what to do. I looked all around the casita and to my amazement she had jars filled with buttons of all colors and shapes, colorful yarn in black and red, spools of thread and needles, as well as fabric swatches and a bag of gently worn socks that could be used for many creative projects.

From the old worn knotty-wood shelves, Mom took a white sock and stuffed it with cotton to make a doll face. The head was round with two black buttons for eyes. With thread and needle, she sewed a little pink pom-pom for the nose. Next, she embroidered the doll's mouth with red thread making a happy face. The doll's face changed my sad mood into a happy one.

Mom said: "She needs a body," and so the sock was once again filled with cotton, making a little protruding tummy. The doll's arms and legs had previously been cut, so I enjoyed filling the arms and legs with cotton, just as Mom had done. The cotton felt soft and comfy. Mom hand-stitched the doll with white thread to keep her together. The doll needed hair of some sort, so Mom braided some black yarn and made two braids. Then she made a dress using a pink piece of cloth with bright yellow flowers and some boots from black felt material. I named my new sock doll, Muñequita, which means little doll in Spanish. She was definitely a work of art in the end.

I was elated to have this sock doll made just for me with Mother's very own hands. She would not just be any ordinary sock doll, but with the love I gave her, I swear she almost came alive. She was better than any doll you could buy at the store.

A Clock Stopped
by Thomas Vaden

Once upon a time in a whirlwind tour of Germany, I passed through a small enchanted village called Baden, Baden, near the Black Forest. The clocks were all abuzz with moving figurines, swinging, see-sawing, colorful birds chirping and peeking out doors and all things magical. Later in life, my wife, Gudelia received a clock, as a gift from her sister. This clock had to have come from Germany, since it had all the bells and whistles one would expect. This clock sometimes stops, and I feel compelled to replace the batteries, for I now need the joy the movement brings to my life. Tempus Fugit. The past is gone and is often recreated sporadically only in memory. Alas, how wonderful the memories! How did I end up in Baden, Baden in February of 1993?

Where do I start? I was authorized to travel to Ramstein AFB, Germany to present a short training module to internal auditors on statistics used to evaluate financial statements. The prior year, the General Accounting Office had flown from Washington to Norton AFB in California to train Air Force auditors on auditing financial statements. During this training, they presented a session on statistics. As the Chief Statistician of the Air Force Audit Agency, I complained to my superiors that GAO had no idea how to use statistics on multi-location audits and were preaching heresy and ruining my programs. GAO came back and requested that I develop and teach the module on appropriate sampling techniques.

Fortunately, I was able to take time to travel and experience the hospitality of the people of Germany. I was determined to see the Ludwig castles in Southern Bavaria. After a terrible drive on ice covered roads in a small rented Fiat that had no window washer fluid, I arrived at a small German hostel in Baden-Baden, a scenic area near the black forests known for its health spas. That evening, I had a wonderful German meal cooked by the owner and enjoyed some great tasting beers at the pub in the basement, along with her family. I spoke only a few words of German, having only one year in high school.

The next day, I visited a beautiful church, a bookstore and a thermal spa not far from the hostel. What a contrast! The church was quiet and beautiful with floor to ceiling leaded glass windows. The bookstore was small with crammed aisles filled with children's books. One book in particular caught my attention. I could actually read the German title *Ich habe einen Teddy* by Gerda Muller. The cover had a young boy kneeling down on his ankles, holding his teddy bear. The book measured 21/2x 5", with only 22 pages and 22 short sentences. The illustrations were lifelike and artistic. I just had to buy this book!

The weather was unbearably cold, so after the bookstore, I decided to go to the spa. What a delightful, awesome experience. I wandered from one room to the next, not sure of what awaited me. One starts the journey by taking off their clothes, wearing only shower clogs and carrying a towel. I was embarrassed when I arrived at the sauna room, which is unisex. A family was sitting there with their young daughter of perhaps 12 or 13. They thought nothing of being without clothes, but I was likely turning a bright Irish red. I was totally self conscious. Afterwards, continuing through other rooms, the massages and warm foot baths were welcomed on this cold wintery day. The final stop was a common pool area where a tribe of giddy Japanese girls, perhaps 18- to 20-years-old were swimming in the nude. I joined them without saying a word. Perhaps they thought I was German and used to this experience. I learned just how ill at ease I have become, molded by my cultural heritage.

The next day, I travelled south to Bavaria through blizzard like conditions, freezing ice and snow. I was determined to see three of the castles of King Ludwig II; Neuschwanstein, Hohenschwangau and Linderhof. Staying overnight in another hostel, I was almost certain that the roads would not be cleared and I would not be able to tour the castles. However, the next morning the sun came up and the roads were open. I briefly stopped at the Linderhof to soak in the wintery landscape and then continued to the Neuschwanstein, perhaps the most well known of the castles. Walt Disney modeled his Sleeping Beauty Castle at Disneyland Park after the Neuschwanstein. I parked at the bottom of a steeply walled driveway and stumbled up the rest of the way, slipping and sliding on the icy stone path. I spent a considerable amount of time exploring the castle and then decided to climb up to a cantilever bridge spanning a Gorge above a frozen waterfall. Perhaps this was a foolish idea since the path was treacherous and the bridge slippery. I have a snapshot of the bridge taken from the castle and a stunning picture of the castle captured from this bridge. Before leaving, I returned to the Neuschwanstein and peered from a balcony across a valley to the Hohenschwangau, majestically rising above a lake.

I wish I had more time to tour the castles, perhaps in a summer setting, but I needed to return to Ramstein to check on the class. I almost forgot that I was sent overseas to proctor the class. During the class sessions, several auditors from the states arrived in Ramstein to share their expertise on financial statements. Some of the instructors were also experts on German landmarks and history, and insisted that we take an afternoon off to see the Heidelberg castle ruins. Rising majestically above the cobble stone streets of Heidelberg's Old Town, overlooking vineyards and forests and the Nectar River Valley, I have seldom experienced such breathtaking beauty.

Occasionally in the evening, we would visit a small German restaurant bar, "ALTE FEUERWACHE," the old firehouse in Landstuhl. Some of the auditors were regulars and personal friends of the owner; and after the bar closed, a select few of us would remain and the owner would then break out his special cache of Schnapps, a wonderful chaser. Wow, one night I really got smashed and somehow, I made it back to my room safely! When the course ended, the class celebrated a grandiose party at the Feuerwache, with perhaps the best home cooked food in Germany.

I stayed a little while longer in Germany. I had one more thing to do before heading home. I had to see Paris, France, regardless of the weather. I prearranged a one-day trip on a tour bus that drove from Ramstein to Paris overnight. We drove through a horrific snowstorm with poor visibility, and I eventually dozed off as we could see none of the countryside. We began our tour early the next morning, starting with a light outdoor breakfast across the street from the Notre Dame Cathedral, and a ride out to the Basilica of the Sacred Heart of Montmartre, which overlooks all of Paris. The basilica's ceilings glittered with gold, red and blue mosaic images of Jesus Christ, Joan of Arc and St. Michael the Archangel. We then returned for a visit to the Cathedral of Notre Dame and the Eiffel Tower. I simply did not have the time to absorb the beauty and majesty that Notre Dame offered. I had barely enough time to ascend the Eiffel Tower and take pictures from the lower levels. The steps to the upper levels were closed due to treacherous icy footing.

In the afternoon, the sun peeked through the mist and we set out on a one-hour river cruise on the Seine, passing by such famous sites as the Louvre Museum and the Arc de Triomphe. When we returned, we had only time to take the bus to visit the shops. The streets of Paris are narrow, leaving little room for maneuvering a large bus! At one point, a small Fiat stuck too far out of its parking place, blocking our path. The bus driver said that he could not get through. I surprised myself as I shouted let's move it! Eight of us jumped off the bus, and with four men on the front bumper and four men on the rear bumper, we simply bounced the car up and down as we slid it sideways into its parking spot. The owner of the Fiat is in for a surprise when he returns. How is he going to get out of his parking dilemma when there is no room to maneuver?

I took a tour of a perfume factory and purchased my wife an expensive bottle of Joy eau de Parfum by Jean Patou of Paris. I also visited a clothing store to purchase a gift for my daughter. I spoke no French and I heard a rumor that if you don't speak French, you are looked down upon; quite a different attitude than the people in Germany who seemed to welcome Americans to their country. A young, exceptionally beautiful, French girl who spoke fluent English waited on me. As we engaged in lengthy conversation, two older clerks were desperately showing their obvious disapproval! I felt hurt by the pressure, quickly purchased a sweatshirt "Vive la France", and exited the store to return to the bus. On the way back to Ramstein, I thought that I should have ignored the older ladies. I enjoyed the conversation, and needed to learn more about life in France.

The time passed so fast that I wished the clock would stop. I needed much more time to experience all the magnificence and beauty that Paris and Germany offered. I am glad that my wife received this clock from her sister. It brings back fleeting memories of a time long ago when I had a brief encounter with a different world.

Pandemic Limericks

by Thomas Vaden

Shelter in place against virus Satanic
Whatever you do – just do not panic
    Staying home alone
    My testosterone
Defended by a wishful fanatic

Young ladies lying on the beach beware
You certainly entice the men to stare
    Virus like a ghost
    Looking for a host
That is something you do not want to share

I sit at home and drink my beer
COVID has turned my life to fear
    Frequent trips to the store
    Always wanting more
Hoard enough Corona to persevere

Pandemic Poems
(a Haiku, a Tanka, a Fibonacci Poem)
by Thomas Vaden

Haiku

Panic fills my lungs

Fear survives and overwhelms

We shall overcome

Tanka

War waged against men

Microscopic enemy

Rampant exposures

Medics battle on front lines

Lives lost – will mankind survive?

Fibonacci Poem

Man

Fears

Hidden

Enemies

Fighting to the end

We shall win, endure, overcome

Human lives must go on – kick the virus in the ass

She Showed the Way ~ Reflections of Francisca Valenzuela Borboa

BY FRANCES J. VASQUEZ

Many people have impacted me deeply in a myriad of positive ways. Some became my heroes — women and men who modeled outstanding attributes in their own unique ways. In my childhood and youth, most of them were women who showed me awesomeness in my own family. My mother's mother, Francisca Valenzuela Borboa became my first *shero*. She was the only grandmother I knew, and people in her Mexican village called her Nana or Nana Pancha in deference to her esteemed position as a *Partera* y *Curandera*. She was everyone's beloved nana in her *pueblito*.

Francisca Valenzuela Borboa was a strong independent woman who lived her life fully and mostly the way she wanted. She was financially independent and supported herself and others on her own meager earnings. She birthed two children: a son, Jose Maria Paredes was born in about 1915. He was her first-born. I called him Tío Chemali. Twelve years later in 1927, my Nana gave birth at the age of thirty-three to her daughter, Rosa Lidia Valenzuela — my mother. Nana took care of herself, her children, and others as a single parent in her *Providencia*.

My Nana was a respected and proficient *Curandera* and *Partera* — a midwife who helped the women in her village give birth. She was a gifted *Curandera* — folk medicine woman who specialized in treating babies and female ailments with her healing massages and special herbal remedies. She usually made house calls to deliver babies and treat women and children.

When Nana was a young single mother, during the Lázaro Cárdenas presidency in the 1930s, she participated in meetings

353

that the federal government convened throughout rural México to develop the *ejido* system of communal land distribution to landless *campesinos*. These were agrarian reforms enacted to implement the Zapatista Plan de Ayala initiative developed during the Mexican Revolution of 1910 to 1920.

My mother recounted early childhood memories of how her mother would take her to the meetings and roll out a *petate* for her daughter (my mother) to lie on and sleep during the evening proceedings. She was one of the few women to participate. As a result, my Nana was granted a parcel of 20 hectares in the countryside near Providencia to grow wheat, soy, and other cash crops to help sustain her family. When Nana died, she left her lands to my mother, including her adobe home. This apparently infuriated my Tío Chemali. But, this was what Nana wanted. Her daughter needed the lands more than her son did — he and his wife, Tía Cuquita already had their own lands to cultivate.

Nana built a modest adobe home near the village square in the middle of Providencia, a *pueblito* located in el *Valle del Rio Yaqui* in the *Cajeme* district near Ciudad Obregón in the norteño state of Sonora, México. The valley is like a small oasis in the midst of the Sonoran Desert. The arid region is made fruitful by the water from the Yaqui River and its tributary canals from a large dam named *la Presa Alvaro Obregón* — named after a former president of México who resided in Ciudad Obregón.

The adobe was constructed hacienda style and featured a hard-packed earthen floor. The front door opened to a corridor with two enclosed bedrooms on either side of the entry. The tiny dark kitchen was enclosed and the adjoining small dining room was attached to a covered but open patio. The porch-like dining room and patio faced a large yard surrounded by a fence built of *Carrizo* — dried bamboo-like reeds. A large earthen, wood-burning oven was the focal point of Nana's backyard. It was made of the same Sonora earth as her adobe.

This was her forever residence and where she dried her *yerbas* and concocted her remedies. Her adobe was situated on a dusty dirt road less than a mile from the main highway connecting Providencia to Ciudad Obregón. It also lead to *el canalón,* a large canal which runs parallel with the highway and where my cousin, Cristina Gutierrez, would go daily to *carretiar agua,* as Nana did not have indoor plumbing. One of Cristina's daily chores was to fetch fresh water in a pail from *el canalón* and carry the pail on her shoulders. One morning, I asked to accompany her out of curiosity — only once. The work was too hard and we had to rise early in the morning before the weather got too hot.

When visiting, we Vasquez children slept with our mother in the bedroom on the right. Nana slept in the room on the left which had a huge battery-operated console radio — one of only two similar radios in the entire village, they say. Nana's *sobrinos,* Jaime and Cristina Gutierrez, lived with her during their youth as *criados* until they married to form their own households. They were Nana's cousin, Josefina Gutierrez's children; she was unable to support them. When we visited, they slept in the patio on woven palm-frond *petates,* which they rolled up during the day.

Some of my fondest recollections of my Nana occurred in my childhood during two long trips to Providencia in the mid 1950s. My mother took us from Highgrove, California to visit her homeland in Providencia — she longed to see her mother, whom she hadn't seen in many years. Imagine a young woman of 27 years traveling with six young daughters in tow: me, the eldest, at age eight or nine, to my youngest sister, a small toddler. Our first trip was by train and the second trip was by bus when I was ten-years-old.

In my child eyes, Nana Pancha was the strongest, most powerful woman in my world. She was head of household and her word was to be obeyed. This image I had of her was confirmed on the day the hog was slaughtered. Nana's big fat pig lived in el *tejabán,* a rustic shed built of *carrizo* (tall bamboo-like dried reeds). It was adjacent to my Nana's adobe home facing the patio. I usually didn't venture too close to the pig's *tejabán*, as she was a big mean-tempered fat pig. I feared it would burst out of her pigpen and bite me, or worse, eat me alive — as if the pig were the big bad wolf.

One day I was surprised to see my young adult cousin Jaime "hog-tie" the pig and hoist it up with a rope, which he suspended over a wooden horizontal beam. He pulled the rope to hold up the squealing pig until it was standing upright on its hind legs. Then, my Nana boldly and swiftly slit the pig's throat with a machete or huge knife. Stunned by this vision, all I could do was stand by with my eyes wide open like tortillas — with my mouth gaping in silent amazement. What an impression! Nana was formidable.

Having come from a family of bakers, my Nana made the most delicious whole wheat bread, and my favorite rolls, called *cemitas*, which she baked in the earthen oven in the far side of her patio. Before baking, she placed the bread dough to rise in our darkened bedroom, where the dough stayed until ready to bake. She learned this skill from her parents who maintained a bakery in Batacosa, *en el municipio del Quiriego de Alamos, Sonora* — her hometown.

Nana Pancha was the go-to Partera in Providencia and its environs. I heard stories of my Nana wading across rivers to reach women and babies living in ranchos and campos to provide her *Partera / Curandera* services. People paid her whatever they could afford for her services. Sometimes they paid her with chicken eggs. This was a new concept for Americana me: the notion that a raw egg was comparable to currency — which one could exchange for goods. The value of an egg at the time was 20 centavos. My Nana's clientele were often poor, so she usually had an ample supply of eggs on her kitchen *trastero* (cupboard).

One day, I committed a bad deed. I stole one of her hard-earned eggs and took it to a nearby *tiendita*, a neighborhood mini-market to exchange the precious egg for 20 centavos worth of cookies, which I ate all by myself — didn't want any witnesses to my crime. I never heard my Nana or my Mamá say a word about the stolen egg; and, I never told anyone about my secret foible — my sin. My ingrained Catholic guilt, however kept me from ever doing it again.

Every time I visited my Mamá in Ciudad Obregón, I always stayed one or two days with my Tía Cuca and her youngest daughter, my *prima* Lupe in Providencia. My Tía had a lucid memory and was a wonderful conversationalist — *la narradora del valle*. During a visit in the 1980s, I visited my Tía's home and spent the night. Tía always answered my questions about family history with clarity and truth. While Lupe was at work at a bank in Obregón, Tía Cuca and I enjoyed cups of morning café and held long conversations about family *chísme*.

I asked her why my Nana never married. She explained that her mother-in-law, my Nana, was a proud woman who never wanted a man to dominate her. She refused offers of marriage by the father of her child. *"Tu Nana nunca quiso casarse pero dejaba la puerta abierta", dijo mi Tía.* However, Nana entertained suitors in her younger days, when she chose to do so. She earned her own living and she and her children resided in her own home. In her day, married Mexican women were obliged to be obedient and subservient to their husbands — my Nana would have none of that. She chose to follow her bliss: maintain a career in which she excelled and was much sought-after.

Another poignant story about Nana's fame was told to me by Tía Cuca. A man from a *campo* went to Providencia in search of la Nana Pancha. He had heard about her expertise as a Curandera who specialized in working with babies. He held his sick infant son in his arms and said that doctors were unable to cure whatever ailed the baby. When he was told that Nana had already passed away, the man burst into tears and lamented that Nana was his baby's last resort.

My cousin Francisca "Panchi" Paredes, who lives in Providencia shared many stories about our grandmother. One was about how Nana liked to bake bread: *cemitas, de panocha, de calabaza*...she would take to her sister Natalia and gave bread away to people. For Día de los Muertos, Nana would take to Cócorit for the celebrations in town and at the Cócorit cemetery. On this solemn occasion Nana also took *café talega* that she had roasted with brown sugar and ground herself. Nana never sold her bread. It was for giving away.

Panchi said that Nana was splendid and generous with people. She always had food on the stove ready to give to anyone who passed her home; it didn't matter to her whether they were rich or poor. When she felt like it, Nana would stand at her door and yell out to people, "*¡Wepa wepa! Ven a comer.*" Come, come to eat, she would say.

Sadly, the land where Nana's adobe once stood is now vacant, barren. During a 2017 trip to Providencia, I didn't see any visible remnants to show that once upon a time, an adobe house stood there to shelter my beloved grandmother — and numerous relatives so long ago. Only broken bottles, scattered rocks, and sparse weeds remain on the property. However, there is progress — the street in front of Nana's vacant property is now paved and has street signs; it's named, "Calle Jose Ma. Morelos" and the cross street is named "FCO. Javier Mina".

I loved my Nana and I was in awe of her for various reasons. I always felt that she loved me unconditionally — confident with the fact that I was her only daughter's first-born daughter. My admiration for her grew stronger as I became an adult and learned more stories about her accomplishments and her perspective as a Mexican woman who survived the brutal Mexican Revolution and economic depression in the 1930s. She experienced a healing profession that fulfilled her soul and benefitted/saved the lives of multitudes of people. My Nana thrived throughout her distinguished career and was beloved by her family and friends and her entire pueblito de Providencia. Doña Francisca Valenzuela Borboa's purpose-filled life is her legacy.

I feel immense gratitude to my Nana who was one of the illuminated people who showed me the way to living an independent life with integrity and purpose. Gracias, Nana.

+ Francisca Valenzuela Borboa — ¡Presente!

Note: Francisca Valenzuela Borboa was born on October 4, 1894 en Batacosa, en el municipio del Quiriego de Alamos, Sonora, México. She died on September 29, 1971 in her adobe home in Providencia en el Municipio de Cócorit, Rio Yaqui, Sonora, México. Tío Chemali frequently offered to take his mother to live in a nicer home next to his house, Nana refused. She told her son, "De aqui, me sacan muerta." Dicho y hecho — after her death, Tío Chemali took her body to his home for the *velorio*. My Nana was buried in Cócorit, one of eight ancestral towns of the Yoeme-Yaqui ethnic Tribe, and the first capitol of Sonora. The government of México and UNESCO declared Cócorit "un Pueblo Mágico" — a magical and historic town.

My Higher Education Journey
by Frances J. Vasquez

University of California Regent Stanley K. Sheinbaum scheduled a visit to our University of California Cooperative Extension office in Riverside in about 1978 or 1979. I was working there at the time, but I don't remember the stated reason for his visit. I don't know whether it was his wish to visit all Extension offices in California. Or, if it was a personal mission to visit Riverside.

I do remember that it was a special occasion for us staff. I regret that the people with whom I worked closely with are no long around to discuss and ask questions about Mr. Sheinbaum's visit to the UC Cooperative Extension office. I left in late 1983 to accept an international position the same year I had graduated with a BS Degree at UC Riverside. I sadly recently learned that Mr. Sheinbaum passed away in 2016.

During the 10 years that I worked for Extension, I don't recall anyone else of his stature visiting our building in the outskirts of Riverside on Box Springs Road at the foot of the Box Springs Mountains. As it turned out, Mr. Sheinbaum was to become a most impactful and unforgettable person. He became a major influence on the future direction of my higher education journey.

When he came, Mr. Sheinbaum first met with academic staff in the morning and later with classified employees, like me. During our group meeting, he informed us of employee fringe benefits that could improve our job performance and classifications — benefits we previously knew nothing about. He had requested a tour of our communities. Our Director, Chloe Beitler asked me to drive Mr. Sheinbaum to visit with some of the people I worked with. My assigned areas were with Chicano communities in East Riverside and Casa Blanca — where I conducted outreach and developed nutrition education classes with groups of children and workshops with adolescents regarding teen pregnancy (or most appropriately — prevention of).

In the afternoon, I drove him through Riverside and around the Casa Blanca neighborhood. I scheduled meetings with Frances Nahas, the Coordinator of the Ysmael R. Villegas Community Center and Glenn Ayala, Coordinator of the center's gym. Sadly, both Ms. Nahas and Mr. Ayala died several years ago, so I can't contact them to brainstorm their perspective of the visit.

I arranged for some of my students and parents to meet us at the center and at the gym. I don't remember whether I had already arranged with Frances Nahas for me to establish an outreach office at the Center on Wednesdays to meet with community members. I have also forgotten whether Glenn Ayala had already asked me if I could develop a 4-H community garden and a small animal project on vacant Riverside County land adjacent to the gym. In any case, Mr. Sheinbaum was visibly impressed with my work in the Casa Blanca community.

I succeeded in obtaining permission from Riverside County Supervisor Norton Younglove to use the vacant land to develop the community garden for Casa Blanca youth. Apparently, County employees complained about the project, and Ms. Beitler directed me to have a fence installed around the 4-H project within a week. This ultimatum was a surprise and very stressful, as I had no budget to handle the expense. My families were primarily low-income, so I couldn't ask my student's parents to finance the cost of the fence.

Augustine Flores came to mind. He was a prominent Riverside businessman with family roots in Casa Blanca. He was an executive with Woodhaven Development Company at the time. I placed a phone call to him about the fence — without hesitation, he said yes — he would help. He had a chain-link fence installed around the property within a day or so — and he financed it himself.

After Mr. Sheinbaum's visit, we were empowered to form a staff development committee — of which I served as chair. We learned that UC Cooperative Extension classified employees in good standing were allowed to take one class on staff time each semester to enhance our job performance. Mr. Sheinbaum encouraged me with this endeavor and we stayed in touch for a few years. He seemed very interested in my college progress.

As a single parent of three school-age children, I didn't want to take classes at night. I worked 75 percent flex time. So, I re-entered Riverside City College to complete my AA Degree by taking an English 1A class at 9 a.m. before I went to the office. The following semester I enrolled in English 1B and a Sociology class. I was on a roll and the next semester I took three classes before I went to work. I took only core classes that were transferable to UC Riverside.

One Saturday evening while my children were watching television, I laid out on my bed RCC and UCR transfer requirements. I realized that I would have to step up the rate of my class load in order to expedite transfer to UCR. I also determined what my major would be — a relatively new program, Human Relations: an interdisciplinary study of Anthropology, Psychology, and Sociology. My aunt, Virginia Vasquez had advised me to take classes that would help me to better understand people.

I earned my AA Degree in about 1981, along with an 80-year-old Sociology class colleague in our graduating class. She always arrived early to sit at the front of the class. I transferred to UCR and earned a BS Degree in June 1983 and that Fall I continued to the Anderson Graduate School of Management at UCR. I graduated with an MBA Degree two years later. It was a rigorous 90-unit program patterned after Harvard's MBA program.

To be sure, Stanley K. Sheinbaum helped motivate me to pursue higher education as a key to the upward mobility of my career path. I thought of him frequently over the years. At the time of our initial encounter, I was unaware of his prominence. I am forever grateful for his mentorship. I recently found an Obituary in the New York Times. Stanley K. Sheinbaum was a former economics professor who worked for liberal candidates and causes. He died at his home in Los Angeles in September 2016 at the age of 96. It stated, "Mr. Sheinbaum was an outspoken progressive not content merely to sign checks. He was a transplanted New Yorker whose family survived bankruptcy during the Depression and who invested well after he went West."

I surmise that Mr. Sheinbaum came specifically to Riverside to do good work — as the late Congressman John Lewis would say. Riverside County Cooperative Extension was not known for a diverse academic and classified staff.

Thank you Mr. Sheinbaum, I am forever grateful for your mentorship. You empowered me to follow my higher education bliss in the most effective way.

Autumn 2020

by Dale Vassantachart

The grey misty glow awakens me.
Shadows melt away.
Squirrels begin their daily search,
collecting, gnawing, burying acorns,
unaware that
over a million earthlings
are of the past
infected by the unceasing COVID virus
which craves more.
Yet,
as the cool breeze whispers,
the honey gold leaf sways,
the cinnamon tea warms,
Autumn comforts and brings hope.
Hope that faces soon will be uncovered
and once again
we can gather together.

Time Is Like the Written Word

BY JOSÉ LUIS VIZCARRA

Every second that goes by is like a single letter.

Every minute that goes by is like a single word.

Every hour passed is like a complete sentence.

Every day lived is like a paragraph.

Every week experienced is like a page.

Every month that passed by is like a chapter in a book.

Every year in the calendar is like a book.

Every person who has lived has written several books.

Every great person has a library full of books that share the author's wisdom

Everyone of you should start writing your own books.

El Último Rollo De Papel Del Baño

by José Luis Vizcarra

Tú eres tan importante pero tan
    menospreciado por la gente
Tantos se burlan de ti
Pero a los idiotas se les olvida
    lo importante que tú eres
Recientemente el virus nos atacó
    y el mundo no estaba preparado
Ahora tú tienes tu venganza
    en contra todos nosotros
Yo pienso que tú y el virus lo planearon,
    ¡Oh pero lo hicieron tan bien!
Todo el mundo les echa la culpa a los chinos
Pero ellos no saben lo inteligentes
    que ustedes dos son
Anoche yo tuve un ataque de pánico
Cuando vi que mi último rollo de papel
    se había terminado
Y busqué en vano por todos lados
Yo ignoré el pánico de la gente
    y me burlé de ellos
Qué estupido fui al no haber ido al Costco
    y a Walmart para agarrar un montón de ti
¡Oh mi querido rollo de papel del baño!
He usado piedras y ramas

Pero mi experiencia sin ti ha sido muy dolorosa
Mi trasero está en un dolor intenso
Ahora nos damos cuenta que tan
    importante tú verdaderamente eres
De hoy en adelante voy a ir temprano a ambas
    tiendas antes de que llegue la muchedumbre
Llame a Amazon pero se les había
    acabado lo que tenían
¡Hay Dios mío! Ahora ya no quiero
    dinero o cosas materiales
¡Todo lo que quiero es una bolsota
    de papel del baño del Costco!

Cadaver In The Desert

by José Luis Vizcarra

I am laying without life on the ground
Somebody left me without food or water
I had to survive for only so many days
Until I eventually ran out of every survival rations
The ones I listened to did not care about my future
Why is it that democrats call Trump racist when he wants us legally
But no democrat would want us in their own homes
Those same democrats accuse President Trump of killing children at the border
And yet they give millions to the abortion centers where minorities live
The coyotes only cared about the money they got paid
They lied and pushed me to come here without permission
Now I find death and desolation in this inhospitable place
For any human being to find survival without food or water
I left family and friends to escape corruption
Evil men who used us to be in power and enrich themselves
With American aide to help our nation
They took the aide and placed it in European banks
They created fortunes and lied to us and did nothing to help us
They don't lack anything and we live in misery
They enjoy champagne and caviar while the people have only misery to feed on
The fleet of new cars transport them, but we have to walk unprotected

Heavily armed soldiers protect their families and we have our bare hands to protect ourselves
They commit crimes and go unpunished
We only think about doing it and we get thrown in jail
Their children have the best schools
Our children don't even have books or pencils
But don't feel sorry for me as now my body serves a purpose
It will disintegrate and all the elements will build something else
Some animals will feast and won't go hungry
So now my body has a purpose for being here

The Magic Farm

by José Luis Vizcarra

Once upon a time, there was a magic farm that could change any predator animal into a domesticated docile creature that no longer hunted and killed other animals. Its fame traveled throughout the world. It was very famous and many came to witness the amazing transformation of the aggressive species.

There were wolves, hawks, eagles, lions, etc. It was amazing how all the animals lived in harmony with one another. The farmer fed them daily and all the animals lived in peace. They roamed the land without any worries. All their needs were met without exception. It was amazing how a chicken was not afraid of the predators. There were different kinds of animals and all of them seemed to be content and without worry. There was no sign of violence anywhere. Each animal just existed peacefully!

One eventual day, an animal behavior scientist who specialized in their behavior came to observe the famous farm. All his experience and training did not prepare him for what he was about to see that day.

The farmer explained to him how he was able to create such a paradise for all the living creatures. He explained to him that by observing human beings he was able to transfer the knowledge he learned to change animal behavior. The scientist was blown away by that response!

'What do you mean? How can you observe human beings and use that knowledge to transform predators into domesticated beasts that no longer killed other animals to feed themselves without your assistance?"

The wise farmer responded by saying, "At the beginning of human existence, man was like a wild animal who used to kill other human beings and animals to survive and to eat. Nobody fed him, so he had to go out and kill or be killed. He started to create skills to survive in such a violent environment. Eventually, he learned to form a group for protection and to be able to hunt, fish and eventually develop farming which started to turn him into a less violent being because he did not have to kill to be able to eat. Evolution of the human species started to build societies and rules to be able to coexist with other groups."

The farmer explained that modern societies devised a system to create docile human beings so that the ruling class will have abundant bodies to do the work and to be trained to consume everything that is produced in their factories and stores. The public education started the mental conditioning and in college the total mental enslavement of the masses completed the process.

Their wisdom created the mighty credit card that will enslave them for the rest of their lives. In return for being slaves they received a salary low enough so that they won't quit being controlled by society with the lie that they had a "good job!"

Many wild animals can be domesticated by feeding them so they are conditioned to be fed without any effort on their part to find their food, because hunting is HARD, like many employees say about leaving their secure jobs and building their own business!

After a few hours of being on the farm, the scientist thanked the farmer for his hospitality. He asked the farmer if he was an employee at the farm. The farmer just smiled and told the scientist that he one day was like any domesticated animal depending on someone feeding him and he observed the wild animals having real freedom with responsibility and real hard work. Those beasts refused to be domesticated by any man. He learned that every wild animal took the risk to fail, but were ready to be up to the challenge.

The farmer mentioned how wealthy people like the wild animals take chances everyday and were not afraid to fail. The scientist just sighed, thinking about all his debt....

Nighttime Walks in the Neighborhood – a Suite of Four Poems

BY HELEN YOUNG

1: Late September Night Sky

Jupiter and Saturn maintain their stance in the southern sky;
    partners for months now - .
The half-moon smiles to stand nearby.
A planet shimmers red and gold in the western sky -
And small planes, blinking red, traverse the heavens.
Beauty manifold;
Calmness, quietude, remain.

2. November Night Sky in Upland

Jupiter and Saturn still in conjunction
Now dipping toward the southwest in a slow-motion dive into the ocean -
    Jupiter sinks lower as Saturn ascends.
Aligned all summer long, they've been good friends -
    Keeping a kindly companionship.
The moon was up earlier this evening to join them,
And Mars glowed reddish orange overhead.

Harmony prevails in the sky above;
We peer up and outward to refresh our sense of stability.

We reach for a deeper truth -

Things are going on outside our own sphere!

3. 10:00 p.m. and All's Well with the World

Quietude falls as night envelopes;

Things calm down; frenetic activity ceases.

The freeway dims to a quiet roar.

Households tuck themselves in for the night – though a random dog barks.

The day is done. The rolling world has turned itself away from the sun

      for its nocturnal sojourn.

4. Listening to the Freeway at Night

Traffic going by on the 210 – with the periodic motorcycle whining by -

Trucks shift into lower gear as they descend the hill -

What is it that's so comforting about these sounds,
      amplified at night when everything else is quiet?

These sounds speak of *activity – quiet,* intentional, peaceful -

People heading back, after a long day's work;

To the respite of home ahead.

Two Triolet Poems
by Helen Young

Triolet poems have a required structure – the rhyme scheme for the lines goes, A,B,A,A A,B,A,B

The Cat Wants In

The cat wants in – the cat wants out –
Is there no satisfying this feline friend??
Its motivation leaves some doubt…
The cat wants in, the cat wants out.
"Make up your mind!" you want to shout! -
To no avail – it won't attend.
The cat wants in – the cat wants out –
Is there no satisfying this feline friend?

Summer Idyll

Echoes from a summer pool
When days are long and sun-enshrined;
The kids are free and home from school –
Echoes from a summer pool.
These sounds unbind me from time's rule
And memories flow, both clear and kind;
Echoes from a summer pool -
When days are long and sun-enshrined.

Author Bios

Elisabeth Anghel is a member of Inland Empire California Writers Club. A retired librarian and an active storyteller, Elisabeth is currently working on a memoir. Some of her short stories are shared with her storytelling fellows. She is a long time Riverside CA resident where she lives with her husband. **[Adventures in Chronologyland with Dr. Carlos Cortés]**

Don Bennett has worn many hats during his life: Deputy DA, private practice lawyer, food bank director, consultant, trainer, husband, father, grandpa, and heart transplant recipient. He found out about the Redlands Joslyn Joy Writers after reading a newspaper article about them, and joined the group's Zoom group last summer. **[Joslyn Joy Writers with Mae Wagner Marinello]**

Brenda Beza is a native of Southern California. Her love for storytelling and history led her to earn a B.A. and M.A. in American Studies from Cal State University, Fullerton, and a M.S. in Educational Counseling from the University of La Verne. She has trained at the American Folk Life Center at the Library of Congress and Smithsonian Institute. **[Adventures in Chronologyland with Dr. Carlos Cortés]**

Beyond fluid movements of Tai Chi Chih, former coastal California artist, **Georgette Buckley**, B.A. Studio Art, fondly recalls teaching painting, attending archaeology lectures amongst Roman ruins and backpacking misty, green Ireland. Selected for the 2007 *Myriad Journal*, she and her husband of 38 years thrive in Inlandia. **[Poetry in Motion with CelenaDiana Bumpus]**

Alben J. Chamberlain was born in San Bernardino, California. He attended San Bernardino Valley College and received a BA in Business Administration from BYU-Hawaii. He earned an MBA degree from the American Graduate School Of International Management as well as teacher's credentials from the University of California-Riverside. **[San Bernardino at the Rowe Branch Library with Allyson Jeffredo]**

Natalie Champion is a poet who lives in San Francisco with her husband Rick and two cats, Princess Tabitha and Milo Morris. **[Adventures in Chronologyland with Dr. Carlos Cortés]**

Richard (Rick) Champion is a writer, photographer, and mathematician in exile. He lives in the San Francisco Bayview where bikes and cars are contending for control of the streets. He enjoys watching local bikes and motorcycles rear up on one back wheel like stallions. **[Adventures in Chronologyland with Dr. Carlos Cortés]**

Sylvia Clarke spent several months this year healing bones broken in her fall but is now able to do nearly everything she did before. She is hiking again and recently returned to Joshua Tree National Park to scramble on some rocks. **[Poetry in Motion with CelenaDiana Bumpus; Colton with Jessica Carillo; Adventures in Chronologyland with Dr. Carlos Cortés]**

Wil Clarke is a retired mathematics teacher who was told by his early teachers to never try to write anything: he was too boring. Thank you, Inlandia, for giving him a second chance! He won a second NaNoWriMo novel writing challenge in November 2020. **[Poetry in Motion with CelenaDiana Bumpus; Colton with Jessica Carillo; Adventures in Chronologyland with Dr. Carlos Cortés]**

Amy Clayton is enjoying retirement! After several decades of teaching she now has the time and energy to read, write, garden, walk, knit, bake, paint, and play solitaire. She awaits the resumption of traveling to distant lands, but until then, shall remain in place, content with life as it is. **[Adventures in Chronologyland with Dr. Carlos Cortés]**

Deenaz P. Coachbuilder, Ph.D., is an educator, artist, writer and environmental advocate. Her poems, commentaries and essays have been published internationally. Her two books of poems, *Metal Horse And Shadows: A Soul's Journey*, and *Imperfect Fragments*, have been received with critical acclaim in the U.S. and abroad. [Dr. M.J. Koerper's workshop, The Art and Heart of Memoir; and Adventures in Chronologyland with Dr. Carlos Cortes' workshop]

Elinor Cohen likes to eat and write. She has a degree in Pre- and Early-Modern Literature that she currently does nothing with. Elinor resides with her family in the desolate desert after decades as an Angeleno, and is obsessed with her rescue dogs Beans and Floof. [Food Writing with Alaina Bixon]

Carlos Cortés is the Edward A. Dickson Emeritus Professor of History and co-director of the School of Medicine Health Equity, Social Justice, and Anti-Racism initiative at the University of California, Riverside. He was Scholar-in-Residence with Univision Communications and is the Creative/Cultural Advisor for Nickelodeon's "Dora the Explorer" and "Go, Diego, Go!" [Riverside with Jo Scott-Coe; Workshop Leader, Adventures in Chronologyland]

Laurel Vermilyea Cortes studied Spanish and Comparative Literature at San Diego State. She retired from the University of California, Riverside, after serving as Management Services Officer in the Department of Literatures and Languages. Laurel always considered herself lucky to be working in the exact environment of her choice. [Riverside with Jo Scott-Coe; Adventures in Chronologyland with Dr. Carlo Cortés]

Barry Cutler has been a professional actor in theatre, television, film, and radio for more than a half century. However, his first loves were writing and . . . baseball. [Ontario with Tim Hatch]

Ellen Estilai lives in Riverside, California. Her poetry and prose have appeared in numerous journals and anthologies, most recently in A *Short Guide to Finding Your First Home in the United States* and *Pandemic Spring*. A two-time Pushcart Prize nominee, she is an Inlandia Institute board member emerita. [Food Writing with Alaina Bixon]

Andrea Fingerson is a writer, a teacher, and child of God. She has taught in the Moreno Valley Unified School District for fourteen years. During that time, she earned an MFA in Creative Writing, with a focus on Fiction from Cal State San Bernardino and studied art at Moreno Valley City College. **[Workshop leader, Corona Public Library]**

Bryan Franco lives in Brunswick, Maine. He is a poet and spoken word artist/performer. He was a member of the Portland, Maine Rhythmic Cypher slam team that competed in the 2014 National Poetry Slam in Oakland, California. He's also a painter, sculptor, gardener, and self-proclaimed culinary genius. **[Poets in Motion with CelenaDiana Bumpus]**

Meryl Freeze is a Los Angeles native. She has a B.A. and an M.A. in Economics, and an obsession for physical fitness. When she is not exercising, she loves learning lifelong skills such as programming and cooking. **[Food Writing with Alaina Bixon]**

Nan Friedley is a retired special education teacher and graduate of Ball State University, Muncie, IN. Her writings have been published in a poetry chapbook, „Short Bus Ride", by Bad Knee Press, Indiana Voice Journal, Inlandia Anthologies, and „Three", a non-fiction anthology collection by Push Pen Press. **[Poets in Motion with CelenaDiana Bumpus; Adventures in Chronologyland with Dr. Carlos Cortés]**

Hazel Fuller resides in Redlands where she attended school and worked in the school library. This experience prepared her for jobs at the San Bernardino County Library, Ventura County Library, and later, libraries for the Dept. of Defense and Dept. of Interior. She enjoys writing, reading, and restoring Victorian houses. **[Joslyn Joy Writers with Mae Wagner Marinello]**

Judy Ginsberg paints, writes, sculpts and does stand-up comedy. She lives in Northern California with Mikey, her well-behaved cat. **[Food Writing with Alaina Bixon]**

Ragini Goel has a masters degree in Sanskrit and a teachers degree in English. People who know Ragini describe her as a Renaissance woman with varied interests. Ragini is an appointed commissioner to the Human Relations Council. Ragini says her best achievements are her two sons Sumeet and Amit. **[Corona with Andrea Fingerson]**

Michael A. Gonzales lived in Casa Blanca during childhood and received a BA from Texas Christian University and a MPA from the University of Southern California. He worked for several Federal agencies and retired as a Social Security Claims Representative for HEW, and from the Air Force Reserves. His passion is family history research. **[Tesoros de Cuentos with Frances J. Vasquez]**

Ralph A. Gonzales was born in the Casa Blanca neighborhood of Riverside and lived/worked in Los Angeles throughout his career. He retired as Superintendent of Finance in the California Air National Guard. He continued his career in Finance as Program Manager for Rocketdyne on the Columbia Space Shuttle Program, among other Corporations. **[Tesoros de Cuentos with Frances J. Vasquez]**

Richard Gonzalez is a native of San Bernardino. He served in the Navy as a Sonarman First Class. He graduated from Fresno State College with a degree in economics. He joined the War-on-Poverty and served as a volunteer in the civil rights movement. He has served on various commissions and civic organizations in the Inland Empire. **[Joslyn Joy Writers with Mae Wagner Marinello]**

Mark Grinyer, Ph.D., has published poems *The Literary Review, The Spoon River Quarterly, The Pacific Review, Perigee, Cordite, Crosswinds Poetry Journal,* and elsewhere. His chapbook, *Approaching Poetry,* was published by Finishing Line Press. He is currently retired, writing and living on the edge of the Cleveland National Forest. **[Redlands with James Ducat]**

Raquel Hernandez is an up-and-coming author. She has taught abroad and enjoys experiencing new cultures and sights. She is an alumna of USF, where she earned her bachelor's in Communication and minor in History with highest honors. When she is not writing, she travels the world as a flight attendant. **[Poets in Motion with CelenaDiana Bumpus]**

Richard (Rich) Hess is a retired physician. He practiced Obstetrics/Gynecology in Fairbanks, Alaska for 41 years. He is now living in Redlands, California with his wife, Marie. He enjoys writing about his medical and other life experiences. **[Joslyn Joy Writers with Mae Wagner Marinello]**

Connie Jameson is a retired teacher, enjoys reading, travel, nature, writing, and theater. She is a 40+ year member of Toastmasters, Int'l. Connie is pleased to have recently published her first book, *Dating 'n' Mating: Wit and Wisdom on Love and Marriage*. **[Poets in Motion with CelenaDiana Bumpus]**

Ann Kanter grew up in Riverside and attended Pomona College and Hastings Law School. She practices immigration law in Sacramento where she has actively supported the arts community. Her bilingual poems have been published in *Voices of the New Sun* (Aztlán Cultural 2004) and *Soñadores - We Came to Dream* (DeepSong/CantoHondo Books 2016). **[Adventures in Chronologyland with Dr. Carlos Cortés]**

Naresh Kaushal is an artist filmmaker & writer based in London UK.Â He has shot moving image works for clients such as the BBC and devised interactive pieces for institutions such as Kings College London.Â He is currently working on his debut poetry collection. www.camerawala.org **[Poets in Motion with CelenaDiana Bumpus]**

Cleone Knopfle is a writer and resident of Palm Springs. **[Food Writing with Alaina Bixon]**

Dr. MJ (Joan) Koerper (MSW, Ph.D.) is a college educator, writer, retired transpersonal psychotherapist (LCSW) and potter. She has published in numerous genres including memoir, creative nonfiction, fiction, poetry, essay, research, plays, scripts, and works for children. **[Workshop Leader, The Art and Heart of Memoir]**

Jessica Lea was a featured artist in Riverside Art Museum's 52 Project 2019 Exhibition. Her poetry and photography are regularly published in Spectrum Magazine. Diamonds and Yoga Pants (2020) is her first book of poems. She is a collaborating artist in a visual Psalter to be published by Elyssar Press. **[Redlands with James Ducat]**

Nina Lewis is from the UK. She has two chapbooks *Fragile Houses* (2016) and *Patience* (2019) published by V. Press. She was Worcestershire Poet Laureate 2017-18. During lockdown she was a Showcase Poet for Stay at Home Literature Festival and a Poet in Residence for Cheltenham Poetry Festival. **[Poets in Motion with CelenaDiana Bumpus]**

Robin Longfield's piece was inspired by her participation in Dr. Carlos Cortes' "Chronology" workshop, a writing prompt to explore our relationship with time. For Robin, that topic was rife with examples of her own notorious lack of understanding about the way time is supposed to work. **[Adventures in Chronologyland with Dr. Carlos Cortés]**

Merrill Lyew is a retired Geographer. After spending a decade in academia, he spent another three decades in the private sector. Frequent business travel to the metropolitan areas of Latin America with sporadic visits to the provinces were engaging, exciting, eventful, full of multitudes of storylines and the subject of some of his storytelling. **[Joslyn Joy Writers with Mae Wagner Marinello]**

A California native, **Pamylla Marsh** worked in education, including California State Polytechnic University, Pomona, and Mt. San Antonio College, Walnut. She also has served as a local reporter/

photojournalist for The Walnut Valley Independent as well as publishing a music newsletter, Quasar Neolithic. Pamylla is a proud mother and grandmother. **[Adventures in Chronologyland with Dr. Carlos Cortés]**

Terry Lee Marzell lives in Chino Hills, California. Before retiring, she invested 36 years in her career as an educator. She earned her BA in English and her teaching credential from CSUF, and her MA in Interdisciplinary Studies from CSUSB. Terry earned an additional credential in Library Science from CSULB. **[Joslyn Joy Writers with Mae Wagner Marinello]**

Phyllis Maynard has been retired for several years, the loving widow of Douglas and mom to Pam, Danny, Mark and Toby. Writing every chance she gets! In 1988, her poem appeared in the *American Poetry Anthology*. She is currently working on an illustrated children's book about four Dalmatians. **[Poets in Motion with CelenaDiana Bumpus]**

Thomas McCabe is an artist and executive coach in Palm Springs. He and Jeff Holloway are opening their gallery, Eminent Design, at The River in Rancho Mirage. **[Food Writing with Alaina Bixon]**

Barbara Ann Meyer was born 8 Oct 1939 in Big Spring, TX. Her family came to San Diego, CA in the early 1940s. She married a young man on 8 Aug 1959 and they were blessed with three children. She and her husband are enjoying retirement in Redlands, CA. **[Joslyn Joy Writers with Mae Wagner Marinello]**

Marvin Meyer was born on 8 Mar1936 in the wilds of western OK. He became a brick mason, a surveyor and several different kinds of engineer. He married in 1959, they had three children, two have survived and one of them presented them with two grandchildren. **[Joslyn Joy Writers with Mae Wagner Marinello]**

Born in Agua Prieta, Sonora, Mexico, **Rose Y. Monge**'s stories of her immigrant and migrant experiences honor her parents' legacy of love and unwavering faith in the "American dream." She is a retired educator and facilitates memoir classes at the Goeske Center. She encourages everyone to leave a written legacy for future generations. **[Adventures in Chronologyland with Dr. Carlos Cortés; Food Writing with Alaina Bixon]**

Mary-Lynne Monroe lives outside Portland, Oregon. She writes poetry, memoir, fiction and non-fiction. Published in *Offerings: Poems Written During Tiferet Journal's Spiritual Poetry Class, Vol. 2* and in *The Power of Our Voices: Sharing Our Story*. Her blog is Unfolding Myths (https://unfoldingmyths.blogspot.com/). Find her on Instagram @mythdancer. **[Poets in Motion with Celena-Diana Bumpus]**

Roberto Murillo is an active member of the Casa Blanca Community Action Group. He researched and wrote about the history of citrus workers' strikes in Casa Blanca. He published a booklet entitled, "Casa Blanca en Huelga" in which he details the community activism that led to ousting a negligent City Councilmember. **[Tesoros de Cuentos with Frances J. Vasquez]**

Cindi Neisinger believes curiosity will lead you to your passions. She did not start off with the intention of writing. However, after many writing classes throughout the Inland Empire, she was hooked. Currently, she is writing micro-memoir, short stories, and a screenplay. She also serves on the Inlandia Institute Advisory Council. **[Poets in Motion with CelenaDiana Bumpus]**

S. J. Perry's work has recently appeared in Cholla Needles, MUSE, and Pandemic Summer. He studied at Emporia State University and the University of Kansas. A retired high school English teacher, he has lived in Southern California since 1985. "MAGA" was written in Stephanie Barbé Hammer's Poet-Try 9 workshop. **[Poet-try 9 with Stephanie Barbé Hammer; Redlands with James Ducat]**

Christine Petzar lives in Riverside and participated in her first Inlandia writers' workshop in 2019. Her career in educational administration involved professional writing and teacher education related to English Learners. In retirement, she is branching out to more personal writing — memoir and creative non-fiction. [**Adventures in Chronologyland with Dr. Carlos Cortés**]

Raymond Price retired in 1989 and moved to Palm Springs in 2010 with his wife Esmé. They volunteer for many Coachella valley organizations including DAP Health, the film society, Desert X, Modernism week and the Palm Springs Art Museum. He enjoys travel, writing, living in Palm Springs, gardening and garden design. [**Food Writing with Alaina Bixon**]

Among **Cindi Pringle's** pastimes are creative writing and illustrating after a career in broadcast journalism and university administration. She is devoted to yoga and volunteering at the Mary S. Roberts Pet Adoption Center, as well as making distributions from Feed America. [**San Bernardino with Romaine Washington and Allyson Jeffredo**]

Randolph Quiroz is a former teacher who's written five novels but has so far only submitted short stories for publication. He won the Top Fiction Award at the 2019 San Diego Southern California Writers' Conference and was a finalist in the 2020 Writers of the Future international competition. [**Ontario with Tim Hatch**]

Kristine Ann Shell lives in Redlands, California. Kristine is a retired school administrator and teacher. She holds Bachelor of Arts degrees in English and Secondary Education. She also holds Master of Education degrees in Elementary Reading and School Administration. Kristine has been a member of the Inlandia Institute since October, 2016. [**Joslyn Joy Writers with Mae Wagner Marinello**]

Stevie Taken loves living in Riverside with her cat Basil. She took up some hobbies and a few habits during quarantine, including enrolling herself in Stephanie Barber's Poetry-9 workshop. For the remainder of the quarantine she'll think about taking a Portuguese class, then take a nap instead. [**Poet-try 9 with Stephanie Barbé Hammer**]

Elizabeth Uter is an award-winning poet, winning the 2018 Poem for Slough Competition in 2 categories. http://www.bringyourownfuture.net/poetry-competition/. She's taught poetry workshops for Farrago Poetry, performed at the Queen's Park Literary Festival, 2019, London; published in: *Bollocks To Brexit* Poetry Anthology, *Reach* and *Sarasvati* magazines. [**Poets in Motion with CelenaDiana Bumpus**]

Gudelia (Delia) Vaden, a retired preschool teacher, earned a BA degree in Liberal Studies with Bilingual-Bicultural Emphasis from CSU San Bernardino. She lives in Riverside with husband, Tom, and has two grown children, Natalie and Patrick. Delia loves writing and has been published in the Inlandia Anthology since 2015. [**Adventures in Chronologyland with Dr. Carlos Cortés**]

Thomas (Tom) Vaden earned a MS degree in Mathematics from the University of Missouri Columbia. Originally from St. Louis, Tom enlisted in the Air Force and spent time in Colorado where he learned to figure skate. He married Gudelia at Castle AFB in the San Joaquin Valley. They now live in Riverside. [**Adventures in Chronologyland with Dr. Carlos Cortés**]

Frances J. Vasquez is native to the Inland region of Southern California and was educated in Riverside Schools, RCC, and UCR. An aficionada of arts and letters, she loves attending and organizing cultural events. She serves on the Inlandia Institute Board as Director Emerita. [**Workshop Leader, Tesoros de Cuentos; Adventures in Chronologyland with Dr. Carlos Cortés**]

During COVID-19, **Dale Vassantachart** temporarily moved to Palo Alto. She appreciates Mae Marinello's perseverance facilitating the Joslyn Joy Writers. Beneath a canopy of oaks and redwoods, Dale and her granddaughter, Autumn, watch squirrels race up tree branches and forage acorns which inspired her poem "Autumn 2020". [**Joslyn Joy Writers with Mae Wagner**]

Jose L. Vizcarra was born in Mexico before moving to the United States in 1963 on a student visa. He was drafted into the Army the week the Rev. Martin Luther King was killed, serving from 1968-70. He received his AA, BA and MA from CSULA and is the author of *Kiss from an Angel.* **[Poets in Motion with Celena-Diana Bumpus]**

Helen Young lives in Upland, CA. An English major in college, she worked as an academic secretary for many years. She recently decided she would love to take up writing again, so enrolled in an online poetry class. She is realizing you have to practice and work to write well! **[Ontario with Tim Hatch]**

About Inlandia Institute

Inlandia Institute is a regional literary non-profit and publishing house. We seek to bring focus to the richness of the literary enterprise that has existed in this region for ages. The mission of the Inlandia Institute is to recognize, support, and expand literary activity in all of its forms in Inland Southern California by publishing books and sponsoring programs that deepen people's awareness, understanding, and appreciation of this unique, complex and creatively vibrant region.

The Institute publishes books, presents free public literary and cultural programming, provides in-school and after school enrichment programs for children and youth, holds free creative writing workshops for teens and adults, and boot camp intensives. In addition, every two years, the Inlandia Institute appoints a distinguished jury panel from outside of the region to name an Inlandia Literary Laureate who serves as an ambassador for the Inlandia Institute, promoting literature, creative literacy, and community. Laureates to date include Susan Straight (2010-2012), Gayle Brandeis (2012-2014), Juan Delgado (2014-2016), Nikia Chaney (2016-2018), and Rachelle Cruz (2018-2020).

To learn more about the Inlandia Institute, please visit our website at www.InlandiaInstitute.org.

Inlandia Books

Güero-Güero: The White Mexican and Other Published and Unpublished Stories by Dr. Eliud Martínez

A Short Guide to Finding Your First Home in the United States: An Inlandia anthology on the immigrant experience

Care: Stories by Christopher Records

San Bernardino, Singing an anthology edited by Nikia Chaney

Facing Fire: Art, Wildfire, and the End of Nature in the New West by Douglas McCulloh

Writing from Inlandia, an annual anthology (2011-)

In the Sunshine of Neglect: Defining Photographs and Radical Experiments in Inland Southern California, 1950 to the Present by Douglas McCulloh

Henry L. A. Jekel: Architect of Eastern Skyscrapers and the California Style by Dr. Vincent Moses and Catherine Whitmore

Orangelandia: The Literature of Inland Citrus by Gayle Brandeis

While We're Here We Should Sing by The Why Nots

Go to the Living by Micah Chatterton

No Easy Way: Integrating Riverside Schools - A Victory for Community by Arthur L. Littleworth